QUINN

Quinn

Seamus Smyth

FLAME
Hodder & Stoughton

First published in Great Britain in 1999 by
Hodder and Stoughton
First published in paperback in 2000 by
Hodder and Stoughton
A division of Hodder Headline

A Flame Paperback

10 9 8 7 6 5 4 3 2 1

A CIP catalogue record for this title
is available from the British Library

ISBN 0 340 75067 7

Typeset by Hewer Text Ltd, Edinburgh
Printed and bound in Great Britain by
Mackays of Chatham PLC, Chatham, Kent

Hodder and Stoughton
A division of Hodder Headline
338 Euston Road
London NW1 3BH

For
Maisie, Lily and Phyllis

ACKNOWLEDGEMENTS

My thanks to Jonathan Williams

PROLOGUE

———◦•◦———

I knew a guy once who pulled off what he thought was the perfect robbery. Then things started to go wrong. So I said to him, 'Noel,' I said, 'take precautionary measures. Don't wait for the law to get on a roll. Know what I mean?'

He ignored me; hoped for the best – he comes up for parole in a couple of years. But my name's not Noel.

Chapter One

So, with a precautionary measure of my own in mind, I met my brother-in-law in town and drove him out to meet a man about work. A pretext. There was no work. It was bullshit.

We got talking on the way, casually, y'know: 'How's the family, Liam?' – crap like that.

'Not bad,' he says. 'The boy's still football mad and you know Molly – still digging away.'

Molly was a crime reporter for the *National Tribune*.

I turned onto the dual carriageway. 'What's she working on now?'

'God knows.' He ran his hand through what few combfuls he had left. 'But by the way she lit out this morning, I'd say it has something to do with Paddy Toner.'

In Dublin Toner *was* crime. And, for the want of a better word, Molly was on a 'crusade' against him.

I'd been with Paddy Toner only the night before – placing explosives near the fuel tank of a white box van where they'd do most damage – when he said to me 'Y'know, Gerd,' (that's pronounced *Jerd*, by the way – not *Gird* – short for Gerard) 'there's nothing more dangerous than a woman without a weak spot. You've nothing to use against her.'

He was referring to Liam's wife.

'Every woman's got a weak spot, Paddy,' I said. 'Even if it's only an electric blanket – you can always electrocute her with it.'

'But we can't kill her, Gerd. Every fucking cop in Dublin'd be after us.'

'No need to, Paddy.' In circumstances like this, y'see, I find *threatening* a loved one is just as effective. But first you have to prove you mean business – that's what this was all about. 'Everything ready?'

'Everything's bugged, Gerd: her office word processor, car, house. If she as much as reaches for toilet paper, we'll hear the perforations separating. Where are you meeting her "electric blanket"?'

'Liam? He goes to the bank every Friday morning for his men's wages.'

'What time do you think she'll find that tape?'

The tape was that 'precautionary measure' I mentioned. On the face of it, there was enough on it to put Toner away for good. We'd planted it for Liam's wife to find. It was gonna backfire on her, y'see. We had to turn her into a demoralized, guilt-ridden wreck. Make her pay for her arrogance, make her question her abilities, make her realize that it was her own vanity, that if she'd only stopped to scrutinize the evidence, a life would have been saved. Neutralize her, in other words. Before *she* got on a roll and did the same to Toner. Which would then lead her to me. Stuff like that.

But I needed her husband to help me pull it off. Not that he knew anything about it. He was too easygoing to ever imagine what I had in mind for him. He was just an ordinary guy who worked all week renovating property, coached a kids' football team – his son kept goal – and lived happily ever after. Marriage was invented for people like him. Wouldn't stray. Boring bastard. Henpecked with it. Sloppy dresser, too – invariably in some worn-out running gear.

He was wearing it in the car.

'Look, Liam,' I said to him, pointing to the white box van I mentioned earlier. It was now parked outside the school canteen. The kids were inside enjoying their dinner. 'See that van? I've to see a man down there in ten minutes about that bit of work. When he comes, tell him I've gone for a packet of fags. Won't be long.'

He went down to the van. I watched him lean against it with his hands in his pockets. Then I drove to a nearby apartment block and went up on to the flat roof.

Toner rang. He was in the back of a Transit, parked across the road from Molly's office, with listening-in equipment tuned to the bug in her word processor. He was laughing as he said it. 'You'll never believe the way she's writing this story of hers. Know what she called me? Sinister.'

'Anyone in that office besides Molly?'

'Ward.'

'Put your phone to that speaker. I wanna hear what they're saying.'

Eamon Ward, Molly's assistant editor, was coming through loud and clear: 'We're not going to print, Moll. Not until the police confirm it's Toner's voice on that tape.'

I could imagine her sitting there, typing away, in her black two-piece suit, white top, hair as curly as an unpicked rope.

'Toner threatened to kill me if I used it, Eamon. That's all the verification I need.'

She believed she had uncovered the tape through her own efforts, y'see. Which was how I'd planned it; or she would have seen straight through it. She was convinced it was twenty-four carat.

'Think about what you're doing, Moll.'

'Look, Eamon, Toner will be in custody by the time this story hits the streets. Stop worrying.'

Ward was sounding pretty het up. 'He can still order you killed.'

'He can try.'

If only it had been that easy. As Toner had touched on: killing a crime reporter like Molly Murray wasn't on. It would be like faxing the law saying she was onto something; telling them to pick up where she'd left off.

'Read the text back to me,' Ward then said to her.

'OK. A man, his wife and his daughter die in an "accident". His only surviving daughter blamed herself. The daughter inherited her father's assets, which she sold to a Dublin drug baron for five million. In cash. The cash disappeared. I have concrete evidence that a man working for the drug baron killed all three people, that the missing cash went back to the drug baron.

'But there is also a third man. The real brains behind it. He is known only to the drug baron. The police do not know he exists. I am close to identifying the third man. I have been threatened. If I don't back off – I'm dead.

'I am not backing off. Nothing will make me back off.'

I'd heard enough.

I was the third man.

Time to change your mind, Moll. Can't let you get to a position where you can identify me.

From the roof, using high-powered binoculars, I made sure I could see straight down into the school. By going to the far end of the roof, I could see down into another school.

Then I rang her. Told her straight and plain. 'There's a bomb in a van in a school in the town.'

She nearly choked. Then: 'What? Oh Jesus! Where?' came back.

'Dial 606784 on the other line and put it on loudspeaker.'

I wanted to hear everything that was said as it was said. She rang the number and a man answered: 'Saint Martin's Primary, Principal speaking.'

Knowing Molly, while she was telling the Principal of the bomb warning she was also waving to Ward to ring the same information through to the Gardaí, like a good citizen.

The Principal, a fat fucker in his thirties, blond crewcut, sports jacket, with a tie the size of a kite, jumped up from his seat and opened his window.

'Tell him to stay where he is if he wants to save lives,' I told her.

'He's watching you,' she told the fat fucker. 'He's watching you. Don't move, whatever you do.'

He didn't.

'Wise man,' I said. 'Ask him what's outside his window.'

She did. 'He says there's a man, the driver, he's not sure, leaning against a white box van at the entrance to the canteen.'

I could see the 'driver' from where I was squatting.

'Tell the Principal if he as much as glances at the driver, I press the button.'

Her nerves were getting to her. I could hear it in her voice as she relayed the message virtually word for word.

'Ask him what time school dinner finishes,' I said.

'He says half twelve.'

'That gives us two minutes.'

'For what?'

5

'Don't be naive.'

'The Principal says the teachers are opening the canteen doors.'

'So I see. Now this is the way it is. If I detonate now, only the driver gets it. If we wait till the kids come out, they all get it. What would you suggest?'

That one got her. '*Me*? You're asking *me*?'

'They're lining up to come out,' said the Principal.

'It's your decision,' I said.

That one winded her. 'Me? You can't ask me to decide.'

'No problem,' I said. 'I'll wait till the kids come out. Then detonate.'

'No! I didn't mean that.'

'OK. So it's just the driver?'

'No!'

'The kids *and* the driver?'

'No!'

'Just the driver?'

'The doors are open,' the Principal shouted.

'What'll it be?' I asked.

'He's making me decide, Eamon. What'll I do? He's making me decide when the bomb goes off! Eamon I can't. Eamon I . . .'

Asking Eamon Ward to take over, make the decision, do whatever it took but please take over the responsibility, was, from what I could make out, getting her sweet fuck all. Some people aren't up to making a decision like that – their hearts'd give out – who lives, who dies. Nothing came back. He may have been her boss. But he wasn't liable for this. She was on her own.

'They're coming out,' shouted the Principal. 'The kids are coming out!'

'Oh my God, I can't decide!' she cried. 'Please don't ask me to. I can't decide!'

'In that case we'll wait,' I said.

'No! No! A . . .'

'Take your time.'

'The kids are coming out!'

'What'll it be?'

Crying, she begged me. 'No! Please don't make me. Please don't make me.'

'Here they come.'

'Pleeeeese . . . I'll do anything you say. But please don't make me do this.' Then came silence. And in that silence she heard the faint sound of children emerging. She had to save them. She had to take the decision. Ward was probably cringing in a corner by now. 'Oh God! Forgive me!' she cried. 'Please God, forgive me.'

'The kids are coming out!' the Principal kept on.

'What'll it be?'

She broke down. But I knew she was up to it. If only because her nephew was amongst those kids. 'YES!'

'Yes?'

'YES!'

She heard the explosion down the line.

About fucking time! Clouds coming in from the Irish Sea looked as if they were being fast-forwarded. I wanted this over with before the rain came on.

It was easy to predict what she'd do next. The story. Everything was the story. Oh sure, she was interested in the human side, but her first instinct was to rush to the scene to get it down on paper.

The place was a madhouse when she arrived: distraught

7

mothers were rushing to the school canteen, smoke and debris everywhere. Automatically she pressed the record button on her microcassette and put it into the top pocket of her jacket as she hit the brakes, intending to rush to the canteen.

But I couldn't let her go to the canteen. If she'd gone to the canteen, the whole thing would have stopped there and then and I couldn't have that. I needed her to be someplace else. I rang her mobile. She grabbed it as she reached for the door handle. 'Stay where you are,' I told her.

'Jesus, it's him! He's still here. He's watching me.'

'Look ahead the whole time.'

But she was looking across at the mangled van, a hundred yards or so away, where she saw who she thought was the driver lying face-down on the grass, the back of his head blown in, children in the canteen crying, broken windows, chaos.

'Drive,' I said.

'Fuck you! The bomb's gone off. You've nothing to threaten me with now. It's gone off, you bastard! Fuck you! You've nothing to threaten me with now.'

'You've the same decision to make.'

'What?'

'There's a bomb in a van in a school in the town.'

'Oh God! No way! You're not putting me through that again.'

'It's your conscience.'

'And it's clear.'

'Then stay here and witness worse later, or drive and save the lives of another bunch of kids. It's up to you.'

'Why are you doing this to me?' she screamed. 'Why? Some sick cause? What?'

'Kids' lives are depending on you. What'll it be?'

Like any mother – and I was counting on this – she thought of her own son, playing in his own school right now, imagined his life at risk. She thought of her husband, how the loss of the boy would kill him. Stuff like that. She had to go. There was no other way. She hit the throttle.

'Where to?'

'Where do you think?'

'What?'

'What school are you thinking of?' I said.

There could be only one. 'No,' she pleaded. 'Not Saint Vincent's. No. Not Liam's school. Not my son's school. Please!'

'Drive.'

She sped through the traffic, horn-blowing, overtaking, jumping lights, and came to the brow of the hill overlooking the playground.

I crossed to the far side of the long roof and refocused the binoculars. She must've been the guts of a mile away, but I could see her well enough across the common. 'Pull in,' I told her.

The car screeched to a halt alongside the high mesh fence. And it was then that she started to really fall apart. Her eleven-year-old son was in goal, his hands on his knees watching his side at the opposite end of the pitch trying to score. In the street, ten feet behind him, parked up tight to the fence, was a white box van. The scenario was a repeat of the last. Only this wasn't a 'driver' we were talking about. To her, this was her son in the driver's position. The question was obvious.

'Will I detonate now?'

'Jesus, please help me!'

9

If she said yes, as she had done at Saint Martin's, it meant that the van would explode, killing her son and thereby saving the teams while they were at the opposite end of the pitch. If she said no, it meant that I would detonate when the players came back up to where her son was. She started to convulse.

'You've worked it out,' I said.

She reached for the door, desperate to run and warn young Liam.

'Stay where you are.'

Recognizing her car, young Liam waved over to her, smiling, proud that his mother was watching him play. It must have been hard for her but she gave a little wave, trying to appear normal for his sake, recalling the sight of the dead man lying face down, the back of his head blown in. There was something about the man, I could see it in her face that she was thinking about him. Which was the reason I had had to stop her getting out of the car back at St Martin's. Something familiar. His clothes, maybe. Running gear. She couldn't quite pin it down. He'd been too far away for her to get a good look. But there was something about him.

It was time to let her know what she had done.

I had two questions for her.

'You know that man you killed?' I said.

It came hard. 'Yes.'

'That's his son you're looking at.'

Chapter Two

⸻◦◦◦⸻

See me? I don't usually get into this sort of thing. I'll give you an idea what I mean, so you'll understand how I got into this position. (By the way, some of what I'm about to tell you came from Molly Murray herself.)

There was this guy called Tom Hassett. He was an ordinary working man who'd done well for himself in the building game. He lived in a big house, The Cedars it was called, in its own grounds with lamp-posts in the drive, eight miles south of Dublin. Money was no problem. He was worth five mil. In fact, the only problem Tom Hassett had was his wife, Bridie. He was worried sick about her. They were both getting on in years, nearing retirement, but still young enough to enjoy life, looking forward to a time of sitting back and taking it easy. But Tom's wife wasn't well. So he took her to see a doctor. And the doctor set up an appointment with a specialist.

They both knew before they went in what this specialist was gonna say: Tom had been reading up on it and he was convinced the news would be bad. But you know how it is; you live in hope.

The tremor in Bridie Hassett's hand was the first thing this specialist noticed. And the rigidity of her face muscles affecting her voice when she spoke was another.

Tom's sitting there holding her hand. The specialist's saying: 'Is the tremor in your hand more pronounced when you're sitting, Mrs Hassett?' Mrs Hassett's answering 'Yes,' and the specialist's taking notes and getting around to this and that, which all added up to one thing: drugs would help, but there was no cure. While all this is going on, Tom Hassett's thinking to himself he'll have to quit work and devote himself to looking after his wife. He can either sell his company or bring in someone he can trust to run it.

The only person he can trust is his son-in-law, Jimmy Byrne, who is in America for eight weeks on his honeymoon. In the meantime Tom Hassett had a company conceal a silent camera behind air-vents in every room in his house. They were connected to a monitor in his office. Now he can sit behind his desk doing paperwork, glancing every once in a while at this monitor so he can keep a watchful eye on his wife. If Bridie Hassett goes into the bedroom, he presses the remote and switches to the bedroom camera; if she goes into the kitchen, he switches to the kitchen camera, and so on. Anything untoward and he can rush home. It was a good system, state of the art eye-in-the-sky, complete with sound, but it wasn't what he wanted.

Hassett's one passion was the races and he went to them as often as he could, sometimes accompanied by his younger daughter Carol.

It was at the track that they met Jimmy Byrne. Byrne was then thirty, tall, dark-haired, with a long, rudder-shaped nose, broken in a kicking during his youth, and deep, gaunt brown eyes. Not what you might call handsome, but he had a certain charm, was well dressed, usually in a suit and tie, and Carol Hassett liked him. And when she began accompanying Tom to the track every chance she got, Tom knew Jimmy Byrne was the reason.

Jimmy Byrne always had a pile of money on him, was extremely lucky, once winning twelve thousand, so the prospect of him being after Carol's money didn't arise.

Tom was happy for them. And he was even happier when Jimmy Byrne proposed.

When Byrne came back from the States with his new bride, he called into the Hassett Property building, near the city centre opposite the Ha'penny Bridge, a pedestrian, silver-railed walkway arching the river Liffey, and was shown into Tom's office on the first floor.

The monitor was the first thing Byrne glanced at, and he commented: 'Office security?' as Tom sat him down and gave him one of the slim panatellas Byrne was fond of.

'Look again,' said Tom and Byrne looked and saw that the screen showed Tom's wife at home in the living room.

Byrne was puzzled.

'Bridie isn't well,' Tom explained. 'She's—' He paused, finding it hard to talk about, and Byrne sensed he was being taken into his father-in-law's confidence. 'She's in the early stages of Parkinson's.'

Byrne was sympathetic, saying how sorry he was and that he had no idea, he had noticed Mrs Hassett's hand tremor on occasions and had put it down to a trapped nerve.

'Neither do the girls,' said Tom. 'And I'd like it kept that way. For as long as possible, anyway. They dote on their mother, you know that.'

Byrne nodded.

'I wanted to install an office at home,' Tom went on. 'I even suggested bringing in a nurse, but Bridie wouldn't hear of it. Then I had a quiet word with her doctor and he explained how some of his other patients' relatives in the same position managed. So I had this installed. She doesn't know about it, of course. If she found out, she'd have a fit. My secretary, myself and now you are the only ones who know. You must be wondering why I'm telling you all this, Jimmy.'

'If there's anything I can do, Tom, I will. But I—'

'I know, Jimmy,' said Tom appreciatively. 'Parkinson's is hardly your field. There is something you can do, though. Help me so I can spend more time with Bridie.'

'How?'

'Sit in this chair. Run things for me.'

'Me? What do I know about the property game?'

'My secretary knows all there is to know. You'll pick it up in no time. You're smart.' Tom tapped his temple. 'Sharp. Besides, if you get stuck, come to me. On top of that, I'd drop in every Friday. Tell me you'll at least think it over.'

Byrne shrugged. 'OK. I'll have a word with Carol. See what she thinks.'

'Thanks, Jimmy.'

Ironically, this was the opening Byrne had been looking for.

Paddy Toner was one of a cartel involved, among other things, in smuggling cocaine over the Colombian border into Venezuela, then on to Trinidad where it was loaded onto fishing boats that rendezvoused at sea with the pleasure craft that brought it into Cork harbour, and from there to Dublin by a front company that delivered food to school canteens.

In white box vans.

Toner's expertise lay in laundering, or 'cleaning' as he liked to call it, the proceeds. One way was by bankrolling bookies, who then falsified their accounts to show winnings. Immediately a race was over, they'd enter the winner's name in the ledger, as if the bet had been placed before the race, then pay Jimmy Byrne his enormous winnings. It would look as if he'd placed the bet before the race on Toner's behalf. Byrne would then take Toner his 'winnings' back. In that sense, Byrne was a runner, an agent, call it what you like. The object of all this was that if some official ever asked Toner where he got his money from: 'I won it at the races, officer. Check with the bookie.' He could prove it hadn't come from drugs.

But there was a limit as to how lucky a 'gambler' could be. So Toner, who also owned snooker halls, nightclubs – or *Nite* clubs, as they're called nowadays – and taxis was always looking for new ways to *clean* his dirty money.

When Byrne took up his new position of manager, he used that state-of-the-art camera system, which was still connected to The Cedars, to spy on Tom to see where he kept the cash he collected each Friday from the office: Hassett went home, removed a large painting from his living-room wall and opened his safe, unaware that Byrne was at his desk, watching him on the monitor that was now attached to a VCR, recording Hassett rotating the dial. Byrne studied the tape, through some fancy image-enhancing gear he'd bought, until he eventually learned the combination. Later Byrne opened the safe and found Hassett's will.

Toner was a big man with red hair, red face and a big gut from all the beer he drank. He liked to laugh a lot. His whole body seemed to join in. He put his size twelves up on the desk, lit the panatella that Byrne had just handed him and then asked him what he was going to do with Hassett Property.

'Sell it. Sure, what would I want with a property business? Interested?'

'What's it consist of?'

'Flats, houses, land, plus a large piece of waste ground in the centre of town. Hassett rents it out for parking, so much an hour, a hundred and twenty spaces. Everything's in cash.'

'If it wasn't I wouldn't be interested.'

Byrne's face lit up. Toner was interested.

To the casual observer, other than the fact that Byrne worked for and wasn't anywhere near as well off as Toner, these two villains, who'd grown up in the same inner-city area of Dublin, might be seen as equals. That wasn't the case at all. Byrne was very much mixing it up with the top man here. If put in military terms: Byrne was a private, while Toner had five stars on his chest. That's not to say that Byrne didn't think he was Toner's equal, or getting on for it. He certainly didn't see himself as a private, or a fool, or a liability, though that was how Toner was now seeing him.

For in order to get his hands on Hassett Property so he could sell it to Toner, Byrne needed to be rid of Tom, and his wife and their elder daughter Annie, so Carol could inherit. Then he needed to get rid of Carol so *he* could inherit. And all without the law becoming suspicious. That required a certain kind of expertise. Which Toner could lay his hands on. Hence Byrne's visit. But Byrne being a minor player automatically meant that he could not be trusted with the knowledge that such a major player had been instrumental in the deaths of four people. If Byrne hadn't been so full of himself at the prospect of getting his hands on Tom Hassett's assets, he might have stopped to think about that. But he didn't.

Now for Toner, the attraction in acquiring Hassett Property lay in the carpark. He could pump in dope money to make the books show that it was always full whether there were really any cars in it or not. Clean money that way. Hit the taxman with a horde of accountants who'd already reinvested the increased profits the extra revenue creates. Increased profits would also make Hassett Property worth more if Toner ever came to sell it on: the new buyer would end up wondering why the takings had suddenly dropped, why the carpark was not full any more. He wouldn't know it was only ever full on paper. This added attraction, the attraction of conning some poor punter, amused Toner. He thought it was funny. A game.

But first he'd have to con this other poor punter, Jimmy Byrne, and to that end he would have to appear to be anything but a conman.

'So,' he said to Byrne, 'I'm not saying I'll buy it. I'd have to look at it first. But let's say I buy it. You reckon it's worth five mil. I'd pay you two for it on paper, and three in cash under the table. When I come to sell it, I'll get the three back cleaned.' Which all sounded normal enough, normal to these two anyway. And of course Byrne was rubbing his hands at the thought of having all that money. Toner was amused by the way he was overcome, telling him to 'Have an anaesthetic and calm your nerves, Jimmy. Pour me one too.'

Which Byrne did, on the tray by the window overlooking the sauna next to the indoor pool (you can see how well Toner was doing for himself), and they touched glasses, Byrne then sitting back, admiring the snooker table and the way the room was done out in oak panelling, coming out with stuff like, 'Think I'll buy me a big place like this. Might even buy the odd leg. Fuck it. Why stop at a leg? Can just see myself in the winner's enclosure cracking open a bottle of champers. No problem,' enjoying himself, acting as if getting his hands on Tom Hassett's money was a foregone conclusion, Toner humouring him – Byrne had moved on from buying racehorses to holidays in the Caribbean – Toner thinking how typical it was of small-time villains to get all excited at the thought of a great idea. Great ideas were one thing, pulling them off was something else.

Pulling this one off was going to require a lot of planning, so, to wrap up this meeting, Toner told Byrne he'd get back to him.

'How much would you want for getting rid of them?' Byrne asked.

'We'll come to that later, Jimmy.'

Byrne was happy with this. Whatever the cost, he'd still be a rich man, he believed. He finished his whiskey, gave a one-finger salute, passed two of Toner's minders in the hall, and was gone.

Toner then contacted me. Gerard Quinn. Though, as I said, people call me Gerd, for short.

Chapter Three

I was having a bit of trouble with the wife at the time. She was hitting me over the head with a brandy bottle. I know I said Molly Murray was a determined cow but Sinead's ten times worse. Runs in their family. I can never understand why people lose their tempers. I always find it's far better to be calm. Calculate the problem, then act. That's how I operate. I'm kipping away and the next thing I know Sinead's splitting my skull. I came to, shouting and flailing, y'know, coming out of a stupor, not knowing where I was, whether I was still in it or where to fuck, and this fucking Hennessy bottle's coming back for more.

'You bastard! You fucking bastard!' Sinead was shouting and I'm going 'Sinead, for fuck's sake, wha' the fuck's – oh, Jesus, Sinead—' WHACK! 'AGH GOD!'

Lucky I caught her wrist or God knows what might've happened. Coulda killed me. She'd lost all control, kicking and bucking and letting fly.

'Wha' the fuck! Sinead! Whattaya doin'?'

'That's it. That's it, you bastard. We're finished. I'm seeing a solicitor. You'll never see your kids again.'

And with that the brandy bottle fell out of her hand onto my head and she was flying downstairs. By the time I got to my feet and saw the blood pouring out of me, I was in no mood to go after her. It was all I could do to catch my breath and put clothes on me.

The phone rang. I let it. I had to get to the hospital. It rang again on my way out. It was Toner.

'Paddy, I can't talk now. I'll have to get back to you.'

'OK, Gerd. I might have a job on.'

'It'll have to wait.'

'No problem.'

I pulled out of the drive into the country lane that led to the main Dublin-to-Wicklow road and headed for the General.

Sinead knew. She had to. How the fuck did she find out? Some bastard had told her. Had to be. If I'd got my hands on him I'd have choked him. Her too, before I'd let her take my kids.

Me and Sinead'd been married eleven years. All right by me, married life suits me. No problems there. Sinead was all right-looking. Considering she'd had a couple of kids. Know what I mean? Took care of herself. Always with the face creams, the exercise machine, horseriding, a decent sort of a figure. Kept it well. No complaints from me on that score. But, well, you know how it is, I'd met this little redhead who worked the bar in Max's, one of Toner's niteclubs. Didn't think for a minute Sinead'd find out. She came on to me, the redhead, Louise. What's a man to do? Not as if I went out with the intention of pulling her. Just happened.

I pulled in at the front, where the ambulances wait, and rushed inside.

'Hello. 'Scuse me. Hello. I need a doctor.'

'Just a minute.'

'Just a minute? Look at the state of me. I'm bleeding to death.'

She looked down her nose.

I thumped the counter. 'Will you put that phone down and get me a doctor?'

She frowned as if she didn't give a shit.

'Hey.'

'What?'

'I need a doctor.'

She cocked her head toward a waiting area full of, I dunno, casualties, that's what you call people waiting in casualty – casualties? I was in a worse state than any of them. I was a priority.

A nurse came over, not bad-looking, saying 'Let me have a look.'

She didn't need to ask twice. 'Ah, thanks. Thank you. What kinda place is this? I walk in here pouring with blood and yer woman there's gabbling away down the phone. Chewing gum like nothing's untoward. Know what I mean? Talking to her bookie, probably. What does the word "emergency" mean around here, anyway?'

'We see an emergency, we treat it; we don't, we don't. Right now we don't. So calm down and take a seat.'

'Take a seat?'

'It's only a flesh wound. Nothing to worry about. Looks worse than it is.'

'You sure?'

'Sit down, you big baby.'

'It'll need stitches.'

'So, it'll need stitches.'

'You're very understanding. Great bedside.'

'How many fingers have I up?'

'Four.'

'What's your name and what day is it?'

'Gerd Quinn, Wednesday, why?'

'Follow my finger with your eyes.'

I did.

'No concussion.'

'You're sure?'

'Don't sound so disappointed.' She led me to a seat. 'We'll get to you as soon as we can. Would you like a cup of tea?'

'Wouldn't mind.'

'Café's down the corridor.'

'Shit!'

'What?'

'Nothin', nothin'.' Molly Murray was coming along the corridor. The last thing I needed was for her to see me and start asking a load of questions. She was two years older than Sinead. Big sister, know what I mean, looking out for little sister. If she'd found out what Sinead must have found out, more than likely she'd lay into me too. A guy in a sports coat came up behind her and they turned off toward the mortuary. I recognized him. Paul Rice. He arrested an acquaintance of mine once. Molly was obviously working on a story. She was gone now, anyway: that was the main thing. Attractive woman, Molly, know what I mean? Small, nothing heavy or loose about her, lean on the bone. Great hair. Little L-shaped nose. She was wearing the same black two-piece suit. Often thought about making a move on her, but a bit close to home. If Sinead caught me at *that*, it'd be more than a brandy bottle. Probably poison me. Definitely be an emergency *then*.

How the fuck did Sinead find out? Louise wouldn't have told her. Fuck it, get Toner to sack Louise, get her offside, deny all knowledge. When in doubt, lie your bollocks off.

'Cup of tea, please.'

'Sugar?'

'Nah. Just milk.'

I thought my luck was in as far as Molly was concerned, but it wasn't. A doctor had given me the once-over and repeated more or less what the nurse had said, and then a different nurse came into the curtained cubicle with a needle and thread and did the business, twelve stitches, then taped a square bandage over it. She opened the curtains to leave just as Molly was walking by. Recognized me right away.

'Gerd? Gerd? Is that you?'

Shit! Things weren't working out for me at all. 'Moll. How's it going?'

She came in, looking all concerned. 'What happened?'

'Ah . . . I . . . a . . . fell. Down the stairs. Had a few too many.' Couldn't let her know the truth.

She shook her head, fussing over me, in loco sisterentis, 'You all right?'

'Ah, yeah. I've had worse hangovers.'

'You're sure?'

Aye. Dead on. Course I'm sure. What else was I gonna say but lies along those lines? 'Just an accident, Moll, nothing to worry about.'

'Sinead with you?'

'Nah, she's in the house. I told her it was nothing to worry about. You know me. What're you doing here?'

'Working. A boy was killed earlier on. Car crash.'

'Since when does a crime reporter cover car accidents?'

'He's the son of a junkie I know, a contact. Man called Sean Connors. You wouldn't know him. He was blitzed out of his mind and hit a tree. His son went through the windscreen.'

Molly didn't know a thing about what I got up to, the

people I knew. She knew I knew Toner. But everybody knew Toner. So there was nothing in that. But the word 'contact' hit me. And I knew who Sean Connors was. He worked for Toner the odd time. For 'contact', see *snitch*. Connors must have been passing on info to Molly, probably for no more than the price of a fix. And now he'd killed his son. Accidentally maybe, but he would have been driving straighter if he hadn't been blitzed out of his mind.

I brought Connors's name up when I saw Toner later that night after I'd got myself fixed up with a shower and a change of clothes. Fuck knows where Sinead had got to with the kids. But I'd find her.

Because of the 'way' I knew Toner, we always met out of the way of prying eyes when he had something important to discuss. A job. We met in a barn on a piece of land he owned twenty miles south of Dublin, out in the country. He came alone. He always came alone when it was to do with me. Other than that, Toner never went anywhere without a couple of heavies. He drove straight in, got out of his blue Merc, closed the barn doors and came into the tack room where I was waiting.

'Gerd.'

'Paddy. How's the crack?'

'What happened to your head?'

'Tripped.'

Toner and me were good mates. If I had a problem, he had a problem and vice versa. It had been that way for over twenty years since I'd left Belfast and come to live in Dublin. Toner wasn't in the big league then. Part of the reason he was in it now was down to me. He knew and respected me for that. Like I say, we go way back, which I'll tell you about later.

Another thing about me and Toner was that if I asked him a question, he didn't hesitate to give me a truthful answer. He knew I wouldn't be asking without a reason. So I asked him if Molly Murray had been reporting lately on anything linked to him.

'Yeah,' he said directly. 'I bought a security outfit's invoice book there a while back. They fit safes. Got the combinations. Everything. Told a coupla lads to go round to every address in the bastard and clean them out and that sister-in-law of yours was waiting with the Gardaí. Why?'

'Sean Connors know anything about it?'

'Has Connors been talking?'

'He's one of Molly's contacts.'

Toner nodded, contemplatively, appreciatively. 'Good man, Gerd.'

'No problem. Now, what's the story?'

Toner leaned against the saddle horse and told me all about his meeting with Jimmy Byrne.

Chapter Four

———⊰⊱———

'What's this guy Byrne like, Paddy?'

'D'you not know him?'

'Seen him around just.'

'He's a user.'

'Junkie?'

'No. Uses people. If he was on a tandem with his granny he'd sit on the back and let her do all the pushing.'

'He wants you to do all the pushing on this one, by the sound of it.'

See me? I'm my own worst enemy. Sure's God I am. Me and Toner'd done so much stuff together over the years, all of which I'd worked out, and got away with it, that we'd now reached the stage where anything seemed possible.

Y'know how it is when you're starting out in life, whatever your chosen profession is, you begin with a feeling deep down in your gut that maybe you're not up to it. You've no confidence in yourself. It might be something minor. Then you pull it off, then you think to yourself, well, that wasn't so hard, what was I worried about? So you take on a bigger job, again with a knot in your stomach that you can't pull it off. But you do. And your confidence gets a boost. Pretty soon you're taking on jobs that are way up in the clouds and you're pulling them off. So you start to think you can do anything. Well, that's not the way I was thinking right at this minute. Because the job Toner was proposing wasn't way up in the clouds. It was way farther up than that. But Toner wasn't looking at it like that. Course, he didn't have to work it out. His trouble was he'd gained so much confidence in me over the years, he thought I could work out anything.

'There's something not right about this, Paddy,' I said, handing him a smoke.

'Why's Byrne doing it, you mean?'

'He's married into money. His mother-in-law's on the way out. He already runs the company. He could milk it till Hassett pops off, then bleed his wife when she inherits her half. It'd probably be worth five mil by then. Why risk losing what'll come to him eventually anyway?'

'He won't wait, Gerd. It's that simple. When he twigged that Carol Hassett liked him, he took one look at what he could get out of it. Saw a result. Marrying her was just the first step towards setting her up. Living with her for any length of time never came into it.'

Strange the way some people carry on. Byrne didn't interest me in himself. Why people do things interests me. From what Toner went on to say, and from what I learned later, Byrne's background was much the same as a lot of kids I'd grown up with. The son of a wife-beater who'd rarely worked and who thought *he* was providing for his family by bringing in a dole cheque every week. Tell him the State was keeping them and you'd take a buckle in your eye. Layabout mentality. Worse – pig-ignorant opinionated drivel.

You hear it all the time in bars from guys who'd made fuck all of themselves, yet are full of advice on what's right and wrong and the best way to make something of yourself. They never stop to think, well, who am I to give advice? What the fuck have I ever achieved? When things keep going wrong because they don't make them go right, they blame their family.

As a boy, Byrne had regularly felt his old man's fist. He'd sat down to eat his dinner, seen Pop coming in in a bad mood, felt the nerves in his throat jump, froze shit-scared of him, couldn't eat a bite, feared for his mother, dreaded the unintentional tone in her voice that would lead to her getting a beating for daring to ask: 'Have you got my housekeeping, dear?' because the bastard had lost it on a horse. Most kids see the hypocrisy of it. Some hone it and perpetuate it to new heights. Byrne was obviously the latter.

So Pop was a cancer in the family. Good reason to want *him* bumped off. In other words, there was nothing in Byrne's upbringing to explain why he was bad. I don't believe people are created by their past. Not to the degree we're talking about here. All this 'he came from a battered home' stuff was invented by solicitors to get their clients off. I've been in this game long enough to know what makes a person bad – himself. The rest of it's all psychological swill.

Byrne had no centre of gravity. He'd pivot whichever way suited him, always for the short-term advantage. Because, for him, there was no long term. A gut-instinct merchant. No class. Show him an iron-clad investment and he'd opt for the poker school. Fuck tomorrow. 'GIMME THE GOODS NOW!' That was Byrne.

Which is all right by me. But I like intellect with it. Byrne didn't impress. He was shallow. Wanted someone else to do it for him. With him it was pure greed.

Me, I do things solely for business reasons. That's the difference between me and people like Byrne.

'Now, Paddy,' I said. 'The way I see it, we're talking about creating "accidents" here. Hassett, his wife, his daughter Annie, all in the one night. Stretching it a bit. Know what I mean? Then there's Carol. She inherits, then it's her turn. Another "accident"? I don't think so. That'd be stretching it way too far.'

'Where'd ya trip?'

'What?'

'Who'd ya trip over?'

'Whattaya mean, who'd I trip over? Nobody.'

Toner was no fool, standing there with that smirk on his face. He knew I was bullshitting. 'Don't tell me if you don't want to.'

'Tell you what?'

'Louise was asking about you. In front of Noreen Bawn.'

Shit! Noreen Bawn was Sinead's best friend. 'You're kidding. The fucking cow! Bawn heard Louise asking about me? How was she asking about me?'

'How do ya think?'

'So *that's* who Sinead got it from.'

Toner thought this was funny. 'Tell me something, Gerd – how can somebody who's so smart when it comes to work be so dumb when it comes to his dick?'

'Bawn hates my guts.'

'She fancies you.'

'Does she, fuck!'

'The wife told me.'

The wife told me. Jesus. See Toner, for such a hard case, he's a real gossip. He loves stirring it up. There's nothing macho about him. He'd cut your balls off for beer money, not because he likes people to think he's a tough guy, that's just the way he is. He can just as easily act the old woman. Especially when it comes to me. The wife told me, indeed.

'Why would Bawn wanna split me and Sinead up?'

'So you'd be available. Why else?'

'Will you stop laughing? This is serious. You're talking a load of crap.'

So Noreen Bawn fancies me, eh? Monster. She can fancy me all she likes for all the good it'll do her. Maybe I could use it against her by making Sinead believe Bawn had told her a pack of lies about me and Louise to get Sinead out of the way, so Bawn could get in with me and have her wicked way. Hmm? Possibilities. It's terribly annoying, though, when somebody who's a monster fancies you.

'Getting back to Hassett. From what you say, his wife's his weak spot. Threaten her and he'll come running. Annie's the problem. Hassett and his wife having an accident in their own house is one thing. Making the daughter have an accident the same night in hers five miles away's something else. And another thing. Annie's husband. If she dies, maybe her slice of her father's will goes to him. Hassett could have inserted a clause to that effect.'

'If Annie dies, her cut goes to Byrne's wife along with the rest, according to Byrne. He read the will. What did she hit you with?'

'What? Oh, a brandy bottle.'

'Stitches?'

'Twelve.'

'Ooouugh!'

'You think this's funny, don't you?'

Toner was trying to keep a straight face. 'Me? What give you that idea?'

31

'Well, it's not. She took my kids.'

'Get her arrested for assault. Say she's not a fit mother. Get them back.' Toner was winding me up. He liked Sinead.

'Paddy, for fuck's sake, we're supposed to be talking business here. It's not funny.'

'I know, I know,' he roared. 'A brandy bottle. Fuck me. The scrapes you get yourself into.'

I dunno what it was with Toner. Maybe because we were so close, he thought he could take liberties. 'You wait till Rosie finds out some of the shit you've been into, too. That little foreign bird you were corking. The one who asked you why they call it a blow job when you don't blow, you suck. Know what I mean? Now quit the fuckin' about. I could lose my kids here.'

'They're staying at Bawn's. Couple of days of that and Sinead'll be begging you to take her back.'

'They're staying at Bawn's? God knows what kinda crap Bawn'll be feeding her about me. Look, I'm in no mood to think straight. This job, know what I mean? Full of holes. Bit of a wobbler.'

'Not for a man of your capabilities.'

'I don't like it, Paddy. Byrne's skint. The pay-off doesn't come till we get rid of his wife and he inherits. If she doesn't croak it in a way that stands up, the law'll come sniffing, and we'll get fuck all for knocking off his in-laws. Bad odds.'

'Have a look at it. That's all I'm asking. An easy five, that's how I see it.'

'Yeah, well. And another thing, is Byrne the type who can keep a poker face while all this's going on? He takes a beamer, gets nervous, all it takes is for one sharp cop to twig and start digging. Then there's that fucking sister-in-law of mine.'

'She doesn't cover accidents.'

'Nah, but she'll turn up for a look. It takes time to figure out if it's an accident and she might figure out that it wasn't. God knows what she'd latch on to. Smart little fucker, Molly.'

I hemmed and hawed. The truth was I didn't wanna be bothered. I'd enough on my mind. But Paddy, being Paddy, kept on and on. Eventually I had him tell me all he knew about Hassett, Hassett Property, asked him could Byrne get keys to Hassett's house, his office, safe combination, a profile of his wife Carol, how she would plausibly react to her parents' and sister's deaths, was it feasible that she could be made to feel guilty for their deaths, so that when she too died, suicide would stand up in an inquest.

'Get Byrne to go through it all again, Paddy. In greater detail. And get it on tape. And keep an eye on Sean Connors. He might have to have a fucking accident as well.'

'No problem.'

'I'll get back to you.'

Chapter Five

Course, I knew what was really behind this. Which was OK. Because if it was good for Toner, it was good for me. But the fact of the matter was the dope business in Ireland was getting to be a little uncomfortable. Toner wasn't what you'd call gradually making an exit, but he was diversifying. Special powers brought in by the Minister for Justice allowed the Garda Siochana to do pretty much what they liked. If they suspected you of dealing in drugs, they could go straight into your finances. 'Where did you get all this money from?' If you didn't have a good answer, your accounts were frozen. Hiding it away in the Cayman Islands wasn't on, either. The Guards were on to everything. They had squads of sharp-witted accountants combing the world's banks. Big names had already fallen and court cases were either pending or well under way.

It had come down to: you're guilty until proven innocent just because you have a few quid in the bank you can't account for. If the law catches you fair and square, then you deserve the consequences. That's the system. But if they catch you by putting the onus on you to prove you're innocent, rather than them proving you're guilty, where's the justice in that? They failed to catch you in the first place and now they're digging into your private affairs, getting banks to squeal, then dragging you into court, taking away your house and assets you've acquired for your family's future. Changing the rules to suit themselves, so they are.

I think it's disgraceful.

Course, even with their underhandedness, Toner was way out in front of them. He had an edge that others didn't have.

Way back in the seventies he'd started buying into legitimate businesses – if you can call it buying – clubs, bookies' shops, stuff like that. So he had something of an answer. 'Where does my money come from? Business. Here, talk to my accountant, officer.' Course, the law knew he'd been inflating profits with dope money but they couldn't prove it. Getting hold of a respectable business like Hassett Property, which he could, on the face of it anyway, buy with money from these businesses, would look legit. It would add credibility to his portfolio, if I can put it that way. That's why he wanted it. Also, it wouldn't cost him the asking price. He'd pay the five mil over, all right, but then we'd steal it back. That's where I came in. We'd split it, naturally, after expenses.

Funnily enough, stealing it was the easy part.

Now, I'm going to tell you a few boring details here. They might come in handy if you ever get into the killing game. In Ireland, that is. I only know about Ireland. The main thing to remember is: know your enemy. The law. A point most half-wits in jail ignored. If the guy you wanna kill is, say, involved in crime, then taking a gun is probably appropriate. It's in keeping with the guy's lifestyle: he mixed with villains, it's not unnatural that he should die at their hands. Chances are the Guards'll be glad somebody shot him. Gets him off the streets. Less trouble for them. Oh, they'd investigate. But their hearts wouldn't be in it. They've better things to investigate.

However, if your target is respectable, a pillar, a decent taxpayer, whose will has to be executed without the law snooping, the last thing you want is a gun. Shooting him would not be in keeping with his lifestyle because he didn't mix with people who shoot people. He has to die in keeping with his lifestyle. No guns. You can give the *impression* you're gonna use them. But that's all.

Another obvious thing is finances. On average it costs half a million to bring a murder case to trial in Ireland. All police forces are overstretched and Ireland is no exception. If a cop sees a clear case of murder, he'll go all the way. If he sees a lot of grey areas, he'll prioritize, run with the cases where the potential for a conviction is greater.

The law in Ireland is so far advanced that they didn't even have a witness-protection programme in place until 1997. They also have only one state pathologist. For the whole twenty-six counties. And that is their biggest weakness.

The guy you have to convince is the state pathologist. If he says my autopsy shows these three people died accidentally, and the scene is clean, who are the cops to argue?

The fact that there's only one SP makes my job a lot easier, I can tell you. The newspapers make my job a lot easier, too. In 1997 they reported that of the previous year's four thousand standard post-mortems, dealing with suicides, road-traffic victims, sudden and unexpected deaths, the SP had time to deal with only eighty. The SP himself was reported as saying that his backlog was so great that a number of murder cases would collapse if he were to die. The papers are effectively telling criminals that if they want to have the cases against them dropped, all they have to do is bump off the SP. If they put as much cash into helping him as they put into chasing illegally held money, my job would be a lot harder.

So the sobering thought is this: if the Hassetts came to look like accidents, the SP won't even look at them. Game, set and match. Brilliant!

Then again, the stupidest of things'll get you caught. A guy carries out the perfect murder, then spits. The cops run a DNA on the spit and the guy's in handcuffs. For spitting. He overlooked a simple detail. So you can never say for sure that you will get away with it.

And of course I've got an even better angle. I won't be at the scene *to* spit. I won't be anywhere near it. My job is to set it up. That's how I operate. Toner won't be anywhere near it. We're managerial. Know what I mean? He comes to me, like I'm some sort of Perry Mason in reverse. Only instead of investigating a crime *after* it happens, I investigate it *before* it happens and iron out the wrinkles by drawing on the same expertise as the police. The methods they use to detect crime, I use to cover it up.

And somebody else carries it out. Who is that somebody? I know who he is. But he doesn't know me. He thinks Toner works everything out. He thinks Toner's the brains. He carries it out the way Toner tells him to carry it out. If he gets caught – and he hasn't been yet – I arrange to have him taken out. Like Molly said in her story, the police don't even know I exist. That's why Toner never brings his heavies when he comes to see me on business. A point that I insisted on.

As you get to know me more, you'll come to realize that I'm a stickler for security. I'm so sensitive about getting caught that I go way out of my way to make sure I am not compromised. As far as my views of policing are concerned, agree with them or not, they have kept me a free man. My fingerprints have never been taken; I've never been questioned. So even if the law come to look at the Hassetts as murder victims instead of accident victims, as I intend them to look at them, the law won't come to my door. Even if things were to go wrong, what have I lost? Time. That's all. The time it took to set it up. Nothing more. Disappointing, I know. But that's business.

And that's the beauty of this set-up. All I lose is *my* time. Not prison time.

So how do you get the law-abiding SP to say 'These three people died accidentally'? I'll come to that later.

Oh, there's one more thing I forgot to mention: surveillance. And I don't mean *by* the law, I mean *of* the law. If you've got the back-up, keep an eye on the bastards at all times while you're at work. They keep tabs on suspects. Do the same to them. Know who they're talking to. Know where it leads them. Know the pattern they're following. Stay ahead that way. Villains pull jobs, then sit around like idiots hoping they won't get caught. If they put the same amount of time into staying at liberty as they do into planning their *whatever*, they would not only be more successful, they'd also stretch the law beyond breaking point. Which would make it better for everybody.

When I pull a caper with Toner, the cops are then watched. If that sister-in-law of mine comes on the scene, she's watched. Toner keeps men on it day and night. That's why he owns the shout in the Arrow Investigation Agency. Expensive? A couple of per cent off the profits, that's all. Business expenses. Don't be greedy. Crime is business. Treat it any other way and it's lock-up time.

Right now it was time to do what I'd told Toner I'd do: take a look at the Hassetts. See what the obstacles are. It would keep my mind off Sinead. She and Bawn and the kids had gone away for a few days, according to Bawn's neighbour. I could go after Sinead. But that might make things worse. Best to let her cool down. Realize what a good catch I am. How it'll affect the kids if we split up. Stuff that'll play on her conscience. It'd be selfish of her to deprive the kids of a strong father figure. She'll make the right decision. She always has before. Course, if she doesn't, I'd have to re-appraise her position. She's not getting my kids under any circumstances. A court can't give custody to a corpse.

Anyway, I stuck on my Marty Robbins tape. I like a bit of Country and Western. Especially the cowboy songs. Then headed out to have a look at obstacle number one: Christy McDermott. He's married to Hassett's daughter Annie. I couldn't have him around when the time came to deal with her. So a way had to be found to get him offside.

I pulled into his garage and he came over and undid the fuel cap.

'Grand day.'

''Tis. Fill her up.'

'No problem.'

Christy McDermott was in his late twenties: oil-stained navy overalls, short dark hair, had the look of a rugby player about him, chewed his nails, liked fishing. He kept a nice tidy garage, forecourt, repair shop, men working for him, a free-standing sign saying 'Petrol pump attendant wanted NOW!', row of clean used cars for sale, CHRISTY MCDER-MOTT in red above the big doors, on a country road just outside the village of Ballinraa.

According to what Byrne told Toner, Tom Hassett used to own this place. Was gonna develop it. When McDermott cornered the fair Annie, Hassett learned that McDermott had always wanted to own his own garage. Hassett put it to him that if he made a go of this one, it was his. Hassett kept his word. Seemed a decent sort, Hassett. Looked after his own.

'That'll be twenty-two quid.'

'Thanks. That's a nice breakdown truck you have there.'

'Not bad,' he replied proudly.

'I see you do twenty-four-hour. I used to be at that game.' I was lying, of course. I wanted to know how much time he devoted to it personally. 'Hard going,' I continued. 'No sooner get your head down and the phone rings.'

'You get used to it. Besides, the lads help me out. Turns apiece. I take Saturdays and Sundays, they do weeknights.'

Saturday and Sunday nights with him out on call meant his wife would be at home alone. That narrowed it down a bit. Helpful sort of a lad. Course, there was always his hobby. 'Any fishing-tackle shops around here?' I asked him.

'There's one in the village. I do a bit myself.'

'Fly?'

'Fly, deep-water. I've a rowboat on Lough Annel. I live just across the road from it.'

'Finding the time's the hard part, though.'

'I know what you mean. Still, I can usually manage the odd night during the week.'

The great thing about fishing is a guy'll leave his wife alone for hours. Of the two, I favoured the breakdown. I couldn't predict what night he'd go fishing, but I could predict what night he could be called out.

A mechanic popped his head out and told him his wife was on the phone.

He looked at his watch and grimaced. 'Christ, I've to take her to the clinic,' he said. 'Forgot about that.'

'Doesn't do to keep them waiting.'

'Tell me about it. See ya.' He ran inside. Cheerful sort of guy, Christy McDermott. You could see it in him. Happy with his lot.

'Clinic' interested me. Maybe his wife was pregnant. Sick, maybe. In this business you're always looking for a person's weak spots. Someone on tablets with side effects – drowsiness, for instance – can be very handy. Nothing more natural than somebody getting up in the middle of the night giddy and falling down the stairs. If there's no sign of a break-in, nothing taken, no signs of a scuffle, nothing incriminating left at the scene, who's to say they were shoved?

Chapter Six

The Long Ranger. That's what the makers call this long-range listening device. It's a camcorder as well. Handy for listening in on conversations.

According to Byrne, these two met in one of Toner's niteclubs. Like the rest of us, they probably hit it off and things progressed from there. McDermott – Christy McDermott, that is – started off his working life straight after leaving school at sixteen in a two-man car-repair shop, while Annie, helped financially by her father, went through college then opened up a hairdressing salon near the city centre.

Smart woman, Annie, by all accounts. I like smart women, know what I mean? I don't just mean smart-looking. In the looks department I like 'em on the light side. No big tubs. No big tits, either. Not mad about big tits. And how some men can cuddle up to those women you see hanging out of magazine covers with hot-air balloons growing out of them is beyond me. Throwing the leg over the like of them must be like trying to fuck a steering column with the airbag out.

No, I mean I like women who can think. They don't have to be scholarly like me, but they do have to have their upstairs light switched on. My mother was like that.

Switched on, I mean. And I've time for men who credit women with more cop-on than men.

Look around the world. Look at the mess it's in. All run by men. Look at crime: all men. High finance: all men. Look at the dictators, torturers, terrorist leaders, religions, leaders: all men. Men are a disaster. God fucked up when He created Man first. I'd say He's probably realized that by now. That's why He's staying away. Probably fed up with this place. Off creating Creation somewhere else, now that He's ironed out the wrinkles, if He's any sense. Giving women the shout. I wouldn't be surprised if a load of women landed on earth one day with crucifixes round their necks. Where would men be then? We'd have twice as many women to play with, for a start. How's that for a divine plan? Wonder what homos would have to say about it? Mind you, I've nothing against homos. They don't fuck with me, I don't fuck with them. Not that I would, anyway. You know me: women are my game.

I remember when I was a kid. I'm going back now to the early sixties. I was coming out of a Latin class one night – when I say Latin I mean Church Latin. I used to be on the altar. Mass was in Latin then. Learning Church Latin isn't the same as learning Latin itself now. You don't end up being able to speak another language. All you do is learn how to repeat the prayers, how to suck up to God, using a sequence of words you don't understand. In effect you're a parrot. That's all. You parrot what the priest says. Waste of time.

Anyway, I was coming out of Clonard Monastery and Protestants were marching down from the Shankill Road onto the Falls Road. They started a riot to get an Irish tricolour taken out of a shop window. Once they got it out, they marched back home.

Did the men of the Falls go after them to get their own back for starting a riot? That I could have understood. But no. They started burning their own road. For a week. Buses, shops, everything went up. All done by men. Women were robbed of transport, provisions, launderettes, by their husbands and brothers and fathers. That's what it amounted to. Where was the sense in that? That was my first lesson in the inadequacies of the male of the species. But what puzzled me was that I seemed to be the only lad who saw it like that. All my mates thought it was great.

So, as I was saying, I'm sitting at the wheel with this Long Ranger aimed at the McDermotts who are coming out of the clinic, laughing and joking, walking hand in hand across the carpark. It turns out there's nothing wrong with her, after all. She's not on medication. Well, I mean, she doesn't look as though she's on anything. No giddiness. Walks with a happy spring in her step. Pity. Still, that's the way it goes.

She's about five-four, light build – more meat on a spare rib – looks as if she'd be easy to hold down, or throw down, if you're wondering why I'm weighing her up – nice red hair. Wouldn't mind having a go at her myself. Christy's helping her up into the passenger seat of that breakdown truck of his. The all-attentive husband. She enjoys being pampered, if that big smile's anything to go by. Like all women. Especially when they're carrying. She's not showing that much, though.

Course, there's an addition here: Hassett, his wife, and Annie here make three. And junior makes four. Byrne didn't mention that. Still, doesn't matter. Not as if there's any more work involved. Annie goes, junior goes with her. No extra planning needed.

I'm hoping they have a little talk before they drive off.

Might find out something I can use. If I'm reading Christy right, he's a man's man. A man's man, by and large, stays in the waiting room – that's it, Christy, get behind the wheel, wind down the window, have a wee talk, tell me what the gynaecologist said – stayed in the waiting room while she went in, I mean. He's chuckling. Something's going on between them. Yes, yes, he didn't go in with her. He wants to know what the gynaecologist said.

'Nothing,' Annie's saying, giggling against the back of her hand. She's teasing him. 'He just asked me if I wanted to know whether it was a boy or girl. That's all. Nothing important.'

'Come on, Annie – boy or girl?'

'Well, he kept referring to junior as *he*. So I said "Why do you keep calling him *he*?" Then he realized he'd let it slip.'

'A boy? You're kidding?'

'Nope.'

Christy's rubbing his hands. He'd been hoping for a boy by the look of him – for MCDERMOTT & SON above the garage door, I suppose. 'Brilliant!' He's leaning across and kissing her. 'Come on.'

'Where are we going?'

'To tell the folks.'.

Well, that was a disappointment. I was hoping something was wrong. Complications. Weak spots. Still, while they're telling the folks, I can have a look at their place.

Nice wee lough, Lough Annel. Very picturesque. Ireland and Switzerland have a lot in common, y'know, the way their lakes are set out.

Just my luck: the McDermotts live in a bungalow, on raised ground above the narrow country road. So much for my 'shoving her down the stairs' theory. Still, there's a staircase in The Cedars. Maybe I can use that one. As long as it's not a winding one. Winding ones are no good. You need a clear roll down to cause the desired effect. I have a theory on death by falling down the stairs. There's a man I need to talk to about that to see what he thinks. He's a forensic pathologist.

Hmm, that's interesting. There's a slipway opposite that leads down to the lake. It forms a fork with the road. A man driving alone in the dead of night could easily mistake that, veer off, find himself in the drink before he knows it. It's wide enough for a car. I'd say this place has a history of accidents. A black spot. That might work in my favour.

There's McDermott's rowing boat, twenty feet out in the water, moored via a line tied to an iron ring in a concrete block on the shore. The boat could be a problem. On a windy night it might get blown over far enough to block the bottom of the slipway and prevent a car going in, or hamper it going in, know what I mean? You have to think of these things.

Farming country, this. Must be a mile or more between houses. The nearest place is far enough away in either direction to rule out a neighbour seeing anything in detail from a distance. And if it's done at night, well, they're all gonna be in their kip.

The McDermotts keep their garden nice, front and back. Nice clean gravel drive, a flagstone pathway around the house, a high hedge flanking either side of the front lawn. Right pair of home-birds. The place is spotless. I'd say she's house-proud. Hate that in a woman.

Now, with Christy out answering a breakdown call and Annie sitting in the wing chair by the front window, she would be able to see the slipway. The hedge isn't in the way.

She'd see a car approaching with its headlights on and skidding into the lake dead easy. She wouldn't have to go out of her way to see it, either. That's important. Everything has to look natural.

There's a photo on the TV of the McDermotts arm-in-arm with Jimmy and Carol Byrne. Wonder what they'd say if they knew what he was up to?

Better check this layout Byrne gave Toner's accurate. Yes, he's got it right: the hall inside the front door, the phone table on the right next to the living-room door, the kitchen to the left, the main bedroom at the back.

Readers, these two, if those stuffed bookcases are anything to go by. Fishing magazine on the coffee table, *Mothercare* magazine. Colour charts. Doing up the spare room for the baby, I'd say. Hmm, yeah, this place has possibilities. Annie sitting reading, sees her dad's car going off the road, runs down to investigate, comes a cropper. Hmm. Course, I'd have to make sure Maguire leaves that magazine of hers open for the police to see, so they can form their opinion that she was sitting reading when it happened. That would tie in with looking natural. I'm a stickler for everything looking natural. If everything looks normal, you're halfway there. Tell you what I mean by that. I could just as easily have decided to have her reading a book the night it happens. But how do I know what she reads? Might end up leaving out one of her husband's books. Run the risk of the cops finding out and asking why was she reading a book her husband liked, not her. A small detail, I know. But like I said: ignore the small details and you increase the chances of things going wrong.

(Maguire – did I mention him before? Can't remember. Anyway, he'll be doing this. Executing it, them – it, them, what's the difference? He does all our work at this level.)

Now let's get a look at this bungalow from the other side of the lake. It's got an island in the middle.

Actually, this lake's bigger than I thought, now that I'm driving around it. A windy old road round it too. A real beauty spot. I'd say holidaymakers pitch tents in the firs and fields bordering this part of it in the good weather. But what could they see from this location? That's what interests me. Not the slipway, certainly. Especially not at four in the morning. Know what I mean? They'd all be under canvas.

Yeah, this place has possibilities all right.

Right. Time to go and have a look at the Hassetts.

Chapter Seven

And what better way than through that monitor.

This is not a bad office. You can tell Byrne's been in it, though – stinks of cigars. Now, put my feet up on the desk, and on goes the monitor.

This'll be the first time I've seen Tom Hassett, you understand. I need to get a look at him and his wife. Weigh them up. Maguire – the guy I referred to earlier who'll be carrying this out – he'll wanna know. Course, it depends on the procedure I finally decide to run with. For instance, if I decide, after talking to people who know about these things, that one of the Hassetts should die from a fall, then, as I say, their body weight'll be a factor: if Tom is twenty stone, then it's unlikely Maguire would be able to carry him back up the stairs to throw him down again, in the event of the first go not doing the trick. Which raises the question: would Forensic know that he'd been thrown down twice?

Switching from Tom's study to the upstairs camera: the Hassetts' bedroom. Actually, this is pretty good equipment. Wide-angle lens. Sharp. I was hoping it wasn't the peephole type where everything looks as though you're viewing it through a magnifying glass. In colour, too. Just an ordinary bedroom, done out in pink, no veranda to get in through.

Switching to bedroom two: the Byrnes'. Crisply made bed, lots of women's creams on the dressing table, soft toys everywhere. Bedroom three, four, five. Nothing special. Made-up spares. Second bathroom above the hall. Let's take a look at the stairs and landing.

Thank God. A straight staircase. I was hoping for that. Bedroom doors on the square landing. Carpeted through-out. That's a pity. Stone stairs are far better for throwing people down. Still, can't have everything.

Switching to the downstairs camera. This is nice. Actually, these people have good taste. Nothing too fancy. Homely, y'know? Telephone bureau, chess set on a mahogany tripod table, game in progress. A penny on the black side to show that it's up to the black to move next. This is one of those houses where a game can go on for a while, I'd say – days, months maybe. Navy bergere chairs, one either side of the tripod. Red velvet chair at the foot of the stairs. A Victorian rosewood spoonback, if I'm not mistaken. There's no an-tiques upstairs or in Tom's study – I'm switching to the living room now – no, none in the living room, either. I'd say they keep the few antiques for sentimental reasons; probably handed down.

There's that big picture above the fireplace Toner was telling me about – the one covering the safe? – of Tom and Bridie when they were younger, mid-thirties, maybe. Taken in a studio, she's sitting, he's standing, against a dusky-pink velour backdrop. All smiles.

Byrne's on the settee, smoking and reading the paper, Christy McDermott in the armchair watching TV, Tom's at the drinks tray – well, it's him if that picture's anything to go by – decanting a bottle of red wine. There's six of everything, by the look of it: brandy glasses, champagne flutes, goblets.

He's opening another bottle of wine, letting it breathe. They must be getting ready to have dinner. Now he's setting out wine glasses on a silver tray. Some sort of occasion, is it? I wonder. Or do they always have a few bottles with their meal? Maybe they're celebrating the news that it's a boy.

Mid-sixties, thinning grey hair, slightly bent – I'd say Tom's got a bad back, the way he's standing – five-ten, eleven stone. Maguire should be able to manage him easily enough.

Tom's carrying the tray out now. Switch to the dining room. Yeah, I was right, he's gone in the dining room. Table's laid for six. You'd get ten around it, though.

Oops! Byrne's wife just came in from the kitchen and banged the door into the tray.

She looks mortified. 'I'm sorry, Daddy.' Apparently Byrne's wife gets all upset at the slightest thing.

Tom looks as if he could choke her, but he's holding his temper. 'It's all right, Carol.'

Plain-looking, this one. Lean and wiry, with straight fair hair, pale skin, shallot-shaped nose, small tits.

Bridie's noticing the broken glass on the floor. She's looking at her husband as if she feels disappointed for him.

'Oh, your mother's glasses,' she's lamenting.

Carol's coming in again with the 'I'm sorry, Daddy.'

Yeah, she's a bundle of nerves, all right, that one. I'd say she's the one the bullies always picked on in school. I wouldn't be surprised if she's accident-prone. Must get Toner to confirm it with Byrne. Accident-prone comes in handy when you're planning accidents. Makes it more believable. I was thinking of suicide for her. Maybe an accident would be better.

Tell you why I'm watching this. I'm interested in finding

out how they get on with one another. Particularly Annie and Carol with their parents. Byrne told Toner a lot about how his wife would react to losing her father, her mother and her sister. In one go, I mean. But Byrne is subjective. Only natural. He's gonna say anything to get the job done. What I need is an objective assessment. That's the beauty of this camera set-up. I can see for myself first-hand.

For example, if I stay with the suicide plan, it has to be convincing. The authorities have to believe Carol fell to pieces because she blamed herself for their deaths. (Sorry, did I mention that Carol has to blame herself for all this? Can't remember. Well, she has.) Then tops herself. If Byrne's right, it'll work. But there's such a thing as Carol blaming herself, then consoling herself with Daddy's millions and going on a spree. Always a possibility. Suicide wouldn't work then. If the cops see her enjoying herself, they'd start wondering if her parents and sister died accidentally or was Carol involved so she could get their loot. She wouldn't top herself if that was the case. And since the object here is to get the cops out of the picture, that would mess things up.

They've settled down to dinner. The mood has changed now, they're all yabbering away as if nothing's happened. Carol's a picker. The rest are getting tucked in and she's nibbling like a sparrow.

Tom's at the head of the table, Carol and Byrne to his right, Christy and Annie to his left, Bridie at the opposite end. Looks a nice bit of beef, that. Wine's flowing. Bottle of Jameson in the centre of the table. This crowd likes a good drink. Except the sparrow, that is. She hasn't touched hers.

'Are you going to call it after Christ?' the sparrow's asking Annie. They're all bursting out laughing. 'I mean *Christy*,'

Carol's correcting herself. Going all red. 'Are you going to call it after *Christy*?'

Annie, for some reason, is taking a deep breath and looking a bit on edge. 'We're calling him after Daddy.'

Tom's stopped his glass halfway up. He's looking at Annie, then around the table. Tom's a happy man. His wife's smiling at him now, knowing this is meaning a lot to him.

Now they are all beginning to look a little apprehensive. All except Carol. 'Déjà vu,' she's saying.

Of course, I'd forgotten – Byrne told Toner his wife had miscarried. If I were a betting man, which I am, I'd say Carol had gathered the family together before to tell them she was going to name her baby after her father. Now Annie's beaten her to it. Wonder if she begrudges her it.

'You don't mind?' Annie's saying.

Carol's shaking her head.

'Your time will come again,' Tom's saying sympathetically. They're all feeling sorry for her. Hard, miscarrying, I suppose. Still, she seems to have got over it.

Carol's lifting her glass, snapping out of it, doesn't want to put a dampener on the evening. 'To Tom McDermott.'

Christy's raising his glass: 'To Tom *Timothy* McDermott.' Byrne's joining in. His is put on, of course. But the rest of them aren't. Wonder why that is.

'Daddy hates his middle name, Christy,' Annie's saying. 'I didn't mean for us to call the baby Tom *Timothy*.' Course, Christy and Byrne wouldn't have known that. Not being immediate family.

'Tom never uses his middle name. He was named after his uncle,' Bridie's explaining. 'Such an old bastard, he was.'

That raised a chuckle.

'Tom will do just fine,' Tom's saying. 'And thanks.'

They're all raising their glasses: 'To *Tom* McDermott.'

'Now,' Tom's saying, reaching for the Jameson. 'Let's have a drop of whiskey. Jimmy?'

'Aye, go ahead, Tom. Good man.'

'Christy?'

'No, thanks, Tom.'

'Would you like a beer, love? There's beer in the fridge.' A woman who fetches for her husband. I like that.

'Thanks, Annie.'

'You can smoke, Jimmy, if you like,' Bridie's saying.

Carol's puzzled. 'You've never allowed smoking at the dinner table before.'

Bridie's shrugging, looking a touch ill at ease. Tom too. Annie's coming back with the can of beer and sitting down. She's noticing Byrne's panatella. Now she's looking at her mother inquisitively.

'What?' Bridie's asking her.

'Nothing.'

This was when I found out that Tom and Bridie Hassett still hadn't told their daughters that Bridie was suffering from Parkinson's. The girls had been suspecting for some time that their mother had been ill. You know how it is with people who are suddenly faced with a serious health problem: trivial things – like smoking at dinner – don't seem important any more. Which is all well and good. But those close to you start wondering why is it suddenly no longer important. Hard to keep serious illness from your own kids, when you come to think about it. They'd been talking about gardening earlier. Carol and her mother obviously share something of an affinity in anything to do with both the garden and the running of the house. I'd got the feeling that

Bridie wasn't showing quite the same level of enthusiasm for an oncoming show that they attend every year, where they usually win prizes for roses. Carol had seemed puzzled by this too, convinced that if her mother wasn't planning for the show it was another tell-tale sign that something was up.

Byrne's wondering why the mood around the table has changed again.

'Have you been to the doctor recently?' Carol's asking her mother.

'No. Why?'

Carol, I have to say, is becoming more and more nervous. As if she wants to know what's wrong with her mother yet dreads knowing. 'Daddy, what are the Parlodel tablets in your bathroom for? Why's Mammy taking them?'

Tom looks drained.

'Carol, why all the questions?' Bridie's asking.

'You said you haven't been to the doctor, yet the label's dated a few days ago.'

Annie's looking resolved now. 'Mammy, you know how we worry about you.'

'I went to the doctor's with high blood pressure. He told me there was nothing to worry about and gave me some tablets. I didn't mention it because I didn't want to worry you. Now, let's drop it, shall we? Tom, tell them the good news.'

'What good news?'

'Your mother and I are going on a trip round the world. We'll be gone a year.'

'When?'

'We're leaving in a month's time.'

'You'll be gone when Annie's having her baby,' Carol's saying. 'Why the urgency? I can't believe you'd not be here for your first grandchild.'

Y'know, I'd say this is one of those family get-togethers where events of the last few weeks are coming to a head, and that Tom's now realizing that the girls aren't going to be fobbed off any longer, that they are seeing the holiday for what it is: if Tom and his wife don't take the opportunity now, it'll never come again. They would go off together in much the same good health as they had always enjoyed. But only Tom would return in good health. Supporting Bridie.

And, of course, probably going through their daughters' minds is, is it wise of Tom to take her abroad to places where the kind of help she might need might not be available? I'd say Tom had long considered that point, but that Bridie had decided she was having one last fling.

'Her fucking swansong!' Byrne later cursed it, when the loan shark he was into wouldn't wait. He needed that inheritance.

The tablets did it. Leaving them lying around for the girls to see was a big mistake. A drugs reference book'd soon tell them what Parlodel's used for.

The nerves in Carol's face are trembling. Annie is squeezing her mother's hand. The question is palpable now. It's hanging over this table like a shroud. Bridie's also realizing that it is impossible to keep the truth from them: they were bound to have seen through it.

Tom looks devastated. Now that he has a few drinks in him, he's finding it hard to keep a brave face on it the way he usually does for Bridie's sake. The girls are picking up on this. They're both fixed on him. It's up to him, he knows that, but it's not easy.

'Your mother . . .' He's looking at her with sadness and love in his eyes. Tom's a sentimentalist. 'Your mother has Parkinson's.'

Annie and Carol are taking it badly. Crying time.

That's not so bad. Based on this, I'd say it's a cert that Carol will take their deaths badly. And, as I say, if I work it so she is made to feel guilty for bringing about their deaths, then suicide is a runner: guilt-ridden daughter tops herself. Hmm, this has been time well spent.

Lot of stuff I can use here.

I had my doubts about this job, but the more I see of it, the more I like it.

Chapter Eight

Now, as with any enterprise, there's a certain amount of clearing up to do when it's all over. Killing is no exception. (You'll notice I use the word 'killing', not 'murder'. 'Murder' is an emotive term. It implies malice. 'Malice aforethought', to quote the legal statute. The statute, of course, is more long-winded, to cover first-degree, second-degree, all that. But there's no *malice* in what I do. I've nothing personal against the Hassetts. They're simply targets: casualties. The law that says 'murder victims' is the same law that exonerates State forces who premeditatedly kill unarmed civilians when they – the civilians – could have been arrested. It's all a matter of selective interpretation. Complex, I know. Anyhow, that's how I see it.) And, since it's my ambition to go through life without getting caught, that means others have to get caught in my place. Should things go wrong, I mean. Rare. Still, you can never account for the Molly Murrays of this world.

Which takes you into the 'blame' factor. If I decide to have some fucker blamed for this, that person will have to disappear. In my experience, it's always best to get rid of the guy you're going to incriminate. If he's not around, he can't prove he was innocent. And the cops think, well, the bastard must have scarpered. Why would he do that if he's not guilty?

Then again, it might suit your purposes to have his body turn up. Full of conclusive evidence. They can't question a corpse. The *conclusive* makes them conclude: fuck it, it was definitely him. Case closed. You get a result that way.

Which means you have to figure out a way to kill him. A gun. A tragic accident. Depends. But you can see the difficulties I have to anticipate. It's not just a question of taking care of the Hassetts and the Byrnes. It's all the affiliated stuff as well. I mean, look at what Molly did to Liam. I had to see that coming. Be ready for it.

I'm always on the lookout for different methods of dealing with these problems. One came to me when I was sussing out some of Hassett's properties. He has a vacant warehouse a couple of miles from his place, out in the country. There's a tree at the entrance to it. And there's a colony of wasps; a fair-sized colony, it is, too, nesting in one of the overhanging branches. (Did you know there are 17,000 different species of wasps? And it's the female who does all the stinging. Typical.) I haven't come to any decisions yet – I'm still working on it – but I'm sort of thinking along the lines of luring someone out there, having them wait at the entrance, in their car or whatever, and then breaking open the nest. I haven't figured out a way to do it yet – so it would look natural, I mean. It would make a great accident.

I remember reading about a case years ago where a family were out for a Sunday drive. It was hot and they had the windows down. They hit a tree where this beehive was. The three of them were stung to death. Down their throats and everywhere, the bees were. Handy, remembering these things in my line of work where you're always looking for new ways to get the job done. So, naturally, when I saw this wasps' nest, the old antenna pinged, know what I mean? Get Nature to do your dirty work for you. I'll keep you posted.

Did I tell you I live out in the country? Came across this place about thirteen years ago. It had been empty for years. Me and Sinead spent a fortune doing it up. Two-storey job on five acres up off the road. Surrounded by farmland. Lovely and quiet.

It's amazing the amount of good ideas you get, living in the country. There was a guy there, oh, years ago now, and the Guards were chasing him. He had dope on him he needed to get rid of. He came across this vacant farmhouse, went in and flushed it down the toilet. City boy, he was. Thought everything that went down the toilet ended up in the Irish Sea. So he's standing there with a big smile on his face. He's got rid of the evidence. He's a happy man. Until the cops opened up the septic tank in the field. Where they found the cellophane bags of cocaine *he thought* he'd disposed of. Which got me thinking.

For those of you from the city who don't know what a septic tank is, well, it's basically an underground hole in a field near the house or premises it's servicing, surrounded by concrete or something similar. It can be as much as ten feet deep by four feet wide. Effluent from the farmhouse runs into it along an ordinary four-inch sewer pipe, then, brims over, and runs out of it along a perforated pipe and soaks away into the ground. But the solids from the toilet are left behind in the tank. They decompose. The bacteria in the tank eat them. These bacteria will eat anything organic. Flesh, for instance. You can see where I'm coming from here.

The bacteria come originally from a dead animal. When

the tank's new, you need a dead animal to get it going, y'see. What you do is, you find, say, a badger that's been hit by a car, drop it in the tank, it decomposes, and anaerobic bacteria form and pretty soon the badger is no more. Its own bacteria have eaten it. Which means the tank is now fully operational. Any solids that go into it from then on get eaten. That's why I was at that vacant warehouse I just mentioned.

I went to check if its septic tank was working. The place has been empty for a while, so there's a chance the bacteria in it have died off. I cleared the grass away from above the tank, lifted the railway sleepers covering it, lowered in a ten-foot rod and gave it a stir. It was full of liquids, but no solids. So I tossed in a dead rabbit. If it isn't working now, it will be soon enough.

You can get a certain amount of this knowledge from textbooks. How long it takes for, say, a rabbit to decompose. A big rabbit takes longer than a small rabbit. Stuff like that. Plus all the technical jargon that goes with it. But there's no info on how long it takes for a *person* to be eaten up this way. No one has done any tests. Except me, that is. I could write a thesis. I'm the only one who knows that it takes roughly ten years for a fifteen-stone man to be eaten away by his own anaerobic bacteria.

A guy who was hassling Toner once – oh, about twelve years ago now – he went missing. The cops probably still have him listed under 'Missing Persons'. (His wife wasn't too happy – the insurance company wouldn't pay out because she couldn't prove he was dead, y'see. I could have done a deal with her, of course, but it might have got complicated. Besides, it would have spoiled my experiment.) I carried out my experiment on him. That's how I know how long it takes.

The wasps and the tank are a couple of extra options to add to the other possibilities I've discussed vis-à-vis the Hassetts. I haven't decided yet who will end up where. But I've one particular customer in mind. Whoever ends up in the tank can rot away to their heart's content. No one will snoop, because Toner will end up owning the warehouse and he'll see to it the tank is left alone. The beauty is that the cops won't raise any eyebrows. Come to think of it, there's room for two in that particular tank.

At one point I was thinking about putting that wanker Liam Murray in it. He came to see me that night and here he was: 'Don't ask me anything about it, Gerd. Don't ask me. I'm under strict instructions to say nothing. I've a list of things to collect for Sinead and the kids. That's why I'm here.'

Lapdog Liam. That's what I call this useless bastard. He's only in the fucking door and already he's telling me he's afraid to open his mouth. I wouldn't be surprised if he's growing tits. His dick's the only thing that proves he's a husband. Everything else about him says 'I'm the little woman'. If you rang his place and asked for Mrs Murray, he'd say 'Speaking'! Somebody should invent a new word for men like him. Henpecked doesn't do it.

'Did I ask you anything about it?'

'No.'

'Then what the fuck are you talking about?'

He backed toward the settee with a 'Fuck-me-take-it-easy, Gerd' look on his face.

What is it with some men? This guy's a builder. He's fitter than a greyhound out of a trap, with all that running he does. OK, he's small enough to be a jockey. Five foot fuck all, to be precise. But if he put his mind to it, he could duck and sting like a bantamweight. Yet he's such a fucking wimp. All I did was raise my voice and he's looking at me as if I'm gonna hit him. Never do time, Liam, that's all I can say. The queers'd be lining up.

'I didn't come here after trouble, Gerd.'

'If the situation was reversed, would I walk into your place with what you've just walked in here with? No. I'd ask you how you were doin'. Maybe ask you out for a pint. Give you the benefit of the doubt. The last thing I'd do is insult you.'

'I didn't mean anything by it, Gerd.'

'Then act like it.'

'Sorry.'

He was too wary not to mean it. Which meant he'd said it out of fear. Therefore he didn't mean it one way or the other; wanted to pacify me. I poured a whiskey. Didn't offer him one. Fuck him.

The list had fallen out of his hand. He picked it up. Looked at it. Then at me. Awaiting my permission to fill it. Christ, did you ever hear the like? A thirty-five-year-old messenger boy, awaiting the indulgence of the country squire, that's how this was beginning to look. 'Take what you've come for, Liam, for fuck's sake.'

Believe it or not, he walked out of the room looking as if I'd just taken a blunderbuss to his status. Maybe there was hope for him yet.

I poured a beer to chase the whiskey down, sat in my chair in front of the fireplace and had a smoke.

I wasn't doing myself any favours here, I knew that. I should have used that daft bastard to find out what Sinead was up to. I dunno, he just caught a raw nerve. As I say, usually I don't lose my temper.

Ordinarily, Liam looks up to me a bit. He's impression-able. All gutless people are impressionable. Easily led. That's what I think, anyway. I hang out with a few known hard cases, guys who can look after themselves. Stuff like that impresses Liam. His mates are a bunch of pub-quizzers. He's in a team, y'know. Their idea of a good night out is sticking their hands up. (And you're not even supposed to.) The odd time he's in my company you can see he's impressed. Likes the idea he's one of the boys. I should have approached him from that angle. Wasn't thinking.

He came back down carrying a holdall. Stood in the doorway looking like teacher'd just sent him to the back of the class.

'What?'

'The, a . . . the kids want me to bring Kipper, Gerd.'

I'd Kipper chained to the cellar wall. Bit of leverage. My two boys'd put Sinead's head away.

'He ran away.'

'What?'

'Kipper ran away.'

'Jesus, they're not going to like that. They haven't shut up about him.'

'I can imagine.'

'They'll think he's gone looking for them. You know what kids are like.'

'He can join the fucking circus, for all I care.'

Liam laughed. It was a sucking-up laugh. Naturally, I twigged right away. My bollocking was getting to him. That status thing again. Didn't want me to think he'd no balls. The tension had eased. He came over and sat down on the edge of the settee.

'Look, Gerd,' he said, leaning over toward me. I could

hear man-to-man stuff coming. 'Sorry about that.' His hand went through what few combfuls he had left. When I first met him it was as long as a pair of curtains. 'Them two sisters. They haven't shut up about this. All I wanted was to get this stuff, get my head showered. Wasn't thinking.'

Here comes the 'Molly's got me so I don't know whether I'm coming or going' routine. Stand up to her, ya piece of putty. Nah, not putty, even putty eventually hardens.

'Every time you two,' he said, then thought about how to put it, '*have a row*' (he meant every time Sinead caught me fucking somebody behind her back and walked out) 'she lands in our place and I end up getting dragged into it. I mean, how many times have I filled that holdall over the years?'

I can't add up that far without a calculator.

'You have to see it from my point of view, Liam. I get a bottle over my skull and I've no idea why. Is anybody gonna tell me? No. Then you come over and I think maybe I'm gonna find out. And what happens?'

'I know, Gerd, I know. I said I was sorry.'

A man for all treasons, our Liam. I'd give odds he swore to Molly he'd come over here and listen to no nonsense from yours truly. Get the holdall, tell me what he thinks of me for how I'd treated poor Sinead if I as much as tried to come the innocent. Don't be fooled by this 'I'm sorry' shit of his. He'll go back to Molly – Molly 'Winter', I call her: she'd grow stalagmites – they're the ones that grow upward, aren't they? – and impale me arse first on them when it comes to her standing up for her sister, and tell her it's still three against one. Fair enough, I'll dress up another pack of lies for him to take back.

'Forget it, Liam. Pour yourself a beer, for fuck's sake.'

If he took the beer, I had his ear. If he refused it, he'd know I'd know he was afraid to go home with it on his breath and have to explain that under no circumstances had it come from me. Tell her you called in for a pint, for fuck's sake.

His manhood won out. He drank from the can. He'd probably eat a case of Polo mints on the way home.

Now, I'm not stupid enough to try to get this eejit to believe my side of the story. Molly wouldn't allow him to, so there's no point. However, letting him think my side's true, not because I said so, but because somebody else said so, might work.

A little ruse I'd figured out in advance. As I work my way around to it, this small talk'll show you what a hypocrite Molly is.

'How's things with you, Liam? How's business?'

'All right. By the way, thanks for putting in a good word for me with The Huntsman.'

See what I mean? She thinks Sinead's too good for me, that I'm a bad husband. But she's not above letting her puppet here take work from me.

'Forget it, Liam.' I'm a silent partner in a pub in town. They're building an extension. I put his name forward. He owes me. 'How's young Liam? Still kicking a football?'

'You know Liam, soccer mad.'

As far as he was concerned, I didn't know who was responsible for having told Sinead that I was carrying on with Louise. No one but me and Louise really knew for sure that I was. Toner said Noreen Bawn overheard Louise asking about me. Based on that, I'd say Bawn told it to Sinead and between them one word led to another and I had been condemned on that. Then Molly got in on it and the war paint came out. But the only opinion that really mattered here was Sinead's. Basically what I'm saying is, if I could discredit Bawn in Sinead's eyes, she might not be influenced by her, or her sister, and see me as the innocent party in this. I didn't want a divorce. For my kids' sake.

'Been in Max's lately, Liam?' He rarely goes to Max's. It's one of Toner's niteclubs.

'Nah. Been up to my eyes in work.'

'Good complaint.'

'Thank God.'

I'd told Toner to tell the manager of Max's to bar Noreen Bawn. 'There was a right carry-on in there the other night.'

'Oh? When was that?'

'The night before I got this,' I said, meaning the bang on the head. 'Noreen Bawn was making a fool of herself. I had to tell her to fuck off.'

'*You* had to tell *her* to fuck off? Why?'

'She was trying it on.'

'*Bawn?*'

'I'm always telling her to fuck off. Ugly cow. Besides, bit close to home. Know what I mean?'

'Sinead wouldn't want to hear that. They're best mates.'

'I doubt she'd believe it.'

'*I'm* having trouble believing it.'

'It's no joke when you have to start fighting off your wife's best mate. Embarrassing, y'know? Still, won't happen again. They barred her for it.'

'They *barred* her?'

'The manager.'

'*Harry* barred her?'

'I'm gonna have a word with him. Don't want anyone barred on my account.'

I left the rest to his imagination. Bawn knew full well that

Sinead had caught me carrying on with other women. (I won't say 'cheating'. I don't regard doing what comes natural as cheating.) It doesn't take a great imagination to figure out that Bawn might have told Sinead I was carrying on with Louise to cover her own tracks. Discredit me before I discredit her. That was the conclusion I wanted Liam to come to. Then carry it back. Whether they believed me or not wasn't important. They'd believe that Harry had barred Bawn. Bawn would say she had been barred for nothing, but Sinead would wonder about that. People don't get barred for nothing. Doubt, y'see. Create doubt. A bit at a time. Nice and easy does it.

'Is Sinead all right for money?' I asked. Playing the concerned husband here.

'I think so.'

'Tell her if she needs anything to let me know and I'll leave it in your place.'

He nodded. Liam left preoccupied with what he'd heard, with luck seeing Bawn as a troublemaker who'd told Sinead a pack of lies to split us up to leave the field clear for herself. Women are not as loyal as men in my experience. Men are stupid when it comes to loyalty, whereas women will stab each other in the back if one thinks the other is trying to screw her husband. And they'll do it without thinking. They're predictable like that.

Course, the beauty about all this was, I knew little Louise would keep her trap shut. Deny everything.

I called Louise. The thought of her walking in the door and pulling her dress up over that mass of red curls and shaking them loose and that delicate little figure of hers wrapped up in nothing but a black V-string was too much to resist.

Men are bastards when you come to think of it. What can you do? That's how God made us. He made the male of each species to service the whole herd. Natural. Then we became civilized. Which was all right because we still had a harem each. Then women went against His laws. Went against Nature. Invented monogamy. And men lost out. That's one of the few things I have against women. How do I know they invented monogamy? Because I know no right-thinking man would have. I'm very religious when it comes to this sort of thing. Stick to what God intended. Good man, God.

The alternative is to go against my sexual instincts. Where would that get me? I'd be walking around with a hard-on all day.

Course, you might be saying to yourself I should honour my marriage vows.

Maybe. But when the priest asked me 'Do you take this woman as your lawful, to have above all others?' and I said yes, I winked at him. He knew I'd no intentions. Shouldn't have married us. Hypocrite.

I knew a guy who was having a bit on the side and his wife found out. He was fifty and his wife was the same age. They weren't having sex any more, but she still wanted him to be faithful. He quit seeing the twenty-year-old he'd been screwing but he couldn't stop thinking about her. For two years he put up with this carry-on, walking around with a hard-on that he didn't want to fuck his wife with because she'd lost her figure and he didn't fancy her any more.

Then he cracked. 'Look at you,' he said to his wife. 'You've turned into a spud. You don't give a fuck that I don't wanna fuck you no more. If you did, you'd have kept your figure.'

She told him to get out.

He went and lived with the bit on the side. I mean, a man

must have his ease, right? Two years later his wife comes to see him. She's lost weight and she's fuckable again as far as he's concerned. She wants him back. She still loves him. All that crap. 'Come back home,' she says.

'No,' he says, 'You've lost your chance.'

I can see Sinead ending up that way if she's not careful.

The moral of this story is: a man can't help himself. Society's changed. But our dicks don't know that. Wives are unreasonable in that regard. They don't understand because all they have between their legs is a gap. And all we have is a plug. Women also know the pleasures of carrying babies. We don't. They're one up on us. Do we complain? Are you fucking mad? We're not unreasonable. Let them have their extra pleasure. But let us have ours. Ours comes in plugging their gaps. That's all we get out of life. We're nothing but a bunch of gap-pluggers. Told you we were no good.

Why doesn't Sinead see it like that? The rest of our marriage is all right.

'Louise?' She isn't into monogamy, thank God.

'Gerd?'

'Get your gap over here.'

73

Chapter Nine

According to Toner, Byrne will soon be running around looking like a mad axeman's chasing after him. It never ceases to amaze me, the way people fuck things up. Byrne sees a great opportunity here, and what does he do? He lays himself wide open to a loan shark. He's got six weeks to pay back fifty big ones or Con Ivers'll come after him. And Ivers doesn't break bones – he pulps them. Ivers is a small-timer. Fifty would be a big number for him.

Mostly he lends to the unemployed, unmarried mothers, petty villains, on the strength of some job or other they're setting up. He gave a woman a heart attack there a lot of months ago. She borrowed a couple of hundred off him to buy the kids toys for Christmas. She was supposed to pay him back twenty a week over thirty weeks. Four hundred profit. Not bad for lending two. She got behind, so he lent her a bit more – a hundred I think it was. So now she was into him for three, which meant she had to pay him back nine hundred at thirty a week. Out of her dole. Naturally, she got behind again and a couple of his boys went round and put a pinch bar through her TV. Course, her kids started squealing they'd no TV. So she borrowed another two hundred to buy another one. That's Ivers's form, y'see. To get her in deeper. Then he took her dole book off her so he could cash it every week to go towards what she owed him, knowing there wouldn't be a bite in the house and she'd do anything to prevent her kids from going hungry. Then he forced her to work the streets. This went on for months until one night the Guards found her lying in the rain where some punter had beat fuck out of her. She cracked and that was that: bang! Heart attack. The authorities stepped in and put her kids in a home. If I know Ivers, he's waiting till she gets better. Meanwhile the interest mounts up.

My old man died from a heart attack. I'm going back a bit now to the early seventies when the Brits brought in internment. Basically what that meant was they locked you up without trial. For anything up to a couple of years. On suspicion of being in the IRA. No charges, no lawyer – nothing. They rounded up hundreds. They came in the night or just lifted you off the streets. Jail enough Catholics and in the swoop you're bound to get IRA men too. That was the logic. But you also get the innocent. Course, Belfast was a madhouse in those days, compared to now. The Brits were trying anything to get the gunmen off the streets. Legal or illegal.

They grabbed my old man on his way home from work. He had fuse wire in his rucksack. You can make detonators out of fuse wire. So he had to be an IRA man, as far as they were concerned. He was Catholic; next-best thing. Whether he was IRA or not I couldn't tell you. But I'd never heard anything to suggest he was. He was a qualified electrician. Hence the fuse wire. Worked all his days.

The Brits took him to an interrogation wing and stripped him. They did this to a lot of men, mind you. It wasn't just him. Course, my mother's running around for days like a lunatic, worried sick about him. The Brits denied all knowledge. They'd no one to answer to, y'see. She thought one of the Loyalist death squads had picked him up. They'd been preying on Catholics too. Bundling them into backs of cars and taking them up onto the Shankill Road. One guy was killed in such a way that people thought it had to have been the work of a doctor, because of the way he'd been cut in order to make the torture last as long as possible: the fleshy parts where there were no veins. Took hours for him to die. I think it was something like a hundred and something different incisions in his body when they found him. And people who were walking past heard him screaming 'Kill me. Kill me. Please, God, please kill me,' it was that bad.

My old man was lucky. The Brits were only using torture techniques they'd developed when they had an empire, in places like Aden and Kenya. Broken glass was one. Y'know, being forced to walk across it with no shoes on. Crude. Any halfwit could dream that one up. It was what came after that was more methodical. Smart bastards, the Brits. You have to give them that.

They made my old man stand in a line. This was after he'd been attacked by dogs and beaten by two rows of baton-wielding soldiers and made to stand on a tea chest and sing 'God Save the Queen'. I don't know how many men were in this line or how many rooms there were with men standing in lines. The object of the lines was to save time and personnel. Torture in groups. It's faster. Then he was told to stretch out his arms with nothing but his fingertips touching the wall. Not his hands; he was allowed to lean against the wall only with his fingertips. If he tried to lean against the wall with his hands or drop his arms, he felt the baton or the cold end of a rifle under his testicles. Then they turned on the white noise. It's the white noise that does it. Like a dentist's drill inside your head. You want to cover your ears. But you can't lower your hands. No sleep. No food. No toilets. Naked. Dark. Light. Disorientation. Time? What's that? All sense of it is gone. Sensory deprivation, they called it.

The never-ending questions come. 'Name names, Paddy.'

'Don't know no names.'

'You're lying.'

They stub out their cigarettes on you.

'Tell us and we'll let you go.'

'But I don't know anything.'

'You know. You're involved. If you're not involved, you know those who are. You live in their communities, you must know their names. Name names.'

Those who knew squealed. Those who knew didn't. Those who didn't know hadn't the luxury of being able to choose. That was my old man's position, I'd say.

They put a black hood over his head and took him up in a helicopter. It went up and flew around. Up and down and up and every which way. Total disorientation.

'Talk or we'll throw you out.'

'But I don't know.'

'Talk! Name names. Who's in the IRA?'

'But I don't know. Please, God, tell them I don't know.'

They booted him out.

He thought he was way up in the air.

He didn't know he was only six feet up.

His heart gave out before he hit the ground.

His name was Gerd, too.

Course, no 'murder' charges were brought, let alone 'killing' charges. No 'malice aforethought' ever came into it.

So I joined the IRA. Not because I wanted to fight for a united Ireland or anything. Just wanted to get my own back. I couldn't give a fuck about a united Ireland. Looking into the North is like watching scenes out of the history books. They're all headers. All sides.

Anyway, you soon get to know what's what if you have any cop-on at all. About how to handle explosives and stuff, I mean. Rigged a bomb inside a sectioned-off part of a bread van that delivered to the army canteen in the barracks where that interrogation centre was and got four of them. They were 'murdered by terrorists', according to the authorities. Then I went to Dublin. Met Toner.

He was just starting off then. Crime in the Republic as a whole wasn't anything worth talking about. If I remember right, there were only five major crimes in as many years leading up to '74. And they'd been carried out by two family gangs, the O'Neills and the Dunnes. And they hated each other.

I spent the first lot of months observing the carry-on of these different outfits. The beauty of my situation was nobody in Dublin knew me. I could move around at will. Just another kid who'd showed up in the capital to get away from the Troubles. Used to play a lot of snooker in those days. Sixpence an hour, old money. Played in Toner's club, mostly.

He only had the one then. Used to watch him and a few of his lads huddled around a table in the corner. Knew they were up to something. Especially if a guy called Kevin Maguire was in on it. Mentioned him already. Course, they didn't know I was watching. And I couldn't hear a word they were saying. But it wasn't unusual to see them splashing money around a day or so after one of these get-togethers. Obviously they'd pulled a job some-where.

One of the things you soon pick up if you get reasonably high up in the IRA is that they know the power of confusion. Confusion is a big angle when it comes to paramilitaries. It can be just as important as detail when it comes to setting something up. 'Confusion' is another word for 'propagan-da'. What people believe, especially in the political situation in the North, is what you make them believe. If something goes down, people in the street don't really know the truth of what happened. They believe their own side's account. Their propaganda. Fuelled by confusion.

To take it a step further, the IRA operates in cells. Each cell is an individual unit of maybe four or five men, operating independently of and not privy to the identity of members of other cells. That way one cell can never inform on the other. Informers are a big problem in the IRA. If information is passed on to the security forces, it's easier for the IRA, or the Ra as it's called, to pinpoint which cell that information came from, and have a better chance of taking out whoever's responsible. These cells might share the same codeword – in my day it was 'Double X' – so the security forces could authenticate an incoming bomb-warning. But that's all they share. If a cell is infiltrated or picked up, and the law interrogate its members about all sorts of things that have gone on, if that particular cell wasn't responsible for the things they were being questioned about, they'd be just as confused as the security forces.

This cell principle works just as well when it comes to everyday crime. And I was about to become a one-man cell, working for – but separate from – Toner. Without him or anyone else knowing about it. Y'see, in Toner I saw what I was looking for. Unlike the families, the Dunnes and the O'Neills, Toner was like me. He wasn't weighed down by the baggage of political causes, religion or feuds. Toner had his own cause in life. And so did I. We both wanted as much out of it as we could get.

Toner was also his own man. He wasn't in charge of a family with all the infighting that entails. Which was another reason I wanted to get in on what he was up to. His was the smallest, but it was also the strongest of the three gangs. They used to call themselves 'gangs'. Not a word I liked. Anyway, the way I saw it was, with the Dunnes and the O'Neills at each others' throats' they were vulnerable. They could be easily confused. If one of the O'Neills met with an 'accident', likely as not the Dunnes would get the blame. And vice versa. Play one family against the other. Know what I mean? That's the way I was looking at it – their respective young bloods would flex their muscles if they believed the other side was trying it on.

My aim was to get rid of the families. With them out of the way, Toner could do what he liked. And some of it would rub off on me.

I was playing a game of snooker by myself late one night. The place was empty. All the other tables were covered up and their lights were off. Mine was the only one still lit. Toner came in to lock up. This was the first time I'd met the guy. He leaned on the table, looking at me. I knew he wanted me to leave. But I kept right on playing. I was in my late teens, and Toner had about nine or ten years on me, so, to him, I was just a kid with a Belfast accent who'd come to Dublin. Someone he'd seen around but didn't know.

'Fancy a game?'

He shook his head. 'Closed.'

Now you have to understand that Toner had an air of menace about him even then. He could intimidate. But was smart with it.

'I'll just finish my game,' I said.

'I said we're closed.'

I got down and potted a long black into the corner pocket. Then came round for a red into the middle. I chalked my cue. Knowing it would irritate him, of course. He came round to where I was getting down to pot this red and stood over me. I looked up at him, never batted an eye, then slowly drew back, took aim, and in it went. I stood up, reached for the chalk and chalked my cue.

'Sure you don't want a game?'

I could see his fists clenching. He knew I was winding him up.

I put the cue down. I didn't square up to him for a fight or anything. This was one guy I didn't wanna fight. Not because I didn't think I could take him. To be honest, I probably couldn't have. My principle in life is, if a guy gets the better of me, I go after him with an iron bar or a knife. From behind. Or whatever it takes. One way or the other he gets to know fists aren't enough. And he never comes after me again.

With Toner, I wanted to get to the stage where we'd do business together. Not fight. But I wanted him to know that I wasn't the type to back down. I wanted his respect. Respect to this guy was somebody who didn't back down. So we're standing there, eyeing each other. I could see the blood rising in him. He was about to let go.

'I'm gonna say something here,' I said. 'And you will never repeat it again, in my company or in anybody else's.'

His eyes narrowed. I was telling him what to do. I was

pushing it. I knew it. But I wanted him to remember this night. I wanted him to remember me.

'See that phone book?'

He looked over at it. 'What about it?'

'I'm gonna open it at a certain page. Then I'm gonna leave.'

'And?'

I shrugged. 'That's it.'

He stood where he was and watched as I went over to the phone, took down the book, opened it and laid it on the snooker table next to it. I didn't circle any names in it, just looked back at him, slung my black bomber jacket over my shoulder and left. The page listed the names and phone numbers of various O'Neills. Including one Hugh O'Neill, painter and decorator.

The next morning a man called Hugh O'Neill was painting the outside of a flat-roofed office building when I kicked his ladder out from under him. He said he saw a man in a black bomber jacket getting into a red Jag and speeding off. He ended up in a wheelchair. This painter was a cousin of Brian O'Neill senior, head of the O'Neill family. He was also not involved in anything to do with crime.

But Roy Dunne owned a red Jag.

So you can see where I'm coming from here. Nothing's proven. But young blood acts on gut instinct. That's their weakness. Drink flows, rumour becomes fact, nobody really knows what's going on. But somebody kicked that ladder, then sped off. Who would do such a thing without a reason? The Dunnes were their enemies. The only ones with a reason. And Roy Dunne drives a red Jag. Had to be him.

No one suspects Toner. No one knows me.

I'm back in the snooker hall that night. Toner had seen

O'Neill's name in the phone book the night before. He's watching me. I finish my game, go to the phone, take down the phone book, open it at the Dunnes' page, Roy Dunne's listed, then I walk out. Toner comes over and looks at the page.

Roy Dunne gets petrol and a lit match through his letter-box in the middle of the night. His wife's running out of the house, screaming 'Save my baby! Save my baby!'

Now the Dunnes' young blood are flexing their muscles. They blame the O'Neills. I step back. Hit follows hit. They have the attention of the Gardaí. Jobs they'd been planning are put on hold. They're damaged; not as strong as they were. I wrap a flask of petrol around the manifold of Pop O'Neill's car. His son's taking him to the races. It goes up. Junior's barbecued. Pop's in intensive. Had to be the Dunnes.

Toner's recruiting the disillusioned from both families who know all there is to know about the families' activities: protection, jobs they'd been planning, details of how they were gonna carry them out. They hand all this information to Toner.

While the families are wiping each other out, Toner's reaping the rewards. Has a free hand. Can take his pick of jobs. He's bigger than they are now. He's reading telephone names to find out who's next. But what did I do? Nothing. Nobody knows me. But Toner knows. He knows I wiped out the families by confusing them, playing one against the other.

Again I'm back potting a few balls. The place is empty. Toner comes up. Looks at me. 'Fancy a game?' Now he's got respect in his voice.

'Sure.'

He takes a shot. Stands up. He wants to talk. I know he does. 'How much of it was down to you?'

'How much of what?'

He eyes me, wondering why I'm being evasive. 'Come on. Between you and me. How much of it was down to you?'

'See that telephone book over there?'

He looks. 'Yeah.'

I miss a red in the corner. 'I don't know a soul in it. And they don't know me. That's the way it stays. You get any prime work, you pass it to me. But you don't know me. Deal?'

He didn't know what to make of me. A spunky kid from the North mixing it with the big boys.

'Name's Gerd. Your shot.'

No one really knew what went on. The law didn't. Toner didn't. The families didn't. So how could anybody prove a thing? Been like that ever since. Confusion.

Speaking of confusion: Sinead rang. I'm still trying to confuse her. Or rather, I'm *continuing* to confuse her. Why that woman refuses to concede that my little extramaritals are only a bit of fun, I'll never know.

Anyway, here was me: 'Sinead, what about you?'

And here she was: 'Don't you "what about you?" me. Fucking typical – talking to me as if nothing's happened.'

'I was only asking how you were doing.'

'Well, don't. I know the way you go about things. I know you remember. Mr Nice Guy to my face and a shitehouse behind my back.'

'Sinead, come on, there's no reason for this kinda talk. How's the kids?'

'Since they're with me, they're obviously fine.'

'Now don't start saying I'm saying they're not fine if

85

they're with you. You know I'd never even think you weren't a good mother.'

'Remember that when we get into court.'

'Sinead, come on. Can't we talk about this, civilized?'

'I'm taking the kids, the house, investments, everything.'

'But that's what we live off. What'll I live off?'

'I want you out of the house today.'

'Sinead, you're not being fair.'

'The kids need to be in their home for when they go back to school.'

'Will you at least tell me what I'm supposed to have done?'

'My solicitor will be reminding you when he serves the papers.'

'Sinead, for Christ's sake.'

'Will you be out of the house today?'

'I'm not leaving my home.'

'So you're forcing your kids out of theirs.'

'I'm not forcing them out of anything. Come home, Sinead. Think of what this is doing to them.'

'You should have thought of that before you went running around.'

'Sinead, please, I wasn't running around. Who's been telling you that?'

'Are you leaving or not?'

'No.'

'Fuck you, then!'

I couldn't figure out why she wasn't believing that pack of lies I'd told Liam. She always had before. If her tone of voice was anything to go by, it was as if she had concrete evidence I'd been carrying on, instead of hearsay evidence. Which, of course, she couldn't have.

Anyhow, the second female approach I had came from Little Louise, or Lou as I sometimes call her. I was in my car, parked at the top of a hill overlooking Toner's place. The Hacienda, he calls it. I'd been keeping an eye on Jimmy Byrne, who'd gone in to see him.

Lou was wearing one of those tight shiny raincoats. Only twenty, she is. She's always got a big smile for me, as if she's genuinely glad to see me. I don't know whether it's just a crush she's got on me or if it goes deeper. Gives you a nice sort of feeling, though, know what I mean?

So, she's getting in the passenger seat, saying 'Gerd,' all smiles, and I'm thinking to myself the smile's put on. Something's on her mind. She's shaking her hair, letting it fall down her back. With me it's the hair. Nothing's more attractive than a mop of wild curly locks – but she's definitely looking a bit guarded.

I ask her how it's going.

She says 'All right.'

I lean across with the old 'C'mere. Give us a kiss. Hmmmwahh!'

'Enjoy last night?'

Women always ask that. I say what I always say: 'What do you think?' She's blushing. Getting all horny just thinking about it. Her, too, by the look of her.

That's the way the conversation was going. Then she asks me what I'm doing.

'Waiting on someone. Bit of business, y'know. You?'

'Seeing about a flat.' She looks apprehensive. 'Have to find something cheaper.'

'Why? What's the matter?'

'Nothing.'

'Yes, there is. What is it?'

'Have to find something cheaper, that's all.'

She looks ready for crying.

'What's wrong?'

'Gerd, you're gonna be hearing some nasty things about me. But they're not true. Honest to God. They're all lies.'

'What things?'

'You promise me you won't believe them? If you believed them, I don't know what I'd do.'

She's such a child. 'Take it easy. You know me. Why would I believe what somebody else says over you? Lou, come on, don't get upset. What is it?'

'Toner rang me this morning and said he'd have to let me go because he'd been hearing complaints about me.'

'What complaints?'

'You promise you'll believe me? They're not true, Gerd, honest.'

'Why would I believe Toner over you? Guy's got the scruples of a hyena. You know what I think of the likes of him.'

'It's just that I wouldn't want you to think I was carrying on behind your back. I couldn't handle that.'

'Why would you carry on behind my back when I'm better at it than anybody else?'

That raised a chuckle. 'That's what I love about you, Gerd. You never take anything serious.'

'Love' stumps me. She says it as if she was just saying it in conversation. She can see it stumped me. The air's getting a bit tingly. She's looking at me with those hazel eyes of hers. She's all nervous. And serious with it.

'I love you, Gerd.'

Christ. Where did that come from?

'You don't have to say anything. I know you don't love

me. And you'd never know I loved you unless I told you. You've got this way of carrying on as if you're unaware of other people's feelings. As if you're immune to them.'

'Me?'

'Oh, I know you don't see it. That's one of the refreshing things about you, you're not hung up on sentimentality. You're so detached. Oh, maybe I'm saying this wrong. I dunno. I didn't intend saying anything and then I saw you and I've been feeling sorry for myself because Toner sacked me and it just came out.'

You know, up until now, I hadn't really thought of Lou as someone I was other than really fond of. Now I'm not so sure. She has a sweet childlike innocence about her which makes you want to fuck her. But love her? No, I don't love her. Are you fucking mad? I like it that she loves me. Might come in useful.

'Know something?' I whispered.

'What?'

'Me too.'

She was overflowing with love. Just thought I'd throw in a corny line.

'You're only saying that, Gerd.'

'Am I? Then why do I wake up every morning thinking about you?'

Her face says *You do?* but she still can't take it in. I hadn't realized I'd had such an effect on her. I'd shown her a lot of attention, you know, to get the leg over, but I never thought for a moment she was falling for me. I must be better at it than I thought. She's waiting for me to say something more. Wonder what way I can run with this.

I told Toner to sack her, of course. I told him to tell her women had been complaining she'd been putting it about that she'd slept with their husbands. That's all I told him to say. No names mentioned. I wanted it left so people could read into it. So anyone hearing it, Molly in particular, would take it back to Sinead and Sinead would think Lou liked making trouble for married men, that Bawn had read it wrong. Create doubt. Make Sinead re-examine her facts. Takes time, though. But I'd say if I keep working on it, Sinead'll begin to see me for the good catch that I am and tell her solicitor to drop it. She won't like living away from the house, either. That'll work for me too. She likes her things about her. The next time she phones it'll be a different story. And in the meantime I can get a bit of comfort from this little lady. Like I say, a man must have his ease. This is working out OK.

Jesus, if she only knew. 'I didn't say I love you before, because I'd never hurt my kids.'

'Oh, I'd never ask you to. I'd never ask you to leave your kids.'

'Can I come over to your place tonight? Talk about this. It's come a bit sudden, y'know? I sort of feel a bit mixed up.'

'Of course.'

'Shall we say nine?' Actually I'm quite a good ham actor when I wanna be.

'Nine it is, Gerd. Bye, darling.'

Darling? Christ – her strings are easily pulled. I watched her walk down the hill, the whistle in her step. Whatta gal!

Byrne came out of the Hacienda and drove off in the white 3-series BM he'd borrowed money to buy. He glanced at me as he passed, panatella in his mouth, arm rod-straight at the wheel. You know how some guys have that look about them, a *spiv* look, shifty, preoccupied, as if they're contemplating something big, yet look worried about it, apprehensive you might say? The spiv trying to work some angle that would lift him up out of the petty stuff. That's how Byrne came across to me. Though he'd as much chance of pulling it off as a photocopy has of becoming an oil painting. His skin's as dry as a photocopy, too.

Time to see Toner.

Chapter Ten

Back centuries ago when it was illegal to be a Catholic, priests in Ireland had to say mass in a field. If the Brits showed up, the priest had to run like fuck.

Picture a small, underground, dungeon-like vault with rough-stone tunnels running off it in different directions, like spokes from a hub. The priest drops down into the dungeon and takes his choice of escape tunnels. They're each a couple of hundred feet long, and come out at different places in the surrounding landscape. Getting caught could mean being 'hanged, drawn and quartered'. (Whoever thought that one up must have been some kind of operator. My kinda man!)

These hides exist today. Though few people – because they're hides – know where they are and how many. Several are listed in some government office in Dublin, others are known only to locals who had the information passed down. The story goes that even earlier inhabitants – Dark Ages stuff, this bit – who lived underground built them, and they were later used to turn priests into rabbits.

There's one below that barn of Toner's. I go in through a concealed tunnel entrance near a river bank. With my head down, I might add. They're not high enough to stand up in. They're dank, rat-infested hovels too. I wouldn't like to be caught in one without a good torch, that's all I can say. So you can fend off the rats, I mean.

Course, if I wasn't so security-conscious, I wouldn't have to go to these lengths to avoid being seen talking to Toner. Which in itself has another downside to it. I like the guy. He's the nearest thing to a brother I've ever had. I'd like to hang around with him and have the crack. But then I'd be known. I couldn't live like that. Knowing the law are watching, waiting for a slip-up. I don't know how he puts up with it. Me, I'm a loner in many ways; can't bear the thought of anyone spying on me. I stay in the shadows. A bad choice of words: denotes something sinister. Which, of course, I'm not.

Incidentally, the hub is a great place for keeping someone tied up in. I've been thinking about using it for Jimmy Byrne when the time comes to figure out what to do with him. The rats are a problem, though. Hungry little bastards. Liable to lick their lips on him.

There's a bolt in the hub's ceiling. I just slide it back, lift the trap, pull myself up into a partitioned-off section behind the tack room, which is locked from the inside so the riding school who rent this place from Toner don't find it, and I'm in.

This was to be our second meeting to do with the Hassett proposal. It was still just a proposal at this stage. I had a lot more groundwork to do before I decided if we could pull it off.

Toner was sitting behind the desk, his feet up, having a smoke. 'Gerd, how's it goin'?'

'Not bad, Paddy.'

He took out a flask, had a swig, handed it across. Jameson it was. Tasted nice. Got the stink of that hide out of my mouth.

94

I told him what I had come up with so far – a sort of progress report: that I had appraised the Hassetts, their daughters, Hassett's business, his secretary Mrs Gallagher, Byrne's part in this, plus a few other possibilities, then asked him why Byrne had been to see him. He told me what I had already suspected, that Byrne, although he had been told that it might take three months to set this up, now wanted it dealt with in three weeks, before Hassett and his wife departed on their trip round the world.

Toner then took a letter out of his pocket.

It was addressed to Hassett Property. A UK supermarket chain was offering five million for a thirty-acre site out on the Belfast Road. They wanted to build a shopping centre. Byrne's wife, who used to be into animal welfare, had, some years earlier, talked her father into letting the land rent-free to a horse sanctuary; green belt, I'd been told.

'They're rezoning, Gerd.'

'Oh?' I pulled up a chair. 'So what's Byrne asking for it now?'

'The same as before.'

I was suspicious. The timing was too much of a coincidence.

'Why, if it's now worth double?'

'Exactly what I asked him. If we hit the Hassetts before they sail, Byrne sees a sure five. If we wait till they return, the situation might have changed. Byrne dangled the letter in front of me and said: "Do it in three weeks and you get an instant five million profit". I said I'd get back to him.'

I was now even more suspicious. Nobody's that generous. 'What's to stop him from using us? He could let us get rid of his in-laws and his wife, then he inherits, sells it behind our backs, cops the ten, and that's the last we see of him.'

'Not with you watching him he won't.'

Which was true. But the job was complicated enough. And even though I didn't rate the guy, Byrne trying to con us out of Hassett Property while *we* were trying to con *him* out of it would make it more so.

'He's got a girlfriend,' I said. 'Did you know that?'

'There's usually a woman involved in it somewhere.'

'Rita Joyce her name is. She has a council flat over in Finglas. Real looker. Out of his league. He's spending Con Ivers's money on her, too.'

'He's taking Carol, and Joyce's taking him, is that it?'

'So it seems. I'd say she's part of the reason he wants what's coming to his wife. It's messy, Paddy. We could be halfway into it, Carol finds out about Joyce, shows Byrne the door, and the whole thing's up in the air. Byrne's going out of his way to make things harder for us.'

'Yeah, but ten big ones, Gerd. Think about that.'

The ten million was important. I'd be lying if I said otherwise. But we both had more money than we'd ever need. So in that sense it was of less importance than the 'game' itself. For, over the years, the 'game' was what it had come down to. There's nothing more satisfying than a result. Stringing together a series of events that lead to a conclusion that fools every fucker – the law, the press – doesn't half give you a high. Better than any drug I ever tried.

Toner loves the con. Always has. Big con, small con; didn't matter. Even when he was a kid and his old man made him join the parish band, he'd bring gobstoppers on a stick, put them down the mouthpiece of his euphonium and sit laughing away to himself at the conductor, who saw his cheeks going and thought he was doing his best. The cunt was sucking a lolly. The kids next to him were doing all the blowing. Never learnt a note. Fuck knows what he'd have done if they'd put him on clarinet. Brought liquorice sticks, probably.

Loves deceiving people.

That's why he likes working with me. I have a very colourful way of doing things. Nobody dispatches people the way I do. He never knows what I'll do next. I weave the strands. I create the jigsaw. He gets a kick out of trying to figure out how the pieces fit. He plays a big part. Enjoys the challenge. He knows I feel the same.

I had another look at the letter.

'What's Hassett say about this?'

'He doesn't know about it. He doesn't even know they're rezoning. Byrne reckons he's too worried about his wife to notice what's going on.'

'I find that hard to believe. Hassett's self-made. He's bound to know if a field just turned into a fortune.'

'What the fuck difference does it make?'

'I'll tell you what difference it makes. Byrne might be handing us five mil without us having to lift a finger.'

'How?'

'What if we tell Byrne we're pulling out, but that we'll buy Hassett Property now? Cut him in if he sets it up. We pay Hassett what he thinks it's worth – five mil – then we sell the thirty acres to that supermarket outfit for five. Get our money back. We'll still have the company. Then cut Byrne out.'

He looked at me as if I'd lost all sense of proportion. 'You want us to pay for a company that we can take for fuck all? Where the fuck's the fun in that? What the fuck's got into you, Gerd?'

'It's still a five mil con.'

'I want a ten mil con.'

'Look into it, ya greedy bastard.'

'What if Hassett won't sell?'

'What if I can't set this up before he goes away? We'll make sweet fuck all. This way we might make five.'

He thought about it long enough to see it as an option. 'Fair enough.'

'In the meantime, we can put a few things in place.' Begin setting people up, in other words, the bit Toner loved best. 'By the way, thanks for sacking Louise.'

'No problem, Gerd.'

'Give her her job back.'

'But I've only just called her a whore.'

'Tell her you're sorry, her having a baby to look after and all, you acted in haste. Offer her a job in Hugo's. Introduce her to Byrne. Drop it into the conversation he rents out accommodation. Tell him to offer her a house to rent. Cheap, so she'll take it. But I don't want anything written down. Nothing on paper. No records. No rent books.'

'Not a word.'

'When she hands him her rent money, photograph it at the point where it's changing hands.'

'OK.'

'I want Lou and her toddler to visit that horse sanctuary. Tell Byrne to tell her he likes her kid and wants to show it the horses. Anything. Think of something. Get her up there when Hassett's there. That's the main thing. I want a photograph of Lou and her baby with Hassett. No one else in the picture but those three. Then I want a similar photograph of Byrne with Lou and her kid.'

'Done.'

'Open a bank account in Lou's name. Tell Byrne to arrange

an eight-hundred-quid-a-month direct debit to be paid into it, drawn on Hassett Property.'

'OK.'

'Now, if Carol's into animal welfare, she must be an animal lover, yet there were no pets in The Cedars. If Byrne says it's because her parents won't have one in the house, tell him to surprise her with a puppy the day before her parents are due to go away on that trip.'

'He can buy her a cobra for all I care.'

'She's supposed to be committing suicide, Paddy.' *Suicide?* He was loving it. 'A cobra might look a bit odd. She's not Cleo-fucking-patra.'

'A puppy it is, Gerd.'

'Tell Maguire to buy a mobile like Byrne's. Exact same model. But he's not to have it connected.'

He was even more intrigued. I was losing him. Quinn the Confuser, he calls me. He, nor anybody else, ever has a clue what the fuck I'm thinking. 'Why the fuck would anybody buy a phone and not connect it?' was written all over his face.

'Which brings us to Mrs Gallagher. She's been Hassett's secretary for fifteen years. And she's honest. Worse still, she knows about that monitor. If what I have in mind for it ever backfired, and she told the police about it, we'd all be smoking roll-ups. We have to discredit her.

'Tell Byrne to count the takings from the carpark and have Mrs Gallagher check it in front of him. She's to put it in the safe just as he's popping out of the office. He mustn't be in the office when she's locking it in the safe. That night he's to go back and take two hundred quid out of it, then have her deposit the remainder in the bank the next morning. When it comes up short, he's to mention it to Hassett and Carol. He's to tell them he feels bad about it and he'll make good the loss himself. But no aspersions are to be cast on Mrs Gallagher. I want it left open to interpretation who took it. People like her don't become thieves overnight. We'll have to make it look good. Did you have Sean Connors followed?'

'I did.'

'Has he been talking to that sister-in-law of mine again?'

'No. But I don't like it, Gerd. Once a squealer, always a squealer. He knows too much.'

'Keep tabs on him. If he goes near Murray, do what you want with him. Other than that, leave him alone. I have a little personal problem he'll come in handy with.'

'Sinead not back yet?'

'Stop grinning, you bastard.'

'Who, me?'

'What was it you said to me: "How is someone so smart when it comes to business so dumb when it comes to his dick"?'

'Sounds about right.'

'I wish to fuck I knew why she isn't believing that crap about Harry barring Bawn.'

'You look puzzled by it, Gerd. Not like you. Don't tell me you're losing your touch.'

'Merely a question of piling on more evidence, Paddy.'

'What've you got in mind?'

'I want no sign of a break-in, so I want you to send a pro, OK, into Noreen Bawn's flat and mix cocaine with her shampoo.'

'Jesus, what're you gonna do – dope her hair?'

'Ah, just working on a little *doubt* scenario. Sinead hates drugs and anybody who takes them. Here.'

'What's that?'

'The makers call it a Secret Safe.'

'It looks like an electricity socket.'

'That's the whole idea. The box at the back's where you keep your valuables. Have one of Bawn's sockets removed and this fitted in its place. Leave thirty or forty deals in it. Heroin, coke, it doesn't matter. Two weeks from now, I want the same pro to go back and remove the shampoo. Then you can hit Sean Connors. I want Bawn's phone number in his pocket when you do, in his own hand. OK? The law'll ask her about it and Sinead'll find out. Create more doubt. I have to get Bawn away from Sinead. She's got too much influence over her.'

'OK, Gerd.'

'I'll be out of the country for a while.'

'Where?'

'I've to see a man about a coffin.'

'A coffin? What the fuck for? You gonna bury Hassett alive? How's that gonna look like an accident?'

'It'll have a hole in the top.'

Should've seen Toner's face. 'A fucking hole in the top! Jesus! I love it.'

'Well, we can't expect him to drive his car into the lake without air. Talk to you when I get back, Paddy.'

Chapter Eleven

―――∞○∞―――

While I was out of the country seeing that forensic pathologist I mentioned earlier, Tom Hassett was indeed asked to sell. I saw an angle in this that would work in our favour even if Hassett decided not to.

I told Toner to lodge a cheque for five million with his solicitor and for Hassett and his solicitor to be made aware of this in writing. That would lend an air of legitimacy to what I had in mind.

Then negotiations got under way. They got under way for three weeks. It was the first business deal me and Toner were involved in that was legit. OK, we were acting on inside information, if you want to call it that, but it was still legit. And the Hassetts would be left alone to get on with the rest of their lives. I had no sentiment one way or the other in that regard, you understand. I'm just as happy making money in business as I am making it with Toner.

But Hassett wouldn't sell. There was something in him that refused to let go of a company he'd built up from nothing. He couldn't sell what was part of him.

I could never understand that kind of feeling in a million years. After all, it was only a business.

'Not worth dying for,' Byrne had said.

I wouldn't have put it quite like that. I don't have Byrne's slanted way of looking at things. As you well know. But that would be the result. Still, that's the way it goes. I try not to get disappointed over these little setbacks. Things usually have a way of working out for the best.

The forensic pathologist was very positive about the whole thing.

I told him I was a writer researching a book: a work of fiction. That the characters in the book got up to no good. That people died in the book and I needed to know how a police forensic pathologist might view their deaths. I also added the sweetener that I would have to include his name in the Acknowledgements – my agent and publisher would insist – for reasons of authenticity.

(By the way, if you want to locate a guy like this, don't ring up police forensic labs. You'll get an FP who will help you. But it might involve you going through the system. In this game you can't afford to be seen by anyone other than the FP himself. I always go to a good library. Old books on the subject, covering crimes that happened twenty or thirty years ago, usually name the FP in charge, where the dire deed was committed, the force to which he was attached. Ring through the phone book for that area until you hit on him. Because the crimes are old, the chances are he's retired and – just as important – living alone. If not, keep looking until you get a one on one. Ultimately, you might have to kill him, y'see.)

Albert Wilson was a widower, in his mid-seventies, with receding white hair, jowls, the look of a warthog about him. He lived in a cottage near the village of Chew Magna, thirty minutes from Bristol. After the initial phone call I watched him for a couple of weeks, to learn his habits, before knocking on his door. In that time he received no visitors and his only outings were to the shops, the post office, the local for half an hour before closing. Basically the guy was lonely. The risk of anyone calling in on him while I was there was minimal.

He served tea and biscuits on a coffee table between two wing chairs.

'Writers make the best killers,' he said to me. 'They can have access to all kinds of sensitive information.'

He was talking on paper, of course.

'I'd say pathologists come a pretty close second.'

'Hmm, you might be right. I've never heard of an FP being handcuffed, come to think of it.' Then he did think about it, and laughed: 'Their little escapades are probably listed under "unsolved".'

I smiled at his attempt at humour.

'So, tell me,' he said, 'what exactly is it you want to know?'

'How a killer in my book can get away with murder. Without someone in your profession becoming suspicious.'

'Ah! The perfect crime. No such thing.'

That's what you think, I thought.

Chapter Twelve

———≫◦◦◦≪———

I now had a decision to make. I'd figured out a way to deal with the first part of the problem: the Hassetts and their daughter Annie. However, I had not figured out a way to deal with Carol. Or Byrne. And bringing about our ultimate goal – Toner buying Hassett Property for fuck all, with the additional challenge of preventing Byrne from splitting it up and selling it behind our backs for double the original asking price – was still very much in the planning stage. Then there was Con Ivers. If things went wrong, could I lump the blame onto him? I had ideas. But for the first time in my life I was faced with embarking on a job with no clear pattern.

It was Friday morning. The Hassetts were leaving in two days' time.

'What'll it be, Gerd?'

'Fuck it, we'll run with it, Paddy. I'll just have to put in a bit of overtime, that's all. Contact Maguire.'

He was delighted. 'Good man, Gerd. I knew you couldn't resist it.'

I wasn't so sure.

As I explained earlier, Kevin Maguire was third in line. He thought he was second in line. He didn't know about me. To him, Toner was the brains behind every job we'd ever pulled. So it was just the two of them. To be honest, it was an open question as to how Maguire'd take it, if he ever found out that I'd been pulling his strings all these years. Proud bastard. Still, I'd enough to contend with without worrying about that.

They met in the back office of Toner's bookie's shop in the centre of Dublin. Maguire: lanky, mid-forties, dark hair, combed back, something shiny keeping it in place, a nose like the front end of a submarine, big and blunt – if you knew him and you thought he could take a joke, you'd hit him with: 'Hey, subnose.' But he can't take a joke. He'd hit you with the head.

He sat, foot on knee, black stonewashed jeans turned up at the bottom, crêpe lace-ups, the sailor's overcoat with only the bottom button done up, fingers ink-stained from betting slips, drawing that hard on the cigarette it was caving in.

Loud fucker Maguire is, deep bellows-like voice, though he's a great mimic and can take off the best of them. He has that peculiarly Irish habit of asking a question while answering it.

'You've work for me, Paddy, y'have?'

'Maybe a couple of months' worth.'

'It's big, it is?'

God knows what Toner thinks of him. To look at him, you'd think he belonged in a dole queue for the unemployable. Yet the guy's been reaping in fuck knows how many ten-per-cents over the years. He just has that I'm-capable-of-fuck-all-but-hanging-around-street-corners appearance. When he walks, the head's always down and to the side. You'd think he was gonna come at you with it. He's a slippery fucker, too. The wife of a guy who owed him money found herself backing into him one night, arse first. She couldn't give the police a description. All she could say was that when she turned and saw him coming towards her in an alley, he moved that fast and that quiet she thought he was a silhouette.

Her husband cleared his arrears.

'How much are we talking about, Paddy? A brave bit I'd say.'

'Ten mil.'

Which put his cut at one. 'Not bad.' He stubbed out the cigarette. 'When?'

'Tomorrow night.'

'How many? A few, I'd say, for that kinda money.'

'Three.'

'Known?'

'No. A couple and their daughter.'

'No shooters, then.'

'Only as persuaders.'

'Any beer in that fridge? I'd say there is.'

'Aye.'

'Give us one.' He lit another cigarette, his cheeks concaving as he drew on it. 'Up all night in an oul poker school, y'know? Terrible drouth on me.'

'Hard oul life.'

'Sure, that's what I'm sayin'.'

He raped another woman one night, a teenager. Though that was for us. Worked out by yours affectionately.

A big-shot printer called Parker comes to Toner and tells him he wants somebody seen to. Twenty grand in it. I saw an angle.

Toner calls in Maguire.

'This guy Parker,' Toner says, 'put in for a printing contract. So has an outfit called McCall Limited. For printing a feminist magazine. Parker reckons they won't be seen dead giving it to a company owned by a guy whose son's in for rape.'

'What's his son's name?'

'Barry McCall.'

We had to set McCall up.

This involved my finding out all about false faces. Barry McCall was blond and had a moustache. So Maguire was made up to look like him, professional job, same clothes, the works. In the dead of night a stranger'd never know the difference.

'So we have to rape a girl and make it look like it was McCall? Isn't that right, Paddy?'

Toner tells him the details, how he was to go about it, stuff like that. 'But you're not to rape just any girl.'

'You've somebody in mind, y'have? No dogs now, Paddy, no dogs.'

'Parker's daughter.'

'Jesus, fuck me. You're a great man for coming up with prime ideas. By Jesus you are.'

Toner shrugs, smiles, nicks my thunder.

Maguire 'borrows' one of McCall's vans, waits for Parker's daughter, bundles her in the back, does the business, boots her out in full view of an all-night takeaway, goes to McCall's flat, leaving the leather jacket he was wearing in the wash basket. McCall has no alibi: all worked out.

Next morning, Parker's round crying, coming apart, can't believe what's happened.

'He grabbed the first girl who came along,' says Toner. 'How the fuck was I to know it'd be your daughter? It was just a mad coincidence.'

McCall does time. Parker gets his contract.

Then he's back, same story: can't believe what's happening. 'That guy's blackmailing me.'

'What guy?'

'Maguire. He's threatening to tell my daughter I was behind it. He wants half a million pounds.'

'I have no control over him.'

'But he works for you.'

'He's on the run. He's desperate. It's out of my hands.'

Maguire sets the time, the place, gets the money, takes his ten points, me and Toner split the rest.

If you do a job – maximize.

Know what Maguire did next? He waits six months or so, til yer woman's out and about, having put it behind her, then chats her up in a bar. He couldn't resist finding out if she'd recognize him without his disguise. She didn't. But she wouldn't wear him either. So he plagues her. Sends her flowers, fakes a scene: gets a couple of low-lifes to hit on her, steps in and tells them to get offside, impresses her, grows on her, starts taking her for Chineses. All to get her into bed to see if she recognizes the feel of him. To put it bluntly: that warped mind of his wanted to know if she could tell one dick from another. She couldn't. He's lying there smoking, looking up at the ceiling, laughing away to himself at the thought of her cuddled up, her head on his shoulder, not knowing what the fuck's going on. He loves getting inside people's heads.

Next thing you know she's bringing him home to meet the folks. 'Dad, this is Kevin.'

There was no talk of marriage or anything. But Parker didn't know that. Though it enters his mind, and the cunt's livid at the thought of it.

But what can he do? He has to sit through dinner making small talk with Nelson-nose.

'You haven't touched yours, dear,' his wife's saying.

'I'm not hungry.'

He'd have choked on it.

Maguire's tucking in. 'So what line of work ya in, CJ? You're making plenty, y'are?'

Parker's seething away to himself. 'Printing.'

'Printin'? Oh. Very nice. Things take a turn for the worse, you can always run off a few tenners.'

Mrs Parker's letting on to laugh, in between firing off a few *Goodness gracious, what manner of lout have you brought home?* looks at her daughter.

After dessert, Parker calls Maguire into his study, makes out a cheque for fifty grand, and says he'll sign it on one condition.

It seems he doesn't want Maguire for a son-in-law.

Some people just can't stop interfering in their daughters' lives.

'But we're in love – Dad!'

Steam's coming out of Parker's ears.

'What if she's pregnant?' says Maguire, folding the cheque away. 'You'll make sure my kid gets a good education, y'will?'

Fuck me, what a carry on!

That's Maguire for you. Heart of gold.

'You'll need a black Transit.'

'No problem, Paddy.'

We had begun.

Chapter Thirteen

———⊰⊶⊷⊶⊰———

Most of what Maguire did from then on came as a result of that trip I'd made. I'll keep it as clipped as I can. And you have to remember that I'm telling it based on how I had instructed it to be carried out and on how it was told to me by Toner, who heard it from Maguire after it was over. I also found a way to get some of it on tape.

Maguire went into Hassett's office and put a VCR into a drawer and connected it to the monitor, switched it to the camera in Hassett's bedroom, and began taping. It was nearly three in the morning and the Hassetts were fast asleep. The monitor showed the darkened bedroom. He then locked Hassett's office, went downstairs to reception, locked the door behind him, put on the alarm, went outside and locked the main door. Then, with a cordless drill, he drilled a hole in the main door near the lock, put the blade of the cordless jigsaw into this hole, cut around the lock, pushed it through to the inside, and opened the door, setting off the alarm. He then took off his surgical gloves and drove out to The Cedars.

Tom Hassett answered the phone beside his bed and heard a voice say: 'Garda Central here. There's a possible break-in at your offices. You'll have to come down.'

Bridie Hassett was on tablets that, according to Byrne, had giddy side effects. The pathologist had told me how to work this in my favour.

Tom Hassett slipped out of bed, grabbed his clothes, got dressed in the bathroom and left his wife a note saying where he had gone.

Maguire passed him on the road on his way to The Cedars.

When Maguire arrived, he got dressed in the car and let himself in by the front door. Then, without touching the banister rail, he went upstairs. He switched on the landing light. He needed the light to shine into the bedroom so the camera could pick up what was happening. However, the surgical gloves he was again wearing had smudged the light switch. He would have to take care of that. Some sharp-eyed fingerprint man asking how come the switch was smudged, when it should carry a fingerprint, know what I mean? Inconsistent. A small detail, I know. But take care of the small details and the master plan takes care of itself. I'm paraphrasing, of course.

Then Maguire opened the door and the light fell on Mrs Hassett. She didn't stir. She was lying on her side, facing the door and snoring, a wisp of hair on her forehead, her lips pursed.

He shook her with his boot. She opened her eyes, shielding them against the glare and saw him standing over her. Maguire had been told that this woman was strong-minded and proud. She might put up a fight. That was the one risk in this. To be avoided at all costs. A struggle, a scratch would leave his flesh in her fingernail and prove she had tried to fight off an assailant. We couldn't have that. For this to work, she had to get up and walk out of the room by herself.

Not a hair from his head could fall on her, hence his black-stocking mask; not a fibre from his clothes could become entangled in her nightdress, hence his heavy plastic body suit. Nothing for Forensic to detect. So the question was: would she put up a struggle? The answer, of course, is so simple it almost goes without saying. But I'll say it anyway: threaten her husband and she'll do anything you tell her.

Which Maguire did, his voice muffled by the mask. 'Do what you're told and he won't get hurt,' he told her. She felt for her husband in the bed. Defiance was written all over this lady. Maguire could see it in her. If she had been in the house alone, my guess is she would have put up a struggle. But she believed her husband was downstairs and was doing what she was told for his sake. Even the revolver pointing at her as she backed out of the room and along the balustrade in the landing didn't make her flinch.

'Close the door.'

She did, leaving her handprint on the handle. This was done to cover the smudge Maguire's gloved hand had made when he had opened it to go in. Next came the switch.

'Turn the light off.'

She did, leaving her print on it, again covering the smudge his finger had made.

'Turn it back on.'

'What?'

'Turn it back on.' On it went. 'Downstairs.'

She put her foot on the tread. Maguire came up behind her with the flat of his hand. She turned as she felt it between her shoulder blades, and let out a scream as he shoved her. She toppled forward, her feet giving out, and fell head first onto the fifth stair and rolled all the way down to the hall. Maguire watched every time her head made contact to see if it hit the skirting or the bottom of the rails. He followed her down. Her head was on the floor, her body from the chest down was still part-way up the stairs. He checked her pulse. She was still alive.

'Stone,' Albert Wilson, the retired forensic pathologist, had told me. 'Make sure the character in your book kills the victim by shoving her down a stone staircase. Staircases are not a satisfactory method. One might survive. Carpet acts as a cushion. Stone does not. The object here is to create the impression that the lady was alone. No sign of a break-in; nothing stolen; no sign of a struggle; no incriminating fibres; nothing in her fingernails; the side effects of the pills leaving her unsteady on her feet. Perfectly natural for her to rise in the night, find the landing light is not working, proceed downstairs in the dark, lose her footing and fall to her death. But the carpet can be an obstacle. Stone is much more reliable. In these circumstances, who is to say the lady did not die accidentally? With no sign of an intruder, the police and the FP would be looking at an accident. Subject to a post-mortem.'

'The stairs are carpeted,' I had told him.

'Do they have to be?'

'They do.' The Cedars was carpeted. I couldn't get away from that.

'And the floor below?'

'Carpeted.'

'If the floor below was stone, the victim's head colliding with it would be much more satisfactory.'

'What if I make the killer throw her down again?' I asked him.

'How can she fall twice?'

'The killer carries her back up and throws her down again to finish her off. Who's to say she fell twice?'

'Novel. In those circumstances, it would depend on the first fall. If, during the first fall, she hit her head against, say, the skirting, the skirting would show signs of collision. If she were to again be thrown, and hit her head on the bottom of the rails directly opposite, that would give the game away. Her head could not hit both ends of the same tread twice. One can't choreograph a fall: that would be your main obstacle. If, however, she fell without hitting either skirting or rails, then a second fall might be feasible. It would depend on whether there was blood. A blood wound to the head would give the game away if the blood stained the carpet of a same tread in different places. Again her head cannot be in two places at the same time. Forensic would spot it a mile off. The same applies to the floor below. If the victim's head stains the floor below at the end of the first fall, then blood from the same wound stains the floor in a different place at the end of the second: that would be inconsistent also. It would strongly indicate foul play. If there is no blood from the first fall, a second fall is feasible without being detectable.'

There was no blood. Maguire carried her back up over his shoulders, stood her on the first tread, and pushed her back down again. He again followed her down. Her head hit the floor below; she gave a slight and final groan. The second fall did it.

He went back up, replaced the light bulb with a dud, leaving the landing in darkness, and left. In the car, he removed his gear, except for the surgical gloves, and drove to the Hassett building.

The Gardaí had met Tom Hassett. They'd checked both floors. But since nothing was out of place, the doors in reception still locked, no sign of entry other than the cut-out in the main door, the only obvious conclusion for them to draw was that a thief had cut his way in, heard the alarm, and scarpered.

There was another reason why Maguire had cut such a chunk. To force Tom Hassett to stay behind and fix it. Maguire needed the time that would take.

The Gardaí had gone and Tom Hassett was in a store room along the corridor getting tools and fixings to do a temporary shore-up job, when Maguire slipped in and went upstairs into Hassett's office.

He switched on the monitor and rewound the video tape to where it showed him entering the Hassetts' bedroom. Then wound it back a further five minutes' play time, closed the drawer and switched the monitor off, took out his mobile and rang the phone on the desk. Tom Hassett came up to answer it. Given the late hour, my guess is he thought his wife had found his note and was checking if everything was all right. As soon as he entered his office, Maguire hung up and cocked the revolver. Hassett stopped and turned.

It always amazes me how people react to guns. You can never really rely on a gun when it comes to a job like this where you can't have a struggle. Some people fall apart at the sight of one and will do whatever you tell them. Others don't. Their blood boils and that can lead to a mad charge. As for Hassett, he seemed wary, not overtly frightened. Angry. Angry that someone had had the audacity to break into his office, lain low until the police had given it the all-clear, and then made a move. I'd say that was how he was reading this. It was how I wanted him to read it. I wanted him to think the man standing in front of him was a pro and not to be treated like some opportunist who had just happened to be passing by and had seen an open door.

Hassett had guts. He actually moved toward Maguire. He told him to get out and he wouldn't call the police. Whether or not he would have made a move on the gun, I can't say. He stopped because what had applied to his wife now applied to him: threaten a loved one.

Maguire, for his part, can be a sarky sort of a bastard on the job if people aren't cooperative. And the fact that this guy was standing up to him annoyed him. Hassett's wife was one thing. A woman standing up to a man is no threat. A man is different. Maguire's macho streak didn't like it. He was always the same.

He cocked his head toward the monitor. 'Wanna watch a little TV, y'do?'

Which threw Hassett. He looked at the monitor, then at Maguire, wondering if he knew what it was for, and what he meant by it.

'See what's goin' on back at The Cedars?' Maguire said. Maguire was overdoing it. Stupid. That kind of behaviour could have riled Hassett. But he was worried about The Cedars and held his temper. 'Get over there and face the wall and she won't get hurt. C'mon, shape yourself.'

Hassett acted coy. 'Who won't get hurt?'

'You coming the cunt?'

Hassett backed up.

Maguire went to the desk and sat down in Hassett's chair. He turned the monitor on and waited. The tape was playing.

Hassett turned. 'How did you know about that?'

Maguire just smirked. The thought of this guy, standing there in a blue suit, shirt half done up, grey hair not combed, having rushed out of bed, demanding to know what was going on, and at gunpoint, seemed ludicrous.

On screen the bedroom was in darkness. Hassett's eyes never left it, repeating, 'I said how did you know about that?' For all the good it did him.

Only Hassett, his secretary, and Byrne knew. Byrne he trusted. Mrs Gallagher he trusted. But there'd been the missing two hundred quid. Open to interpretation. Byrne hadn't taken it, he knew that. Byrne was well-off. Byrne had just bought a thirty-grand BM. Byrne hadn't taken it. Two hundred was nothing to Byrne. Mrs Gallagher? Nah. She was honest. She hadn't taken it. But one of them had. Suddenly this was important. Was one of them setting him up? Somebody had told about the monitor. Had to be one of them. After all these years, Mrs Gallagher? No. So how did this guy find out about the monitor? Why did he *want* to find out about it?

Proving Mrs Gallagher was in on this wasn't important. Doubt was. Hassett was beginning to doubt. The guy in his chair had inside information. It had to have come from Gallagher.

Hassett was bound to try and work out how this stranger knew so much about his private and business life. He wasn't stupid. Maguire had been told to say things to Hassett that would *imply* that his secretary was conspiring to rob him. Hassett had to be made to believe that this was a robbery with menace, but that everything else would work out OK if he did what he was told.

'You own a carpark, y'do?'

'What about it?'

'Making plenty, y'are?'

'Why?'

'Ah, sure, y'know yourself: few pound comes in handy. From what I hear, you don't bank it all.'

How did he know that? Only two other people knew that.

Maguire began typing a letter. This letter was a back-up. Whether I'd need it would depend on Hassett's daughter. Hassett watched him type it, his eyes veering from the screen to the typewriter.

'You've a key to that safe, y'have?'

'There's no cash in it.'

Maguire cocked his head for Hassett to open it, then ushered him to the one side with the gun and had a look inside. No cash.

Maguire sat down again. 'Fair enough. We'll look in your other safe.'

On screen, the bedroom door opened and light from the hall shone in on Mrs Hassett. Maguire, on the threshold, wakened her with his boot. She stirred. The drugs she was on meant that her head wasn't clear. She took a little time to come round, to focus on the figure in black standing over her with a revolver in his hand.

Hassett was beside himself. 'What are you doing? Tell me, please tell me, what are you doing?'

'Checking your other safe.'

On screen, Mrs Hassett raised herself up on her elbow, her left hand shielding her eyes against the light, then recoiled from the intruder.

'Don't hurt her,' Hassett pleaded.

That sarky streak of Maguire's raised its head. 'I'm not touching her.'

Mrs Hassett turned in the bed to see if her husband was all right.

'Downstairs,' Maguire said to her, his voice muffled by the stocking he was wearing. He raised the gun. 'I said down-stairs.'

'Don't hurt her. Please don't hurt her. I'll do anything you say. She's not well. Please.'

'I haven't put a hand on her. It's *him* you have to convince.'

'Get downstairs and open the safe. Move,' said the Maguire on the videotape.

Mrs Hassett got out of bed, reached for her dressing gown and put it on. She tied the belt as she skirted the bed.

Tom Hassett cried, 'Leave her alone. Please . . .'

'There'd better be money in that safe.'

'There is. There is. I'll give it to you. All of it. It's yours. Only please don't hurt her. She's not well. Please.'

The screen was very effective. Hassett's face watching it was just as I imagined it would be. He'd have done anything to save her. The slight grogginess in his wife's face, unsure on her feet, these were things he would have noticed much more than a stranger. He saw she was holding up – that defiant streak, that pride. But how would she cope with the stairs, the strain? Would she remember the combination of the living-room safe, her mind muddled from the pills? What if she couldn't? How would that go for her? How would the intruder react to that?

'She knows the combination, she does?'

'Call your friend. I know it. I'll open it. You can have it all. Everything. But please call your friend. She's not well.'

'There's plenty in it, there is?'

'A hundred thousand! More than a hundred! It's yours. All of it. Just take it and go. Not a word to the police. I promise.'

'A hundred?'

'At least.'

'That's too bad.'

'But—' Hassett started trembling. He was inconsolable. The hundred had been his way out. Now it wasn't.

'Need more. Expenses. Y'know?'

'I can get more. Tomorrow. From the bank.'

'They're closed till Monday. How are you gonna get over this problem?'

Hassett was coming apart.

Maguire covered the text of the typed letter. 'Sign here.'

'What? What is it?'

'A beggin' letter.'

'But there's no need for a ransom. I'll give you whatever I have myself. You don't understand. My wife wouldn't be up to coping with the like of this. My daughter's away. I'll—'

'Write "The police must not be involved in this", then make your mark.'

Hassett did so.

On screen the light shone on the packed suitcases. The trip was to begin the next morning. Hassett watched his wife go out of the bedroom. He saw the beam of light die on the cases as the door closed.

(I viewed the videotape afterwards to see if this part of the plan could've been improved any. All in all I was happy with it.)

Maguire opened the rucksack. 'Put these on.'

'What? But my wife—'

'That guy hasn't my good nature. Hates being kept waitin'.'

Tom Hassett put on the padded gauntlets. Maguire bound his wrists with tape.

Maguire drove. Hassett was in the passenger seat. He was in a bad way.

They came to the country road leading to the lake opposite the McDermotts' place. It was dry and visibility was good.

The first thing the law would look for was skid-marks on the road. Maguire jammed on the brakes and as the car screeched and fishtailed, he swerved onto the slip leading down to the lake. Up ahead in the headlights, a box lay at the water's edge.

Hassett saw it. Whether he could tell what it was in the false light against the dark of the lake, I couldn't say. But Maguire later told Toner that Hassett nearly went into convulsions at the sight of it. Maguire pulled a heavily-padded balaclava over Hassett's head, pushed the door lever and told him to get out.

'But my wife?'

'Out ya get.'

He kept looking at the box through the slits in the balaclava. The box terrified him. He began pleading. 'Please. Look, I'll—. Plea-ease . . . plea-ea-ease. What are you going to do?'

Maguire went round and manhandled him out. 'Walk.'

Maguire killed the lights. The sharp angle of the box now stood out against the grey water like a tablet of stone.

Maguire pushed him toward it, the gun in the small of his back. They reached it. Maguire wrapped foam around each of Hassett's legs and ankles and bound them with tape. Then taped his arms to his sides. Hassett was crying and shaking involuntarily at the sight of the box.

'In ya get.'

'But my wife? Your money?' he sobbed uncontrollably.

Maguire put the gun to his head. 'Ya wanna save her – get in.'

No man in his right mind would have got into that box, unless it was to save the one he loved. I'd figured he'd do anything for her, the night I saw them having dinner.

So Hassett had no choice.

If I was reading this right, he was thinking this was part of some plan he didn't understand. But everything would be all right as long as he did what he was told. They'd get the cash from the safe and everything would be all right. The ransom note, he thought. *They wouldn't be making me sign a ransom note if they were going to kill me.* This was all part of some plan he didn't understand, he kept telling himself.

'But how will I breathe?'

'It's air-conditioned,' said Maguire, pointing to a hole in the lid. He cocked the trigger. 'Get in.'

'Now, wait a minute, for God's sake, man.'

'Get in to fuck or I pull the trigger.'

Hassett looked up at the cottage on the hill where his daughter lived and saw that it was in darkness. Maybe he was hoping the light would come on or that she'd rush out and Maguire would see her and think she had raised the alarm. Maybe he was in his own way saying goodbye because in his heart he knew this was the end and that he'd been fooling himself thinking everything would be all right. It's hard to say. He was desperate, that's all I can say.

Tom Hassett needed help to get in the padded coffin. He looked up through the eye-slits. He pleaded for some sign that it would turn out all right. There was none. But there was the hole. *He wouldn't go to the trouble of it if he didn't want me to live.* The alternative reason for the hole was too much to bear and he couldn't contemplate it as a possibility without going mad. Though I'd say he contemplated it. Maguire closed the lid, bolt-clamping it tight.

Keeping hold of the rope attached to it, Maguire slid the bottom half of the coffin into the lake. He took out a compact recorder and held it over the hole in the top half which wasn't in the lake. Hassett felt the water coming in the bottom half and began to scream. He called out his wife's name. He called it out like it was a farewell, full of regret and sadness that he would never see her again.

Maguire filled the measuring can with water from the lake and poured it in through the hole. Hassett screamed 'Oh Bridie, oh Bridie.' He gulped against the water from the can coming in through the hole. Maguire kept filling it. He poured it again. Taping the spurting and the gulps and the lamenting tortured wail 'Oh Bridie. Oh Carol . . . Annie.' He was lamenting his own death and calling to those he loved. I'd say that's what it was.

Maguire lit a cigarette. He smoked the cigarette and when he was done he was still on his hunkers pouring and Hassett was still fighting against the water coming in. Maguire had it all on tape. I needed ten minutes on tape. But it only took eight minutes to fill the top half of the coffin with the measuring can through the hole.

The tape was a back-up measure. I wasn't sure if I'd use it. It all depended on Carol Byrne. If I did use it, it would come before the letter. The letter and the tape formed part of a sequence I was working on.

'The killer in your book,' the forensic pathologist had said. 'He carries the victim out of the box, removes the padded hood, et cetera, then puts the victim behind the wheel of the car, puts the car in automatic drive, and sends it into the lake?'

'Yes.'

Maguire did this and watched the car sink. Then he carried the coffin along the road to his van and drove up to the McDermotts' cottage on the hill. He took the coffin out of the van and placed it beside the garden hose. Then he rang the bell. The lights came on and Annie McDermott opened the door in her dressing gown. He had his back to her. He turned and aimed the revolver at her stomach.

'Your next victim is pregnant?' the FP had asked.

'Yes. The gun is pointing at her baby. So she'll do what she's told. She's afraid for her unborn child.'

'What does she say to the killer?'

'She asks him what he's doing.'

'She probably thinks he's come to rob the place.'

'She's supposed to think that.'

'It's amazing.'

'What is?'

'When police interview killers, they invariably say their victims had begun by asking the killer what he is doing. What the victim is actually asking, of course, is: Will you not harm me if I do what you say? It's ironic, really, asking someone who is threatening your life not to harm you. Why put your trust in a person who is holding a gun on you? The victim is hoping everything will turn out for the best, of course. Still, it has a certain irony to it.'

'That's fear for you.'

'This dying-in-a-box theory of yours. That could prove to be difficult. The victim would scratch violently against the inside of the box. Inconsistent.'

'The killer gives her a pair of padded gauntlets. She puts them on. He binds her wrists.'

'She would go mad trying to get out. Bruising would occur, on her head, feet, knees.'

'He places a padded hood over her head. He pads each of her legs, then binds her legs together. The inside of the box is heavily padded. Nothing to impact upon. No bruising. He carries her to the box and places her inside. He then bolts the lid shut. She is now inside the box. And she can't move.'

Maguire did this.

'The cause of asphyxiation is your problem,' said the FP.

'How?'

'Drowning is to be the cause of death.'

'So?'

'The victim might wedge her padded hands against the inside of the hole in the lid. This would stop the water coming in. It would also stop air getting in. She would suffocate through lack of oxygen. Not drown.'

'The killer has bound her arms to her sides. She can't raise her hands to the hole.'

'That would take care of it. If she cannot plug the hole, then water can enter her lungs. Then what happens?'

'The killer places the hosepipe in the hole and turns on the garden tap. The box begins to fill.'

Maguire did this.

'But I thought you said she is to drown in the lake.'

'She is. It will look like she drowned in the lake.'

'Then your killer has made a big mistake. Tap water is treated. Lake water is not. The water found in her lungs must be untreated.'

'Her death takes place in the country. Water pumped from lakes is common. The water in the hosepipe comes from the lake.'

'Tell me, why is it so important to have so many "accidents"?'

'The killer is a medical professor. He knows all there is to know about how the body responds. He runs a sort of a Betty Ford clinic. His patients are totally dependent on him and they're loaded. He's in their will. If the FP sees an "accident" the professor's in the money. He's after their money.'

'Well, I must say, you seem to have ironed out all the obstacles. If I were the FP, and I saw these corpses, not a mark on them, no sign of foul play, skid-marks on the road, I'd say he's in the money too. Even if there were some bruising, I might put it down to the victim trying to force his or her way out of the car. How does he get caught?'

'He doesn't.'

'But I thought the bad guys always get caught.'

'This book is true to life. Bad guys are walking around even as we speak. They didn't get caught. They didn't kill anybody. No bad guys. No murders. "Accidents." Nothing to investigate. Tragedies. Nothing more.'

'And in what genre is this? Thriller or chiller?'

'A *Do It Yourself. How to Kill*.'

He laughed; thought I was joking.

'Told from the killer's point of view,' I said.

'You will spell my name right in the Acknowledgements, won't you?'

Albert Wilson's not that hard to spell.

The hosepipe kept filling. Maguire did not tape Annie McDermott's screams. I had no reason to tape her dying.

Maguire left the hosepipe. He went to the phone in the hall and dialled The Cedars. The answerphone came on and he hung up.

The coffin was overflowing when he came back. He unbolted the lid, removed the padding, carried Annie McDermott to the back of the van and laid her on a sheet. He emptied the water out of the coffin and put it next to her, then drove down to the slip. He carried her down and waded in. The car was fully submerged. He went under-water and opened the driver's door. Tom Hassett's body was slumped over the wheel. He lifted Hassett's body halfway out of the car and laid Annie McDermott's body across it.

Of course, the beauty of all this was motive. I couldn't see anyone getting caught for this. Everything had gone smoothly. But even if it did go wrong, who were they going to suspect? The one with motive. Carol Byrne would inherit everything. She had motive. It was an unlikely scenario that Carol Byrne would commit such acts. Or have others commit them for her. But police always suspect a member of the family. That's the way it is. I don't know the actual statistic but, more often than not, murder *is* committed by next of kin. As I say, I couldn't see it coming to that. Besides, as an extra precaution, I had insisted that Carol Byrne and her husband were out of the country. They had an alibi. It wouldn't have suited my purposes for the Byrnes to come under suspicion. They were in a hotel in London.

Byrne was laughing when he told the story to Toner.

He and Carol were in bed when a knock came to the door. Carol was smiling and looking back at her husband in the bed where they had just made love. He winked at her and she giggled.

Then she pulled on a dressing gown, opened the door and saw a fresh-faced constable. He asked her if she was Mrs Carol Byrne. She said she was. The constable looked as though he himself had just received bad news. He probably thought he had to look like that. He said he was afraid he had bad news.

'All three are dead,' was all she heard before she collapsed.

Byrne, of course, in the role of the concerned husband, jumped out of bed, overcome, and rushed to her side. He said she never suspected a thing.

I never saw anything funny in it. I'd say he was laughing because he was really full of nerves that it had actually happened. That, and a bit of sucking-up to Toner. I suppose Byrne couldn't believe his luck. He was closer to getting his hands on his wife's inheritance. That's why he was excited. I never liked that guy.

By the way, I saw another expert while I was away – a psychiatrist.

Chapter Fourteen

Now I had to sort out my own problems. Sinead.

I went along to the *National Tribune* the next morning to see Molly Murray. She wasn't in the best of form, I have to say. All that reporting must take it out of her. Nah, I'm only joking. She loves her job, really. Nosing around in other people's business. What woman wouldn't? I'd say she was in bad form because I'd come to see her.

Naturally, I was wearing my sad face. Wanted to give the impression this business with Sinead was getting to me. The old soft-soap approach. 'I need to talk to you, Molly.'

She looked at me as if I was some sort of disease. Stick together, these sisters, that's the worst of it. 'How'd you get in here?'

'They know I'm your brother-in-law, Moll.'

'Not for much longer. Divorce came in last year.'

'What kinda talk's that?'

'Gerd, I want to say something very important to you.'

'What?'

'Fuck off.'

'Molly, I only want to talk.'

'Wrong office. Adultery's along the corridor.'

'Molly, for Christ's sake.'

'You've been dirty-dicking my sister.'

'Molly—'

'What's the matter, Gerd, too crude for you?'

'I'm being condemned without a hearing, Moll.'

'You'll get your hearing.'

'But I didn't do anything.'

'*Louse* with an "I".'

'What?'

'I believe that's how you spell it. A parasite. Feeds off husbands. Ring any bells?'

'Look, Moll, let me tell you what happened. I go out, have a few drinks, come home, get a bottle over the skull—'

'Sit.'

'What?'

'Sit.'

I did.

'Now,' here came the finger-waving, 'you're a respectable man who makes his living honourably. You're successful. You drive a top-of-the range BM; home like a palace. You're good to your wife and children. They want for nothing. You're OK. Right so far?'

'Well, you know me, Moll – not one to brag.'

'But you have a dick.'

Stumped me a bit, that one.

Mind like a calculator, our Moll. You can see it in her, digiting away. She has this way of summarizing details into darts; then she throws them at you, aiming below the belt, of course. She also has that direct, school-marm way of talking to you as if you've just failed your exams and you're out the door with her boot up your arse. A real turn-on. She's wasted on that wimp Liam.

'At the hearing you may or may not be given the opportunity – I don't know, I don't cover divorce – to say whether your dick has been where it shouldn't. You'll say "No". Why? Because that's what men say. Divorce courts are full of innocent men. Right so far?'

This will give you some idea of the sort of crap I have to take from Sinead's sister. OK, I'm guilty. But they don't know that. They only think it. I'm being condemned on hearsay. No evidence. If you don't get caught, you shouldn't get condemned. Otherwise what's the point in going out of your way not to get caught? I think it's disgraceful.

She straightened the jacket of the red two-piece suit she was wearing; white top, black tights. Or maybe suspenders. Hmm, nice! Whoever invented tights should be shot.

'You see, Gerd, what you, and all men like you, don't realize is this.' (Oh shit! She was definitely in her lecturing mode.) 'The days of the dinosaurs who still believe in the old "Anything goes as long as you get the leg over" mentality are gone. It's a state of mind that only men have. I'm bringing myself down to your level in saying this, you understand. It applies to those who absolve themselves of guilt on the grounds that God created them to procreate and, on that basis, they'd be going against God's will if they failed to procreate at every opportunity. They're very selective, of course. It's a "man" thing. They believe that "Thou shalt not commit adultery" applies only to wives – their wives – not those whom *they* seek to adulterate.

'When they're caught out, whether it be in the office or on the shop floor, they say: "Oh, you can't flirt with a woman these days or you'll be accused of sexual harassment. Why are they getting all legal about it?" And when they get caught cheating in niteclubs, they concoct the biggest pile of lies to get themselves off and when no one believes them, they feel aggrieved because the case against them is not proven in the face of all their "evidence", even when they know that they themselves manipulated the facts. Am I getting through to you, Gerd? Am I convincing you that your coming in here with "I'm innocent" written all over your face will fail to elicit one iota of understanding? Hmm?'

Jesus, poor Liam, fancy having to live with that! Hope this is not one of her good days.

(By the way, I meant to tell you my good news. I told Toner not to remove that shampoo bottle from Noreen Bawn's flat after all. In fact I told him to keep topping it and future bottles up. I also had him arrange for the odd pinch of cocaine to be sprinkled around the flat, and in her clothes. I want her smelling of the stuff. One of his dealers has also taken to doing business across the road from her place. So junkies congregate there from time to time – well, every night, just about. Nothing's been levelled against Bawn. That would be too obvious.

In my experience of setting people up, it's better to just create situations where things can be open to interpretation. Then, when she's arrested, everything'll click into place. I have to get her out of the way, y'see. As I say, she's a bad influence on Sinead. That's my problem.

But the good news is that a dog handler who works for the GNDU – that's the Garda National Drugs Unit – has a thing for Bawn. He obviously likes his women rough. Skinny, gawky-looking fucker he is, with a turn in his eye, by the name of O'Reilly. They used to go together a few years ago. Anyway, it seems he's back on the scene. They were seen together in Hugo's the other night. It's only a matter of time before he bumps into her in the street wearing his uniform – gives her a hug, contaminates himself that way, know what I mean? It'll be some crack when the sniffer dogs start sniffing around *him*. His mates in blue'll be giving him some funny looks. Course, it'd be even better if he came across Bawn when Bonzo's with him. It'd be all over her. It'll think she's a walking joint. After a while O'Reilly's bound to start wondering why it is that every time he hugs Bawn, his dogs are sniffing dope on him. With luck something'll come of it. I'll keep you posted.)

'I hadn't realized everybody had such a low opinion of me, Moll.'

'Just me and Sinead. We both think you're . . . what's the word I'm looking for?'

'Too broad-minded?'

'Try warped-minded.'

'Kick-Gerd-when-he's-down time. I see.'

'Excellent. I'd hate to think I was wasting my breath.'

'How's the kids?'

'Fine.'

'No, I mean mine.'

'So do I.'

That disappointed me. I was hoping they'd be applying pressure. 'How are they taking this?'

'They're not leverage, Gerd.'

'Who said they were?'

'You did, when you kept their dog.'

'It ran away.'

'Bollocks!'

'You're not being fair, Moll. I'd never use my boys that way.'

'You did before. They're why she took you back before. And before that and before that and before that.'

She answered her phone. I got the gist of what she was

137

saying about the Hassetts. The car had been found. No mention of Mrs Hassett, though. She stood up and slipped a microcassette into the top pocket of her jacket. She had that excited, suddenly preoccupied look about her that said a promising story had just broken.

'I need to see Sinead, Moll.'

'Try her solicitor.'

'I just want to talk to her. See she has enough money. Look, tell her I'll meet her any time, any place. Tell her to ring me. Surely she can do that.'

'I'll tell her.'

'Thanks.'

'And by the way – that tale about Noreen Bawn – nobody's believing it. Sinead knows you've been cheating on her, Bawn or no Bawn. Stick that up your arse and choke on it.'

Hmm. So much for dialogue aimed at conflict resolution.

Chapter Fifteen

Women! Fuck me – they must think we're all idiots.

You take Sinead. For somebody who's trying to steer clear of me, she's going a funny way about it. I mean, let's say you went away, you know, from your old man, split up, wanted a divorce, didn't want him to find you, all that. Would you take your joint cheque book? Write cheques in the area you're staying in so he can go into your bank and say: 'Here, who's been writing all these cheques?'

'Your wife, sir.'

That's what I did. I asked the bank. That's how I found out she had rented a house in Wicklow town. A holiday home. She'd used her credit card as well. I read the statements while I was watching the news. Sinead knows me. She knew I'd pick up on stuff like that. So why did she do it if she doesn't want me to find her? Simple. She wants me to go after her and get down on one knee. Beg forgiveness. Know what I mean? Trying to make me believe she doesn't wanna know me, while leaving a trail for me to follow.

The newsreader was saying that the Gardaí had cordoned off the area round the lake.

I'd say Molly Murray got on the blower to her as soon as

I'd left. What did he say? Bla bla bla. And then what did he say? Bla bla bla. And what did you say?

A Garda was being interviewed at the top of the slip, a TV reporter asking him if he suspected foul play. 'Too soon to say. We've set up an incident room.'

Wouldn't worry about that; that's normal, y'know, for *potential* witnesses to ring in if they'd seen anything. Mobile crane arriving to lift out Hassett's car.

They cut to The Cedars. Onlookers. Police tape. Ambulance. Bringing out Hassett's wife's body. At this stage, the law would keep an open mind. You know how it works: talk to the friends and neighbours, hold post-mortems, suss it out. They usually give an indication if they suspect foul play. They weren't giving any on this programme. Good sign, that. Reporter gave a little background: Mr Hassett was a Dublin businessman; he and his wife were due to go on holiday; survived by their younger daughter, Carol. All pretty tame. Good night's work, actually, on the face of it.

Step one had been accomplished.

Step two had begun.

'Kipper. Here we are, Kipper.' Kipper's the kids' red setter. I had him in kennels while I was away. I'll blame what I have in mind for him on them. Beef and onions and wild mushrooms. Looked them up in a mushroom-and-toadstool guide in a book called *Nature's Poisons*. This type grow in under cedars. That's why I chose them.

Poisoning a dog's not as straightforward as you might think. Certain rat poisons don't work on them. Anything that eats dug-up old bones is hard poisoned. So whether this would work or not, I couldn't say. If it did, I'd have a use for the ones growing in the garden of The Cedars. That way it wouldn't look out of the ordinary when Carol Byrne came to use them. 'There, boy, that nice? Munch munch.' Gave him a good helping. Couple of days, then liver and kidney failure occurs. Or was it heart failure and asphyxiation? Still, soon find out. They look much the same as ordinary mushrooms. Easy for a person to confuse them with the real thing. That's the beauty. 'There's a good boy.'

All this was aimed at that pup Byrne had bought his wife, just in case you're wondering. Not that she was gonna poison it. That was Maguire's job. She'd only *think* she'd poisoned it.

I'd already worked out another little idea to do with her. To do with her bath plug, as it happens. Ever notice how long the chain on yours is? Course not. Start noticing things like that, you're leading one hell of a mundane life. I mean, would you believe me if I told you I know how long mine is? Why the fuck would anybody want to know such crap, you'd say. Well, a plug on a long chain will not accidentally go into the hole when the water's running, if you must know. I've tried. A plug will only go into the hole accidentally if it's on just the right length of chain. Then the slightest trickle will push it in.

When the time comes, Byrne will have a bath. Carol will clean up after him, then she'll go out. Maguire will go in, adjust the chain – maybe take a few links out of it, doctor the overflow, whatever – fill the bath, leave the tap on and no more: Carol comes back to a flood. She'll think she went out and left the tap on and the water forced the plug into the hole. If it looks right, she won't question it. That's why I'm boring you with all this shit. Another small detail, I know. But as I said before: everything has to look normal in this game. You have to use the facilities at hand. Don't go getting technical when you're using everyday things. It will look out of place.

I had to explain it all to Toner, so he could explain it to Maguire. As usual, Maguire was in his sailor's overcoat, and sucking the life out of a cigarette.

'We're talkin' about the upstairs bathroom, Paddy, we are?'

'The one directly above the entrance hall where they keep that chess set and antique furniture. Seen Con Ivers lately?'

'Haven't, Paddy, no. Haven't seen him about this good while.'

'He's our scapegoat.'

'You're jokin'! Con? Con's on the way out? Fuck me. Ya want me to handle him, y'do?'

'Thought that'd make you happy.'

'Can't wait to see his face.'

'I'm waiting to see yours when you tipple to the bonus behind it.'

'What bonus is that?'

Toner grinned.

'What?'

'Think about it.'

Maguire twigged. Now he was grinning. 'Fuck me, Paddy, you're one shrewd cunt!'

'You see it?'

'Sure, who wouldn't?'

'Isn't it a cracker?'

'By fuck, it is!'

'You gonna go for it?'

'Fuckin' right I'm gonna go for it, Paddy.'

'How much?'

'Dunno. Much d'you think he'd wear?'

'He lent Byrne fifty.'

'You're kiddin'?'

142

'Sure's God.'

'If he lent Byrne fifty, I have to be good for a hundred. I'm a better risk. You're lookin' a wedge, y'are?'

'It's all yours.'

'Fuck me. Even better.'

Ivers didn't have a hundred. He had eighty. Maguire borrowed that. Handy borrowing money from people when you know they're not gonna live long enough to collect.

Chapter Sixteen

———◆◇◆———

Byrne wants to know when his wife's gonna commit suicide. Doesn't give you much of a chance, does he? We've only just done his fucking in-laws. Course, I know what's happened here. Whenever we pull a stroke like this, y'see, Maguire turns on that radio scanner of his and picks up what the Guards are saying on their car radios. That way we get a progress report, y'know, the Hassetts' autopsies came up clean, stuff like that. When Byrne heard that, he said he wanted the autopsy on his wife.

I told Toner to tell him to fuck away off. Carol doesn't commit anything till she sees a shrink. Byrne says she's refusing to go. Well, of course she's refusing to go. People don't just *go* to shrinks. Especially someone as shy as Carol Byrne. Shy people are the last to go and see shrinks. It's all a question of persuading her to go. For the suicide angle to work, you have to make sure a shrink hears from her own lips that she blames herself for her parents' and sister's deaths. That way, when the shrink gets called and the Inquest hears that owing to her low mental state, bla bla bla, suicide was a strong possibility, you have an impartial expert opinion working in your favour. Could take months before we get to that stage. Byrne'll have to wait.

I'd say Byrne's been taking comfort from Molly Murray's coverage of this as well. Molly wrote what I wanted her to write, which was that phone records showed that Annie McDermott rang The Cedars to check on her father when she saw what appeared to be her father's car skidding into the lake, then went to help him and died trying. Molly concluded her piece by speculating that the phone call woke Mrs Hassett and the machine clicked in before she answered it. She saw her husband was gone, got up and fell in the dark.

Molly's no fool, though. She actually rented a silver Audi with a white stripe like Tom Hassett's and had someone drive it toward the lake at four the next morning, when visibility was just as good, while she watched it from the McDermotts' cottage. She could see it clear enough to recognize it, and decided that that was the way it must have happened.

There's a couple of question marks over Christy McDermott's activities that night. That rowboat of his wasn't at the slip when Hassett's car went in, for instance. I'm still trying to clear that up.

McDermott seems to be holding up well, though. Can't say the same for Carol Byrne. She's still roaring her eyes out. They were in the back of the first car, along with Byrne. A coffin in each of the three hearses behind. Just turning into the cemetery. Family plot, by the look of it.

My mobile sounded. 'Hello.'

'Gerd?'

'Sinead?'

'Gerd?'

'What's the matter, Sinead?'

'Gerd?' She sounds in a bad way. 'I . . . I've . . .'

146

'You've what, Sinead?'

'I've been arrested.'

'Arrested? Why?'

'Can you come down? I'm in Store Street station.'

'Where are the kids?'

'With a welfare officer.'

'A *welfare* officer? What the hell's going on, Sinead?'

'Just come down, will you? I need your help.'

They're getting out of the funeral cars now. Byrne's helping Carol to the grave. She looks ready to faint. McDermott's being comforted by, I dunno, relatives, I suppose. There's a good turnout. The Hassetts must have been well liked.

'You better tell me what's going on, Sinead. Sinead?'

She hung up. Must have been hard for her to ask me for help. I'd say that's part of the reason she's crying. But I knew she'd ring me. She always turns to me when things go wrong. Most people ring their brief. But Sinead knows I'll take care of everything. Things are working out OK.

The priest's getting ready to do his bit. McDermott's in bits at the sight of his wife's coffin being carried to the grave. Byrne's got his arm round Carol's waist, holding her up. Fuck this, it could take half an hour to lower those three in. I rang my solicitor and got going.

See me? I've always been lucky. Luck's something I put great store in. Many's a one can try till doomsday to get something going, but me, I dunno, it always just seems to fall into place. I suppose it's because I never rush at it. Patience, y'see. I'm a great believer in doing things bit by bit. You read about people who get caught conspiring against some poor fucker. The m.o.'s often the same. They leave a trail any halfwit cop could follow. You never read about the ones who don't get caught. Course you don't. Their hand in it is not to be seen. Makes you wonder when you read the papers what the *real* truth is. And I'll tell you something else: being too smart can get you caught just as easily as being stupid. I'll explain what I mean by that.

Sinead got caught. I don't know how. And I don't need to. But I'd lay odds some cop went looking for Noreen Bawn to ask her why her phone number was in Sean Connors's top pocket when they found him shot in the head, found traces of cocaine in her flat and convinced himself he had a case. Bawn'll deny everything, of course. She'll say it's a plant. But that's what they all say, isn't it? If a cop has evidence, he has a case. He's not interested in investigating conspiracy theories. He doesn't see no *master plan*. Sinead must have been with Bawn when she was picked up. Wonder what they're charging her with? Doesn't matter. I have the mother of my children mixed up in it. If she goes ahead with this divorce, the judge'll take that into account when I sue for custody. That's the important thing.

'Michael, it's Gerd Quinn. I want you to go down to Store Street station for me. Sinead's been arrested.'

'For what?'

'I don't know. Probably back-lipped a traffic warden.'

'She must have back-*kicked* him if they arrested her for it.'

'The thing is, the kids were with her.'

'Ah, I see. Leave it to me.'

'What way does that work, Michael?'

'If they hold Sinead, which is unlikely once I arrange bail, if it even comes to that, they'll release the kids to you, you being the father, a solid citizen of good character and all that.'

'Thanks, Michael.'

*   *   *

148

I contacted Toner and told him to get me one hundred deals of cocaine.

Then I drove to that house Sinead had rented in Wicklow town. The name of it was on the credit card statement. I looked up the address in the tourist accommodation book for the area. It was simply a case of picking the front-door lock and going inside. I then went up to the bathroom, took the lid off the cistern and put the cellophane-wrapped coke inside. Then I went to Store Street Garda station in Dublin.

Michael – grey pinstriped suit, slanted-line tie, fox-coloured hair – was at the desk waiting for me. He took me to one side. You should have seen the look on his face. 'Gerd,' he said, 'I've got extremely bad news. I'm still having trouble believing it myself, knowing yourself and Sinead as I do.'

'What is it, Michael?'

'You're not going to believe this.'

'Believe what?'

'Sinead. They're holding her for being in possession of drugs.'

'*What?*'

'Gerd, is there something you're not telling me? I'm your solicitor. You can tell me anything. That's my job. I deal with this sort of thing every day. I just hadn't expected to be having to deal with a case concerning anyone to do with you.'

Michael usually handles my business affairs. Crime never comes into it.

'Look, Michael, Sinead walked out on me five weeks ago. There's nothing else to tell. As far as this is concerned, it's a mistake. They've got their facts wrong. Sinead doesn't do drugs. End of story.'

He thumbed his moustache. 'What about this Noreen Bawn?'

'What about her?'

'Sinead was in her flat when they were arrested.'

'They arrested Bawn as well?'

'Yes. That will go in Sinead's favour. The drugs were found in Bawn's flat. Sinead can argue she wasn't to know, she was just visiting.'

'There you are, then.'

'It's not quite that simple as far as my own position is concerned, Gerd.'

'You've lost me.'

'Sinead tells me she instructed another solicitor to serve divorce papers on you. I can't act for her here. There's a direct conflict of interest. You're my client. I can only act for you.'

'Surely you can arrange bail for her.'

'They won't grant bail yet. They're arranging for a warrant to search a house in Wicklow.'

'What for?'

'For more drugs, of course. Look, Gerd, I appreciate you're not too au fait with this. Let me explain how it works. They found thirty deals in Bawn's flat. A dealer's quantity. Not a user's quantity. On the face of it, it looks as if Bawn was dealing. However, if they find more drugs in Wicklow—'

'They won't.'

'If they do, Sinead will have a hard time proving that she knew nothing of it, when it was she who rented the house.'

'Sinead wouldn't have anything to do with drugs. Believe me, Michael. I know her. She detests drugs.'

'All we can do is wait.'

'Where's my two boys, Michael?'

'I've arranged for them to be brought over.'

'Thanks.'

Michael then lowered his chin and came at me as if he was about to divulge a state secret. He was half-whispering as he said it. 'You know, Gerd, this might give you some leverage.'

'What?'

'In the divorce.'

'There won't be one. She'll come to her senses.'

'She seemed adamant.'

'I know her.'

'OK, then hypothetically. All right?'

I nodded.

'If it comes to a divorce, Sinead would get custody.'

'I'd have something to say about that.'

'I know. And I'd do my best for you, you know that. But the fact is, she can't get custody if she's in prison.'

'Jesus, Michael. *Prison?*'

'They come down hard on dealers these days. Even first offenders. And divorce is a messy business. She'll drag up the dirt against you. And you'll have to do the same to her, if you want custody. If she goes up on a drugs charge, and even if she doesn't do time, we can still blacken her with it in a custody battle.'

'I hadn't thought of that. But—'

'I know. I know. You don't want to play dirty. Think about it. That's all I'm saying.'

I sounded reluctant. 'OK, if that's your advice. Listen, I'm gonna wait outside.'

'Don't you want to see Sinead?'

'Yes. But I'm not going to today. I'm not having my boys stay here longer than I have to.'

Chapter Seventeen

Naturally every father wants his sons to grow up like him, and I'm no exception.

Now, you take my eldest, Steven. He's eleven. He's like his mother, soft. His mother behind bars is getting to him more than it is to Gerd. Gerd's a year younger. Emotionally he's the stronger of the two. He's more like me. I'd say he'll grow up to be like me. Steven only picked at his tea when I brought them home, whereas Gerd got tucked in. Steven was the first to ask about Kipper. He wanted to know whether he'd come back. I told him he had. But that he'd run away again. Steven was ready for crying, whereas Gerd shrugged, said they'd go and look for him in the morning and had another spoonful of baked beans.

'You have to go back to school in the morning,' I told them. 'You've lost enough time already.' I didn't want the bother of looking after them, y'see. I'd things to do.

'Can't we go the next day, Dad?' Steven asked me. 'Please.' He was all upset. Maybe Kipper was lying in some ditch somewhere waiting on the cavalry. 'We can find Kipper tomorrow and go the next day.'

Actually, Kipper was in that septic tank. The poison

mushrooms did the trick. I figured I'd put him to good use, help me get it going faster.

'Yeah, we can go the next day, Dad,' Gerd said.

I laughed to myself. If I knew Gerd junior, he was using Kipper as an excuse to miss school.

'I've your education to think of, kids,' I said. 'Know what I mean? I'd be failing in my responsibility.'

'One day won't make any difference.'

'It might. They might be teaching you geography tomorrow. They might be teaching you what an ice cap is. That question might come up in your exams. You get it wrong. You think it's for a hangover. Get bad marks. The whole exam might hang on that one question. But if you get it right, you'll pass; get a good job. You'll thank me one day. You'll be sitting at your desks in some flash office making a fortune, and you'll say to yourselves: Dad was right. If we'd failed our exams, we'd be digging ditches. Thank God he didn't shirk his responsibility. Thank God we knew what an ice cap was. There but for the grace of geography go I. Know what I mean? Pass the salt.'

'You don't half talk a load of crap, Dad,' Gerd said.

'Go on, Dad,' Steven persisted. 'Can we, please?'

'Yeah, go on, Dad. We find Kipper, we go to school with peace of mind, we learn more. Psychological. Know what I mean?' That Gerd, he's got an answer for everything. 'Besides, Dad, we can be here for when Mammy comes home. She'll like that.'

'Yeah,' said Steven. He meant it, whereas my namesake was *using* it.

'OK, you can look for Kipper tomorrow.'

'Thanks, Dad,' they said.

'Now, boys, I've got a little problem. Will you two be OK

by yourselves in the morning for a couple of hours, while you're looking for Kipper, I mean? You don't need me to come with you, do you? I'm not much good searching through fields.'

'You'd slow us down.'

'That's what I thought. I've to go and pick up your mother's car in case it gets clamped. Where did she park it?'

'Round the corner from Noreen Bawn's flat.'

'Good. Now, I've to go out tonight. I've got a babysitter—'

'We're not babies!'

'Sorry, I've got a young lady coming over to mind the place. Leaving you alone for a couple of hours tomorrow's one thing, but that doesn't mean I can leave you alone at night. Her name's Mary. You'll like her.'

I'd phoned Lou earlier and explained that her name was now Mary. What the kids don't know won't bother them, I told her. We can get them off to bed, then get ourselves off to bed. She was very reluctant, didn't wanna use the kids just so she could be with me. She's sensitive like that. I spun her a yarn.

She was trembling when I opened the front door. She'd dressed down for the occasion, jeans and sweater. 'Ah, you must be Mary,' I said.

She grabbed my arm and pulled me outside.

'What's up?'

She spoke under her breath. 'I'm shaking like a leaf. That's what's up.'

'Why?'

'Keep your voice down.'

'Why are you so nervous?'

'I'm nervous about meeting your kids.'

'Don't be daft. They're only a couple of lads.'

155

'Yeah, but they're *yours*. I want to make a good impression.'

'You're only supposed to be babysitting, Lou. If you start trying to make a good impression, they'll wonder why. Now calm down. Take a deep breath. Come in and sit down and keep your mouth shut. They'll think you're just shy. I'll do all the talking.'

'OK.'

'Right.'

'OK.'

'Why are you tensing yourself up? Look at you.'

'I'm steeling myself.'

'You're *steeling* yourself?'

'Stop laughing.'

'Lou, you're not going on a *mission*.'

'Shut up. And stop calling me Lou.' She pushed me indoors.

Gerd was in the hall. 'Gerd, this is Lou-ou—' Lou froze. '—lou-oook. Look at the time Gerd, this is Mary.'

She smiled at him.

'I thought you said she was a nice person, Dad?'

Lou looked uncomfortable. She thought he was saying she wasn't.

'What's that supposed to mean?'

'You said she was very nice. Then you opened the door and said "Ah, you must be Mary". Which means you've only just met her. So how did you know she was nice?'

'Get in there, you little scoundrel. I meant she came highly recommended.'

He ran into the living room, laughing. Sharp as a scalpel, that little fucker.

Steven came out. He looked at Lou. She smiled. His face lit up. 'Auntie Molly,' he said.

I turned and saw Molly Murray in the doorway. I don't know what my face looked like but you shoulda seen Lou's. She looked as if she was hoping a stone would appear so she could crawl under it.

Molly looked like just such a stone.

'Molly,' I gulped. 'What . . . brings you here?'

'Gerd, Auntie Molly's here,' Steven called to his brother. They both went to her, asking whether she'd heard any more about their mother. 'No,' she said. 'Your mammy's coming home tomorrow. This has all been a terrible mistake.' She may have been talking to the kids, but it was me and Lou she was looking down her nose at. Poor Lou, she didn't know where to put herself.

Now, if I knew that wife of mine, she wouldn't have told the boys a word about my *alleged* indiscretions. She wouldn't have dragged them into it, in other words. And neither would Molly. Her look of contempt suggested that she might explode into a tirade of abuse – how dare I bring my fancy woman here, stuff like that. But she was controlling it. For the boys' sake. She knew I knew that. They're into that 'Keep it from the kids' stuff, her and Sinead.

The kids saw her staring at Lou. 'That's Mary,' Gerd said.

Molly let go one of her darts. 'Oh? *Mary?* Must be your middle name.'

'She's come to mind us,' Steven said.

Then another. 'Is that what they call it these days?'

I glanced at Lou. She looked mortified. She'd convinced herself she was about to be condemned as a harlot before my sons' very eyes. Which didn't really fit in with her wanting to make a good impression on them. She'd never live it down. I had to help her out. 'Actually, Molly, I'm glad you came.'

She cocked her eyebrows. That snooty school-marm expression at work again. 'Oh?'

'Yes. I wanted to talk to you about helping Sinead.'

'I'm all ears.'

'In my study.'

She threw in another look of contempt at Lou for good measure, then patted the boys' heads. 'I'll be back in a few minutes, lads.'

I stepped aside, let her go first, winked at Lou, then whispered, 'Put the Movie Channel on and turn it up. I don't want the kids overhearing this,' went in after Molly and closed the door.

The fact was I was glad Molly had come. I wanted to wipe that Miss Prim smirk off her face. She'd always been stuck up when it came to me. Oh she'd wear a smile when it suited her, when she'd seen me at the hospital, for instance, when she thought me and Sinead were getting on well together, to keep the peace, y'know, that way. But deep down she thought her sister was too good for the likes of me. To be honest, I'd have liked nothing better than to have pulled that black skirt of hers up round her waist, spread her on the desk, let her know what a real fuck tasted like, then booted her out the door. Some women like that kind of treatment. I'd always suspected she would have.

She squared up to me for a row. 'So you brought your "toy" home. And in front of your own sons.'

'You're not welcome here after tonight.'

'What?'

'Fuck you!'

'How dare you!'

'It's my house. I can dare what I like. You lorded it over

me because you knew I'd put up with anything rather than lose my kids.'

'I lorded it over *you*?'

'Judge and jury rolled into the one package. Well, you won't judge me again. I'm cutting all ties.'

'What's that supposed to mean?'

'Your sister can have her divorce. That's what you wanted, isn't it? Now you've got it.'

Now she looked smug. 'Fine. I won't say I'm sorry.'

'You will be.'

She raised that stuck-up eyebrow of hers. 'Oh? And what can you do?'

'You're a crime reporter. You figure it out.'

'What's that supposed to mean?'

'Tell me, when you're covering Sinead's case, will you mention that she's your sister? Or will she be an embarrassment to you?'

'Sinead will never be an embarrassment to me.'

'Good. Then you can begin your piece by saying: *My sister's doing time for drug dealing.* How's that?'

'That'll never happen.'

'Oh? You got some leverage?'

'She's innocent.'

'Then you've nothing to worry about. Of course, if she's found guilty, you will write about her like all the other junkies.'

'I can't believe I'm hearing this. Sinead's not a junkie.'

'A dealer, then. Worse still.'

'You bastard! Who do you think you are?'

'I'm a man who's gonna get custody of his kids when his ex-wife goes down.'

She laughed. Sarcastically, as it happens. 'You're out of

159

your mind. Sinead's not going anywhere. Drugs were found in a flat she just happened to be in, that's all. I've been in that flat myself. Does that make me a dealer? Am I going down too?'

'My solicitor rang me an hour ago. They found cocaine in Wicklow. One hundred deals.'

'*What?* You're lying.'

'Some of Sinead's clothes were in Bawn's wardrobe. They found traces on them.'

'Never!'

It was my turn to be sarcastic. 'So the cops are lying too? Is that it?'

'Sinead's no dealer.'

'Oh, I see. It's all a big conspiracy. The cops planted it.'

'She's no dealer.'

'Prove it.'

That winded her. Boy, was I savouring this moment. I came in close. Close enough to kiss her. I could feel her breath on my lips, the sweat on her brow, the panting of her breasts, the fluttering of her stomach. She was seeing Sinead's life torn apart.

I said it softly, and I said it as if I understood the way she was now coming to terms with the unthinkable. 'You're like me, Moll. We're both so smart, we didn't even have a clue what was going on behind our backs.'

Now she was conciliatory. Now she was looking at me differently, looking up at me, her lips were trembling, her cheeks were trembling, she was trembling, coming round, questioning, reappraising Sinead's innocence. And there was more. She wasn't drawing back. She was holding her ground.

She was whispering. 'Don't take her kids, Gerd. Please don't take her kids.'

And I was whispering back. 'But she wants a divorce. You said so yourself.'

'No, she loves you, Gerd.'

'But I'm no good. You said that too.'

'No, Gerd, I didn't mean—'

'Yes, you did. You were right. I'm no good. You said so. I've got a dick. Remember?'

'Please, Gerd, please.'

'Molly, you can do one of two things here.'

'No, Gerd, please, no.'

I could almost taste her. 'Molly, I think about you.'

'No, Gerd, no, please.'

'I do, Moll. I think about you.'

'No, Gerd, this isn't right.'

'I think about you, Moll.'

'No, Gerd, no, I—'

'Yes, Moll.'

'No, Gerd, I—'

'Oh, yes . . .'

It came like a shunting train, her knee, full force, right in the bollocks. I reeled, legs gave out, and landed on my ass in agony. 'Aagh God!' The bitch had led me on. Teased me. Took me right up to the hilt, then *whack!* Bollocksed me. I'd never known such pain.

She, calmly and slowly, loving every minute of it, the cow, straddled me.

'What's the matter Gerd?' she smirked – no, 'smirked' doesn't do it. Call it what you like: sarcasm, reproach, mocking, jeering; they were all there on her face, all rolled into one superior 'I just got my own back for all the years you cheated on my sister' smile.

'You fucker!'

'Why, thank you, Gerd.'

I mean, what manner of woman actually leads you on, just to make you squirm? I hated her. I detested her. If I'd been able to get up, I'd have choked her.

Here she was: 'I knew you'd make a move one day. It was only a matter of time.' Then she bent down, tapped my cheek, and with a look of triumph in her eyes, savoured every taunting syllable: ' "I think about you, Gerd".' Threw my own words back at me. Then, with a sardonic grin on her face, started to make an even bigger fool of me. 'I'll never forget this moment as long as I live. Passion unrequited. This dear sweet moment of a love that was not to be. Alas, that's the way it goes. Fuck face!' She blew me a kiss, stuck up her middle finger, added: 'Bye, darling!' and was gone.

She'd planned the whole fucking thing. Had been waiting, years probably, to let me know how it felt to be on the receiving end. Well, she'd gone too far.

I was seething. 'Right, you fucking barbarian! What was it old boxers used to say? *Put up your dooks!* You wanna play games, Moll? Fair enough. *Games it is.*'

Later, Lou was full of herself. Couldn't believe her luck. Telling me what had been happening while I was away. Toner had given her a new job and he'd introduced her to a man called Jimmy Byrne, who had rented her a detached house in Finster Avenue. This Jimmy Byrne character had brought her and her kid up to some horse sanctuary. Her kid had had his photograph taken on a horse. She and a man called Hassett had held him in the saddle. Mr Hassett had died tragically. He was such a nice man.

'So you didn't miss me while I was away?'

She snuggled up to me on the settee. 'Course I missed you, Gerd. I love you.'

I kissed her. 'I love you, too.'

'I still can't believe you do.'

'On my kids' lives. You know I wouldn't say that if it wasn't true.'

'Oh Gerd.' She laid her head against my chest.

'Lou, tomorrow I'm telling the kids I got your name wrong. I wasn't thinking right when I said your name was Mary. I sort of had it in the back of my head that Sinead might have told them about you. Now that you'll be seeing a lot of them, it's best to be honest. I hate deceit.'

'Gerd, are you sure you want to break up with Sinead?'

'Yeah. Why?'

'The kids. It's bound to affect them.'

'I know. But this is Sinead's doing. Let's change the subject.' I kissed the top of her head, then turned on the charm. 'Lou, I want to ask you something.'

'What?'

'When this dies down, how would you feel about moving in with me?'

She didn't answer, gave me a squeeze, looked up, and nodded. Her eyes were filling up.

Sweet little thing, Lou. Innocent as a white butterfly. If you married her and she caught you playing around, she'd pretend not to notice, put up with it, for the sake of the marriage, that sort of a kid, y'know? I liked that. Not that I was thinking of marriage. But living together's the same thing. I liked her sparkle. She made me feel good, made me feel full of life. The boys seemed to like her too. Course, that would probably change. If she usurped their mother, I mean. Still, cross that bridge when I come to it.

Right now I had the best of everything. I'd have Lou over and let the kids think of her as their regular sitter. Let them get to know her better, become fond of her. Fuck her while they're asleep. Means smuggling her out every morning. Still, wouldn't worry about that. I'm an early riser. Course, she'd need a car, living this far out. Couldn't keep getting taxis. I had already thought of buying her a car. She could quit her job. Look after my two. Save me the trouble.

I also had another use for her. 'Race week starts tomorrow. Fancy going? Bring little Liza.'

'Shall we go to bed, Gerd?'

Stupid question.

In bed I found that I was able to keep a hard-on longer. Which surprised me. I'd thought that cock-cruncher had ruined me for life.

Lou's like a little snake in bed, writhes up and down. Course, she was making love. Me, I was just fucking.

I had a smoke afterwards. Lay looking at the ceiling, her head on my shoulder, sleeping like a baby.

I lay awake until about two. This was the night of the funeral. Two was the time for Byrne to begin playing that tape Maguire had made of Tom Hassett dying.

I'd told the psychiatrist I'd visited in England that the female character in the book I was writing had, among other things, to feel responsible for her father's death, and that I needed to plot a sequence of events – several of which would include the use of the tape – that would drive her to suicide.

He was very helpful. He asked me to explain the first of these scenes as I would write it. I did – changing the names for his ears only – and it went exactly as planned.

Byrne had the recorder under a loose floorboard beneath their bed. A tiny remote in his hand which he could slip into his trousers pocket after he'd played it. His wife had dropped off about one. Sleep wasn't coming easily to her, naturally.

The tape came on. Low volume, resonant. The sound of her father pleading for his life, calling out to his wife. The sound of the water coming in. Splurting, gulping, gasping. Calling out to Bridie, Annie, Carol, God. It played on her ears, her eyes twitching, nose twitching, working away on her in her already unsettled sleep, resounding in the room, becoming part of the room, the fabric, filling her head, stirring her unconsciousness. *Bridie, oh my God, Carol, Annie, help me.* Byrne staring at the door, perspiring, himself trying to get away from it, even though he had brought it on, but can't. *Bridie. Help me, Bridie. God help me. Annie. Carol.* A nightmare in progress.

She bounced up, panting, 'Dad-dy?'

Byrne hit the remote and cut it off. Closed his eyes and ignored her trying to wake him to comfort her. Four o'clock was next. Every two hours. Let her get back to sleep then hit the remote again. Byrne wasn't hearing it. He wasn't waking up. He couldn't hear it. Only *she* could hear it. *Was it in her head? Did he hear it? Had* she *heard it?* Night after night. *Help me, Carol.* Funny things, minds. Like that white noise I was telling you about. Get enough of it and it becomes part of you.

By the third night, she was waking up screaming. *'Daddy? Is that you?* Jimmy! Jimmy! Jimmy, wake up. Oh please God, wake up.'

Byrne's bleary-eyed. 'What is it, Carol?'

'It's Daddy. Didn't you hear him? Please tell me you heard him.'

'I never heard a thing.'

'Jimmy, I think I'm going mad. I keep hearing Daddy begging me for help.'

'Carol, I never heard a thing.'

Now she's afraid to go back to sleep. Back to that. And every morning, Byrne's suggesting for her own good that she should see a psychiatrist. But she won't. Not even for the baby she's now carrying. It'll pass, she believes, once she can stop feeling so guilty.

But it doesn't pass.

'Subliminally,' the psychiatrist I had visited told me.

'What does that mean? Plain English, please.'

'Existing below the threshold of consciousness. Let me give you an example of what I'm trying to touch on; it may help you with your characterization. A person goes without sleep and food for a period of days; that person may then become susceptible to sleepwalking. Asleep, he may get up, go for a walk, and end up standing in the middle of a busy road in the early hours of the morning, convinced he's queuing up for a hamburger. A car whizzes by, snaps him out of it, but several seconds may pass before the smell of food actually leaves his nostrils. And in those seconds, he's still convinced he's seeing and smelling the hamburger van, may even ask a passer-by where it went. The only thing that will satisfy his hunger is food.

'Now, the character in your book,' he continued. 'The trauma, the guilt she is feeling over the death of her father, can be assuaged by the passing of time, with professional counselling, rest and medication. However, without these she can become the sleepwalker. But she has a different hunger. She is seeking her father; his forgiveness. The tape? She needs to believe that his calling out to her is her punishment. She needs to be punished. She has a spiritual affinity with his spirit calling out "Help me" to her, because the fact that she had *not* helped him had brought about his death. But her inability to help him – that, in a person in a state of disorientation, can drive her to the brink. So deprive your character of sleep and medication, apply the other pressures you have already mentioned, and when she finally succumbs and visits a psychiatrist, the psychiatrist will not rule out suicide at the subsequent inquest into her death. Murder will not come into it.'

Fancy having *that* bastard inside your head!

Chapter Eighteen

———∞∞∞———

The next morning got off to a good start. The previous night had given me a few ideas. First on the agenda was Sinead's car. Sinead drives a brand-spanking-new 3-series BM. A blue one. Before going to see her, I traded it in for another new one. Midnight pink. To go with Lou's red hair. I could've given Lou Sinead's blue one but I didn't know how that would go down with the kids, Lou driving their mother's car, I mean. That was the difficulty I faced, y'see. So from now on Sinead *used* to drive a 3-series BM.

She looked wretched when she came into the visiting room, dark shadows under her eyes, cheeks puffed up from crying. Looking at her now as she came over to the table, fidgeting with her hands, not knowing where to put herself, given the way she had treated me, taken my kids away, threatened divorce, it was hard to imagine the same person being capable of wielding a brandy bottle. Though, to be fair to her, it *had* been the first and only time. Wonder what drove her to it. I had always looked after her. She had never wanted for anything since the day we were married. Getting married was all she had ever wanted.

She wasn't a career woman like her strong-minded sister. She'd grown up in a council house and worked behind the counter in a ladies' clothes shop until I came along. Ours was a marriage where she took care of the kids and ran the house. Everything else fell to me. She had an open cheque book, not a worry in the world. She was the mother of my kids. And nothing was more important than my kids. I had her on a pedestal. I would never have divorced her. I had held up my end of the bargain.

And now she was in trouble she needed my help, as always. But she had become the enemy.

Given the way things were between us, she didn't quite know how to begin.

'How are the boys?' was the obvious one.

'Fine.'

'How are they taking this?'

'Fine.'

'Oh?' She was disappointed. She thought they'd be taking it bad, crying their eyes out. 'Did they go back to school today?'

'They're going back tomorrow. They were too upset to go back today.'

'Ah, I thought they'd be too upset to go back today.'

'They wanted the day off to look for Kipper.'

'*Kipper?*'

'He came back in a terrible state. I fed him and fixed him up. Then he ran away again. I think they blame themselves.'

'So now it's *my* fault.'

'I didn't say that.'

'You never say anything, Gerd. You insinuate.'

'What's that supposed to mean?'

'If I hadn't taken the kids away, Kipper wouldn't have run away to try and find them. That's what you're saying. It's your hallmark. You always put things so I can draw the worst possible conclusion.'

'Oh, I see. Now I'm being blamed for how a dog thinks.'

'There you go again: twisting it so I'll feel bad. I didn't say I blamed you for how a dog thinks.'

'You insinuated it.'

'*I* insinuated it? I asked you how the kids were taking this, thinking they'd be upset because I'm in custody, and you start telling me they're more worried about Kipper.'

'I didn't say that.'

'You insinuated it.'

'*I* insinuated it? You asked me if they'd gone back to school and I told you the truth. You want me to *lie*?'

'No, I don't want you to lie, Gerd.'

'Good. Because I don't lie.'

The guard made a move. I put my palm up and nodded that everything was all right, under control, no need to worry.

She calmed down. 'I don't want a row, Gerd.'

'Then why are you starting one?'

She flared up again. 'I'm starting one?'

The guard came over and put his hands on the table. 'Look,' he said. 'Any more and I'll have to end the visit.'

Sinead slouched back in her chair, exasperated, blowing her hair back off her face, acting as if I'd provoked her. Me? Can you believe that?

'We'll keep it down. I apologize. She's upset. Her first time in a place like this. She's not used to it yet. First offence.'

Sinead was seething. 'First offence? I haven't committed *any* offence. You think I committed an offence?'

I kept my voice down. 'Sinead, don't shout at me. He's the one who said you committed an offence. Not you personally. I mean this place. You know – the law.'

'It's all right. I know what you meant. Now, miss, I'm going to have to insist you be civil.'

Civil! This guard was a peach. *Civil* infuriated Sinead. She was ready to burst. She was thinking the guard was regarding me in a better light than he was her. One of the ways Sinead used to try to insult me was by saying I had a plausible tongue. *You've a plausible tongue, you bastard. Mr Nice Guy. You make everyone think you're so nice.* People who can't win an argument always come out with shit like that. I never used to take any notice of her. *So now you've even got the guard on your side* – that was the way she was looking at me.

'Look, officer,' I said. 'We'll keep it quiet. Sorry.'

'All right, then.' He looked at Sinead as if to say 'I'm watching you', then went back and stood in the corner.

She folded her arms, still in a huff. I lit a cigarette.

'Look, Sinead, I honestly didn't come here for a row. I want you out of here.'

She glared at me as if everything I said was a pack of lies.

'Sinead, come on.'

'Don't *Sinead, come on* me.'

'*Now* what have I done?'

'If you hadn't treated me like shit, I wouldn't be in here.'

'*Me?*'

'You don't see it, do you? You never see it. Living with you is like living with two opposites. You're a walking contradiction. One minute sweet, the next minute bitter. And you're so fucking opinionated. I wouldn't mind if you were firm in your opinions. But they change by the day. And you treat me like dirt. You've no appreciation of my feelings. You've no appreciation of anybody's feelings. People are cardboard cut-outs to you.'

Fuck me! I won't be asking her to put in a good word for

me anywhere. Even the guard was cringing at the way she was talking to me. I'd say he too had to put up with shit like this from his missis.

'Look, Sinead, you in here affects the kids. I don't want that. At least grant me that.'

She rolled her eyes, then started to come round, realizing it was getting her nowhere.

'Smoke?'

She sat up straight and took a cigarette.

'How's your head?'

I shrugged it off. 'Need anything?'

'Out of here.'

'What's your solicitor say?'

'He won't know until they've finished "investigating". Maybe this afternoon; tomorrow at the latest.' Her eyes started to water. 'Gerd, I'm frightened.'

'They'll get to the bottom of it.'

'What if they don't?'

'Sinead, you're no drug dealer. You don't even like drugs, for Christ's sake. You've never even been near drugs.'

'That's what I said.'

'There, then.'

'They said everybody's got to start sometime.'

'That's bullshit. They mean every *dealer's* got to start sometime. You're no dealer. The whole idea's a joke.'

I was waiting for it. It was due any second. Whatever Sinead thought of me, she knew I was capable. I got things done. Big houses and BMs. I was an achiever, a successful businessman.

It came: 'Gerd, can you get me your solicitor? Mine doesn't seem up to it. He only usually handles—' The next word lay between us. Right now she wished otherwise, wanted me on her side. At least until she got herself out of this mess. *'Divorce.'*

I let the word linger in the air. Let her think that I was thinking that she didn't want me when things were smooth, but now that they weren't, she wanted me. Wanted to *use* me. I looked both hurt, yet resolved to help her out. After all, she was my wife – we'd had good times together, for the kids' sake, for old times, stuff like that.

Y'know, it's funny the things you think about at times like these. But an idea came to me. Maybe I *should* get her freed, get the charges dropped. Take her back.

A mate of mine was once in a situation similar to this. His wife wasn't in custody. She was in the house. And that was his problem. He wanted rid of her so he could bring in his new bit of stuff. His wife knew his BOS. She even liked her: known her years, got on well together. The only thing she had against her was her age – she was eighteen. She couldn't compete with that. And she loved her husband and knew she was losing him. She was desperate. And my mate, he was soft, sentimental, y'know, the idea of booting his wife out wasn't sitting too well with him. He still loved her. So he said to me one night over a pint, Gerd, he said, I want the pair of them. I want to live with the pair of them. How can I do that? So I said to him, Fra, I said, you're making a big mistake. Fuck the wife out the door and enjoy yourself. You've only one life. Don't let convention live it for you. I know, he said, it's all right saying that, but I can't bring myself to fuck her out. Not now it's upon me. She means too much to me. Sex isn't everything. It is where women's concerned, I said. But the wife's also my best friend, he said. She's good to me. I like her company. Besides, she's a great cook. That other article couldn't boil an egg. I want the pair of them. You and the wife still at it? I asked. Ah yeah, he said. She's dick mad. Easily worked up? I asked. Very. Straight sex or anything goes? Anything goes. That might work in your favour, Fra. How, Gerd? All right, Fra, I said. This is what you'll do. Get them spending more time together in the house at nights with you in it. Get a few drinks into them. Work it so they end up sitting on the same settee. Start fooling around, innocent stuff, y'know – jokes, tickling, on your knees in front of them – then reach up and kiss the wife, but have your hand on the girlfriend's leg while you're doing it. See if the wife objects. She wants to keep you. She might compromise. Then the next night, do the same thing again, but move your hand further up your girlfriend's leg. The next night, a bit further up. See if they vie for your affection. Test the water. If you sense that the wife isn't objecting to you touching up the girlfriend in front of her after having got away with it three times, plant a kiss on the girlfriend. But have your hand on your wife's crotch. Some women like threesomes. They just need you to take the lead. If you sense you've got them, reel them in.

He did. And it worked. The girlfriend moved in. He bought a big bed. He was happy. Then things started to go wrong. Jealousy set in.

When his wife went shopping, she used to rush back in case the girlfriend was getting screwed and she was missing out. The girlfriend used to run home from school in case the wife was getting screwed and *she* was missing out. If one was getting more than the other, the other made him make up for it. Poor Fra, he was fucked. Worn out. He never took up with any more women after that. And it was this that was making me think.

SEAMUS SMYTH

Sinead had her good points. She was a right little goer in bed, too. She was also a great cook. I was forgetting about that. Lou was a dead loss in the kitchen.

Moving Lou in and the three of us living happily ever after was now seeming like a good idea. Fra didn't have my stamina. I could manage two easy. But what happens when I take up with somebody else? That's what was bothering me. Would I be able to move her in as well? Foursomes. Then another. Fivesomes. I mean, even I couldn't run to that. That was my problem, y'see. End up in hospital.

'What's up with him, Doctor?'

'He's fucked. Literally.'

Know what I mean?

I mean, I'm a great believer in harems, as I said. But, most of that harem carry-on was back in the old days when wives lived on a bowl of vegetables and what their old man could bow-and-arrow. These days they want the best of everything. A car each. Stuff like that. Then you might have the bra-burners after you. And you'd need a dining table the size of the Last Supper. Have to build an extension. The place'd be crammed with women, all wanting attention. I'd be aching from morning till night. They'd be taking it in shifts. I mean, one dick can only go so far. Six months of that and you'd need a transplant. Nah! I don't think so. Hard luck, Sinead. My mind was running away with me there. You're on your own. Harems are a bad idea after all.

'I already asked him to help you, Sinead,' I said. Which pepped her up a bit. My man was the best in Dublin.

'Thanks, Gerd.'

'He refused.'

She looked disappointed.

'This will interfere with the divorce, he reckons.'

'But how, Gerd?'

'I'm not sure. But he can't act for two opposing sides. He says you'll be suing for half of everything.'

'Can't we put that behind us till this is over?'

'He says I can't tie his hands.'

'Please, Gerd.'

'He told me I had to do certain things to protect myself.'

'Such as?'

When we met, Sinead was skint. I wasn't. Since then my hard-earned money had paid for everything. So everything was mine. 'I've emptied our joint account. It's all in my name now.'

'But how will I feed the kids?'

'Feed them where? You've no home. You left. Besides, you're in here.'

'I'll get out.'

That guard was too interested in this to stop it.

'I can't have my kids walking the streets, Sinead. They stay with me.'

'Molly will put us up.'

'No dice.'

'I'll sell my car. It's worth thirty thousand. That'll get us going.'

'I've sold it.'

'You sold *my* car?'

'It was in my name. I paid for it.'

She was raging. Anger is a great defeater. Anger your opponent and you have a weak opponent. 'You can't take my kids!'

'The divorce was your idea, Sinead.'

She rounded on me. 'You'll never get my kids. I'm the

mother. Custody always goes to the mother. Especially when the judge hears what you've been up to.'

'My solicitor said you'd play dirty.'

'*I'd* play dirty?'

'He said you'd put Lou on the stand.'

'Too right I will.'

'Then he'll play dirty. He'll put Molly on the stand.'

'*Molly*? What's Molly got to do with it? Molly hates you.'

'That's all a front.' Molly was a great influence on Sinead. Molly was also smarter, more resourceful. She would advise Sinead. I needed them at each other's throats. 'She hates me to *your* face. It's a different story when you're not around.'

'I don't believe you.'

'You don't see it, do you? You live in a world of your own. You're always so busy blaming me for everything, you never look around you. Wake up, Sinead. With you and me split up, Molly has a free hand.'

'You're fucking mental. My sister wouldn't do that to me.'

'Look into her eyes when you ask her. You'll be able to tell whether she's lying or not.'

'*You're* lying!'

'Then ask the kids. You'll believe them if they tell you Molly was alone with me in my study last night.'

She was ready for convulsions. 'No, no, no, not Molly. No, Molly wouldn't do that to me. Molly wouldn't do that to me. Not our Molly. No. No. Aw no. No way.' I could tell it had come as a shock. 'You bastard!'

'You're violent. I've got stitches to prove it. You're a drug dealer. I'll have your record to prove it. I'd say the judge'll take all that into account. Especially when he sees you in handcuffs.'

'You fucking bastard!' She lunged at me, fists flying. The guard had to restrain her. 'You fucking bastard! Let me at him! Let me at the fucking bastard!' I was glad there wasn't a brandy bottle handy.

'I'll tell the kids you were asking.'

Chapter Nineteen

—————◦◦◦◦———————

Carol Byrne was doing very well as far as I was concerned. What I mean is, she was acting the way I had hoped she would act.

She'd fallen asleep at the kitchen table by the time Byrne came down the stairs.

Here he was: 'Fancy a game of chess, Carol?' He picked up the bishop. 'Carol, fancy a game of chess?'

That poodle puppy Byrne had bought her sprang up out of its basket and stood wagging its tail at him. A white poodle, it was, both affectionate and trying. Byrne had bought it for Carol the day before they'd gone to London. At this moment in her life, she could well have done without it. Which, of course, was the reason Byrne had given it to her. By the same token, she, as much as was likely in her grief, had grown fond of it. Which was another reason Byrne had given it to her. Its death would affect her.

'Carol. Fancy a game of chess?'

She started to come round. 'Whaaa?'

'Game of chess?'

Carol looked half-doped. Half turned-on. As if she'd been on Valium and wasn't quite tuned in. She looked up from the table, trying to focus in on where her husband's voice was coming from.

'Don't touch that, Jimmy.' Her voice was slurred.

'Why not?'

'Daddy and I were playing that.'

The unfinished chess game on the walnut tripod table was just as Carol and her father had left it. This was part of the process of breaking her. And she was helping us to break her. She was turning the place into a shrine. So, naturally we used that against her. I'd worked out a few other of her weaknesses, based on what I'd learnt that night the Hassetts and the McDermotts were having dinner. If she drove us to it, we would use them against her, too. It all depended on how stubborn she was.

'But I thought we might have a game,' said Byrne.

'I don't want anything of Mammy's and Daddy's touched.'

'I didn't think it applied to a chess set.'

'Jimmy, please.'

'All right, all right,' said Byrne, replacing the bishop. 'No need to get excited.'

She hadn't the energy to get excited.

'Did you give any more thought to the new kitchen?' Byrne asked.

'What new kitchen?'

'The one you were talking about yesterday.'

'I don't remember talking about any new kitchen. There's no way I'm changing Mammy's kitchen.'

'Then why did you bring it up?'

'I never brought it up.'

Byrne looked baffled. Carol came out into the hall. She tied her dressing gown and yawned.

The phone rang. It was Maguire. He was ringing on Con

Ivers's phone, I might add. Maguire did the odd bit of work for Ivers. Not enough to inspire any loyalty. Byrne didn't know he was phoning on it, though. He didn't know that we were setting Ivers up as well as setting him up. Whether the law would ever check Ivers's phone records when the time came, I couldn't say. But it was likely. And if they did, everything would fall into place the way I wanted it to. I was making sure I was ready for it.

Byrne answered the phone while Carol went about in a daze, straightening her mother's favourite chair, a Victorian buttoned spoon-back, beside the telephone. Incidentally, this furniture and chess set were in the entrance hall below the bathroom.

'Is she there, she is?' Maguire asked.

'Yeah. Hang on a minute. It's for you, Carol. Something about carpet cleaning. He wants to know if tomorrow's OK.'

'For what?'

'For carpet cleaning, I suppose.'

'What carpet cleaning?'

'Someone here wants to know if tomorrow's OK for cleaning the carpets.'

'I didn't arrange for a carpet cleaner.'

'You must have.'

'I didn't.'

'You must have the wrong number,' Byrne told Maguire, keeping up the charade. Then he handed the phone to Carol. 'He wants to talk to you, Carol.' He stood to the one side, as she took over the call, looking at her as if he was puzzled by her behaviour. Doubt, y'see. That's what this was all about. Simple everyday things. Nice and easy does it. Gradually make her think that she's going round the twist. Bit by bit. This stuff was just for openers.

'Who is this?' she asked Maguire.

'Is that Carol Byrne?'

'Yes, I'm Carol Byrne.'

'Ah, I thought I had the wrong number there for a minute. We can clean your carpets tomorrow, Mrs Byrne, as discussed.'

'I'm sorry. I don't understand.'

'Maybe I have the wrong Mrs Byrne. Maybe it was your mother who made the arrangement yesterday.'

At the mention of her mother, she simply, and forlornly, hung up.

Byrne looked at her wondering what was going on.

This was the third appointment in as many days that Carol had *apparently* forgotten she had made.

'Jimmy, I didn't ring any carpet cleaner.'

'All right. It's not important. You were talking about it the other day so—'

'I wasn't talking about it.'

'All right. After what you've been through, it's understandable you'd forget the odd thing or two.'

'But I didn't.'

Byrne raised his palms. 'All right, all right. I said I'm sorry.'

She went through to the living room and sat down. The puppy jumped up onto her lap. It wanted attention, got on her nerves. 'There, Ginny, there. Settle down now. Mammy's tired.'

'Carol, what would you say if I brought in a manager to run Hassett Property? I'd pop in every day to keep an eye on things.'

'I don't care what you do with it! If Daddy hadn't gone to it that night, they'd still be alive. I hate it.'

Byrne sat on the arm of the settee. He was full of concern. 'Look, Carol, you're going to have to snap out of this.'

She put her head in her hand. 'If only we hadn't gone to London, Jimmy. You would have answered that break-in; not Daddy. They'd still be alive.'

'I know.'

As the then new manager, Byrne had been responsible for Hassett Property, including answering alarms going off in the middle of the night. To be fair to Carol, she hadn't wanted to go to London. Her parents had been due to leave Dublin the following morning to catch the Cunard liner in Southampton. Byrne had suggested they go to London, then on to Southampton to see them off. Carol had reluctantly agreed. If she hadn't, Byrne would have been in Dublin to answer the alarm. That's how she was seeing this. Feeling guilty. Course, we had a lot more guilt lined up for her if she persisted in being stubborn.

'It's all my fault.'

'You can't keep blaming yourself, Carol. You'll have to snap out of it. For the baby's sake as well as your own. Look, why don't you get some professional help?'

'No.'

See what I mean? Stubbornness. This would have stopped there and then if she'd said yes. The dog licked her face and she stroked it.

'Carol, I hate to see you torturing yourself like this.'

'I'll be all right, Jimmy. If only I could get some sleep.'

Sleep was out of the question. Snatches of it, fair enough. But I had to act on that psychiatrist's advice.

Carol was turning out of the drive, dark glasses on to hide the black rings round her eyes, her puppy on the passenger seat, when the phone in the hall rang. Again it was Maguire.

'You can start work in the morning,' Byrne told him.

'No sign of a shrink, no?'

'She won't go.'

'I thought you'd clout.'

'I can't make her go.'

'You're lettin' the side down, Byrne. Where is she now?'

'The cemetery, I'd say. She usually goes there when she wants to think. She likes to talk to them. I'm just on my way after her.'

What Byrne did next surprised even me. He started acting on his own initiative. He followed Carol from the cemetery to the local garden centre, then back home. He went out to the greenhouse and saw that she had bought a bottle of stuff for getting rid of greenfly and a mushroom kit.

Within minutes he was back in the same centre buying a bottle of weedkiller and a mushroom kit. He dumped the mushroom kit on the way home, went back out to the greenhouse, poured the greenfly solution into the weedkiller bottle and poured the weedkiller into the greenfly bottle. Then he swopped her receipt for his receipt. As I say, this was his idea, not mine, applying pressure, to drive her to breaking point quicker. Good thinking on his part. Bridie Hassett's garden had been her pride and joy, y'see, and Carol was turning it into a shrine as well. That made it useful. That was Byrne's thinking behind this.

Later that afternoon, Carol mixed what she thought was the greenfly solution and began spraying the flowerbeds. Bloom by bloom she sprayed, keeping the nozzle high so the force of the spray wouldn't dislodge any petals, treating the flowers like royalty. Her mother had planted most of the perennials, shrubs and stuff. Carol was tending them in her memory.

Chapter Twenty

Course, Sinead told Molly I'd said I'd been fucking her in my study. I was quite looking forward to our little talk, to be honest. I love gloating. And treating 'Fuck face' to a dollop of her own medicine wrapped up in a generous helping of sarcasm. Well, who could resist it?

It was after midnight, Nicolas Cage and Sean Connery had just knocked the crap out of the bad guys in *The Rock* on Sky and I was on my second whiskey, when I saw her car drawing up. She rang the doorbell. I let her in without so much as looking at her, and went back to my chair beside the fire. Didn't offer her a seat or a drink, of course; just let her stand there behind the settee.

This was one of those rare occasions when you know you're about to say something that has ramifications that could be blown out of all proportion. Call it what you like: sticking the knife in; putting the frighteners on; whatever. That ticking off she'd given me in her office, plus damages to my epicentre; know what I mean? I had to have compensation. I was gonna put in a claim that would leave *her* reeling. And I was going to enjoy every minute of it.

Here she was: 'I went to see Sinead.'

'Asking about me, was she?'

'Just who do you think you are, telling her that pack of lies about us?'

'Which pack was that?'

'Try "scurrilous".'

'I was thinking more like *scandalous*. For the divorce hearing, y'know? Sinead calls her witnesses: Lou – to tell how I've been cheating on her, y'know? I call mine: you – character witness. Lovers often stick up for one another.'

I'm not sure at what temperature blood boils, but if the look on Molly's face was anything to go by, I'd say she had a brave idea.

'Course,' I continued, 'you broke it off when you found out I was cheating on you with Lou. Then Sinead found out about Lou and sued for divorce. Then Sinead found out about us.'

Now a head of steam was building up inside her. If she'd been a kettle, she'd have whistled.

'Hard on Liam, though. Still, that's the way it goes. Anyway, you told me henpecked husbands aren't real men. They don't take the lead. Their wives never really know what it's like to have a *real* man give them what-for. The cock who doesn't rule the roost doesn't rule the bedroom. He's afraid to give his wife a good hard fucking in case she tells him off. It's a status thing. If he gets away with dominating the bedroom, he might get ideas above himself. And Liam's a classic. You came to me because he wasn't enough for you. That's how I'll tell it. I'll look at him from the stand, y'know, shrug "I'm sorry, Liam". He's only human. Doubt, y'see – bound to creep in. And doubt has a way of festering. *He* will have grounds for divorce by the time I'm through with you. He'll be a laughing stock. Don't look so shocked, Moll. I'm only getting my own back. You bollocks me, I bollocks you. Anyway, I thought you wanted to see me in court.'

She couldn't believe what she was hearing. Then she broke out in a fit of laughing. She laughed that loud I thought she'd waken the kids. Actually, this wasn't going according to plan. Tears were leaping out of her. But they weren't tears of desperation. The cow was enjoying herself.

Then here she was: 'OK, you've had your monologue – here's mine: Go to court. Call me. We'll all have a good laugh. You see, what you don't realize is, I can prove you're lying. And while I'm at it, I'll throw in my twopence worth. I'll even write it up. Might even sell a few more newspapers. A nice juicy tale for the reading public. Of course, I'll have to see what I can dig up on you. You threaten me; I threaten you.' She clicked her tongue. 'That's fair, isn't it? I'm going to do a little investigative journalism on you. I wonder what I'll find?

'For instance, I've often wondered how you managed to do so well for yourself. I mean, take this place – a palace. You want for nothing. Where does all the money come from? You're successful. But are you *this* successful? Or are there a few shady deals swept away under your carpet? You came to Dublin in the mid-seventies, didn't you? From a working-class background. Where would dipping into that take me, I wonder? Then maybe I'll have a word with the taxman. I've thrown him the odd helping hand over the years. He'll be delighted to reciprocate. Your start-up money must have come from somewhere. But was it clean? I've never known you to do an honest day's work to earn any.

'And who did you mix with when you came to Dublin? Where did you hang out? What possibilities will that raise? None? Well, I can always bend the truth a little. Do it your way: "Look, Your Honour, my brother-in-law knew I was looking into his background. Based on evidence from a paid informant, I discovered that he came into funds linked to . . ." I don't know what yet but I'll think of something. "And when he found out I was going to expose him, he made up these allegations of an affair to blacken my character. He's using this hearing to get at me".'

She went on. What she said about the taxman didn't bother me. Hot air. My accounts were well manicured. But the consequences of a 'crusade' against me were not to be welcomed. Immediately after doing jobs with Toner over the years, I'd used the proceeds to make substantial investments. Dates might coincide in that head of hers and she might get to thinking. Dig deep enough, and she'd find out that on occasions Toner had been known to be keen to buy into two of the city's top pubs. He'd then backed out without explanation. And I'd silently bought in. Nothing illegal in that. But Toner backs out for nobody. He'd done it as a favour to me. If Molly made a link like that, to a guy I've always avoided in public, where would that lead? If not today, in a few years' time, if my luck changed and a series of coincidences, together with fuck knows what else she might dig up, formed a pattern. I'd misjudged her. I wished I'd kept my fucking mouth shut. She was smart. And she might get on a roll.

Chapter Twenty One

━━━◦○◦━━━

That monitor was still coming in pretty handy. Maguire had it on day and night. Every word was reported back to Toner, who then informed me. Some of it was even on video, which I analysed.

Carol Byrne had told her husband that she hated Hassett Property so much she never wanted to see it again. She wanted it sold. I wasn't sure where this might lead. Would she instruct an agent herself? Would she find out about that offer from the UK? Would she find a buyer before Toner got his hands on it? I didn't like it. I told Toner to step up the pressure.

In other words, Byrne was told to have a bath.

While Carol Byrne was cleaning the upstairs bathroom after him, Maguire was back on the monitor watching her. Byrne called up from downstairs and she turned off the hot tap and came down.

'You ready?'

'Jimmy, I don't want to go.'

Today was the day for the reading of her father's will. It was a foregone conclusion, so I won't repeat what you already know.

Maguire watched them leave, then let himself in, doctored

the plug's chain and the overflow outlet, and turned on the hot tap. When the bath was full, he turned the tap to a trickle.

On their return, Byrne dropped Carol at the back gate. She came in through the garden.

The roses were dying.

They were the first she noticed, the prizewinners. She seemed to search every flower in every bed: the hibiscus, impatiens, carnations, petunias, they were all on their way out. Petals were strewn all over the place. She made for the greenhouse.

The brown-glass bottle was still on the bench where she had left it. But it was labelled 'Weedkiller'. She distinctly recalled buying an identical bottle labelled 'Greenfly', and a ready-to-grow mushroom kit. She stood staring at it, racking her brains, going over it again, the man handing her the bottle in a brown paper bag, the receipt . . . The *itemized* receipt? She searched the bin and found the bag. The enclosed receipt said 'Mushroom kit' and 'Weedkiller'. She had bought weedkiller by mistake. Her mother's prizewinning roses, everything, she had sprayed them all.

She rushed to the phone in the kitchen and dialled the garden centre. 'Anything? Isn't there anything I could try. Anything at all?'

'Sorry, miss. Nothing that I know of. I'm afraid you've lost them.'

She – and she alone – was responsible.

She sat down at the table and cried.

The puppy jumped up at her. Her hand went to it, patting it, and then, feeling its paws were wet, she looked down and saw the floor. Water was coming in over the door saddle from the hall. She pulled the door open. It was raining down on the furniture. Her mother's furniture! The chess set was upturned and the ceiling plasterboard had been brought down. She looked up. The bathroom was directly above. She ran upstairs. The bath was overflowing, the cold tap was off, the hot barely running. But she *had* turned it off. She'd used the hot tap to clean the bath. She could clearly recall turning it off.

The bedside phone rang.

'Is Mrs Byrne there?' He saw her on screen. The state she was in.

'Speaking.'

'Kevin Maguire here, Mrs Byrne. Damp old day.'

'Mr Maguire, I'm very busy.'

'Won't keep you. I'm going through the company's bank statements here and they show a regular monthly direct debit of eight hundred pounds and I can't trace who the money is going to.'

'I'm sorry, Mr Maguire, I can't help you.'

'I also need to clear up what's happening at a house at Finster Avenue, number forty-seven.'

'Look, Mr Maguire, I—'

'Mrs Byrne, are you all right? You sound a bit flustered.'

'I've just come back home to find the place flooded. I . . . I must have left the bath running. I . . .'

Maguire zoomed in on 'must have', pleased she was questioning her own actions. 'Leave it to me, Mrs Byrne. I'll send some men over right away. One of the joys of owning your own building firm. We'll have it sorted out in no time.'

Maguire called maintenance, switched off the monitor, then buzzed his secretary, Mrs Gallagher; she who had been Tom Hassett's secretary for fifteen years. She who had known about the monitor in Hassett's day. If this ever went wrong, and she told the police about the monitor, I couldn't say where that might take us. She had to go, and in such a way that only Carol could sack her. Toner's hands had to be lily-white in this when he took over. This was small-detail stuff, I grant you. But I always take care of small details.

'Mrs Gallagher, I've just been going through the deeds to that thirty acres the horse sanctuary uses and I can't find their public liability insurance policy for it.'

'It's not insured.'

Maguire knew that already. He was picking holes in it. Thanks to yours truly. 'But if those horses got out and caused an accident, Hassett Property would be liable.'

'Mr Hassett and Carol always dealt with it. Letting the land rent-free was more Carol's doing than her father's. Being a charity, and PL insurance so expensive, he merely insisted on good fencing and left it at that.'

We had to get rid of that sanctuary, y'see. So we could sell the land. That was part of the thinking behind it.

The mess had been cleared away and a man was drying the carpet with an industrial vacuum cleaner when Byrne returned home that evening.

Carol was mopping the bathroom floor when he came up. She looked worn out. Byrne was understanding, taking her in his arms. 'No one's hurt. That's the main thing.'

'But Daddy's chess set, Mammy's furniture; it's all ruined.'

'It can be fixed.'

'It's not the same.'

She started sobbing.

'Try not to be so upset.'

'Jimmy, what's happening to me?'

'I don't know, Carol. I only know I love you and I want you to get better. And I'm worried about how this will affect the baby.' He left it at that.

When it came to backing horses, Byrne was a dead loss. But Carol didn't know that. She and her father had thought he was the luckiest gambler they had ever met. But this was just another ruse of mine, to draw her attention to the safe. I needed it registered in Carol's mind that that safe of her father's hadn't been opened since before his death. So I had Toner tell Byrne to come home with a wad of cash, tell Carol that he'd won it, then ask her if he could put it in the safe.

'I don't know the combination,' she told him.

'You mean Tom was the last one to open it?'

'Yes.'

'What's in it?'

'Don't know.'

'Would you ring someone who specializes in that sort of thing and have them open it?'

She nodded.

Chapter Twenty Two

——————◆◆◆◆——————

Here was Jimmy Byrne: 'Oh fuck! Oo-ooh fuck!' when one of Con Ivers's *crunchers* slammed him against the alley wall. The fifty he owed Ivers now stood at eighty, interest included. Byrne had gone to Toner for a loan to pay off Ivers, y'know, a bit of refinancing, just until his 'inheritance' came through. Toner knew Ivers's form, that he'd kick the crap out of Byrne on a regular basis until he came across. Which suited what I had in mind. So Byrne was out of luck.

'No can do, Jimmy,' Toner told him.

'Paddy, at least give me some of that hundred you got out of Hassett's safe.'

'Went on expenses, Jimmy.'

'All of it?'

'You had the cream working for you that night, Jimmy. The cream costs money. And I'm *still* out of pocket.'

'Well, what about the takings from the carpark?'

'That's going towards expenses, too.'

Maguire had been put in to run Hassett Property to prevent Byrne robbing it, selling it behind our backs. We couldn't trust him. Anyway, keeping the pressure on Byrne meant that it would show on Carol. That was the beauty of it.

'Fuck's sake, Paddy, have a heart. What am I gonna tell Carol?'

'Tell her you fell.'

'I can't *keep* telling her that.'

'Work one of my pitches for a while. Tell her you bought it. Tell her that's why you wanted out of the property business. She knows horses are your game. She thinks you're loaded. She won't turn a hair.'

'But why would I do that?'

'Jimmy, you asked me what were you gonna tell Carol. Have I got to explain every detail? You know the way sore punters work. Besides, it'll fit in with what I've got in mind for her.'

'What about that tape?'

'What about it?'

'She's stopped going to bed.'

'Where's she sleeping?'

'All over the place. The kitchen, mostly. She's getting too much sleep.'

'The kitchen's below your bedroom, isn't it?'

'So?'

'So the tape's in the ceiling between your bedroom and the kitchen.'

'So?'

'Jimmy, did you ever hear of a guy called Isaac Newton?'

'No.'

'That's what you get for mitching school. Look, Jimmy, what goes up must come down.'

'So-oo?'

'So what *plays* up, must *play* down.'

Idiot! Comes to something when you gotta start teaching people physics.

Con Ivers is one of these wee men who runs about with a leather overcoat on his shoulders, never puts his arms in the sleeves, wears it like it's a cape.

'Jimmy, how's it goin'? Long time.'

Byrne's twitching, eyes darting, he knows how this works. He says *Oh hello, Con. How's things?* But his voice is cracking. 'Con,' comes out in syllables. 'How's things?' in spasms. The two crunchers, one on either side of him, like columns, grin *Byrne's got no balls*. They're awaiting instructions, they're keen to earn their pay.

'What've you got for me, Jimmy?'

'Con, I was coming to see you,' he blurts out.

'Go-oood.' Ivers puts out his hand. 'I'll save you the trouble.'

Byrne's knees buckle, as if he's trying not to wet himself.

'What's the matter, Jimmy? You don't look too good.'

Did you ever see those guys who're on TV sometimes who contort their faces? Gurners, I think they call them. I looked up the word in the dictionary once but couldn't find it. Well, that's what Byrne was looking like. He should've taken up gurning, with the faces he was pulling, pleading faces, y'know. Woulda won prizes. The crunchers found it entertaining; they were a good audience, pulling faces back at him, joining in, good sports. *Byrne's got no balls. Byrne's got no ba-alls.* Those sort of faces.

'Jimmy, I can't stand here all day with my hand out.'

Nothing came back. All Ivers was getting was a face full of pleas for mercy. Ivers shook his head – his own head, I mean. He was a disillusioned man; was deeply hurt. He had put his trust in this man to pay him back his hard-earned money, plus the fifteen grand interest per month, and here he was not honouring his part of the deal at the appointed time.

What's the world coming to? Ivers shook his head, Byrne's this time, to convey his heartfelt disappointment. Then he shook his own head again, y'know, letting Byrne know he didn't want to do this. But what could he do? Byrne had forced him to do it. This was Byrne's idea. Ivers looked at the crunchers. They grinned crocodile tears back at him. Both at the same time. I'd say he'd choreographed these two.

Ivers sniffed. Byrne looked like the Philistines were upon him. Each of the crunchers stamped a boot on Byrne's foot. He crumbled. They held him up. Ivers sniffed. Two fists, one each side, crashed into Byrne's face. He crumbled. They held him up. Ivers sniffed. Two knees crashed into Byrne's calves. Crumbled. Held. Sniff. Two heels crashed into Byrne's shins. Crumbled. Held. Sniff. Two knees in the side of Byrne's hip. Crumbled, held, sniff. Two heads butted the sides of Byrne's head. CHS. Two fists, one in the bollocks. CHS. The second fist in the bollocks. CH. They looked at Ivers. *No sniff?* Ivers was darting his cuffs. Smart dresser, Ivers. *No sniff?* Ivers shook his head. Byrne crumbled. He had them choreographed all right.

'Got a cold, Con?'

'Touch of hay fever.'

'Should get it seen to.'

'I intend to.'

'Case it gets worse.'

'It worries me.'

'I mean, what if you started sniffing one day and couldn't stop?'

'My thoughts exactly. Be seeing you soon, Jimmy.'

Maguire had his eye on Carol Byrne. She was doing her best to hold up under pressure. Which wasn't easy – the sight of the flowerbeds was enough to make her cry every time she looked at them. She had taken cuttings from the prize-winning roses and had potted them in the greenhouse, hoping they would take, y'know, hoping the weedkiller hadn't affected the main stem, trying to salvage what she could. I don't know what way that works. My guess was she was desperate, trying anything. But who knows? Maybe they would take. Then she weeded in under the row of cedars, where those wild mushrooms I was telling you about grow. Gathered the lot into the wheelbarrow, before wheeling it down to the vegetable patch where she picked some carrots, the pup wanting to play at all times, running between her legs, messing around every time she bent down.

Byrne arrived. One look at the state of him and the carrots fell from her hand into the barrow. She ran up, was all over him: 'What happened, Jimmy?'

'Help me get inside, Carol.'

'But what happened?'

'I "fell".'

One of Carol Byrne's good points was her cooking. Byrne loved her cooking. That's why I had the idea for the mushrooms. She had an old mushroom kit in the greenhouse as well as a new one as back-up.

She had no sooner helped Byrne up the stairs and onto the bed when his mobile rang.

'You're there, Byrne, y'are?'

Byrne asked Carol to make him a cup of coffee to get her out of the room.

'Ya fancy a pie, Byrne, y'do?'

'What?'

201

'Tell her to make you a pie for tea. A nice beef, carrot and mushroom one. Yum yum.'

'Why?'

'What's the matter – you don't like pies?'

'Yeah, I like pies.'

'Well, don't eat this one.'

'Look, what is all this fucking crap about pies? I don't understand all this. Why can't we just deal with her tonight?'

'She seen a shrink?'

'No.'

'Then there's your answer.'

'You don't realize the pressure I'm under here.'

'Leopardstown starts at five. Be there.'

'For fuck's sake, I can hardly walk. Con Ivers jumped me and—'

'Do it. Now switch off your phone. So it can't take any incoming calls.'

'Why?'

'Look, Byrne. Toner tells me what to do, I tell you what to do. That's the way it works. You don't like it, take it up with him. You want this job done, you switch off your mobile.'

Byrne was on his feet when Carol came up with the coffee.

'What are you doing, Jimmy?'

'I've to go to work.'

'But Jimmy, look at you. Your face is all swollen. You can't go.'

'Harry'll be waiting for me.'

'Call and tell him you're not going. Please, Jimmy.'

'I'm all right, Carol. Now, why don't you make me one of your nice pies for when I get back? Beef and mushroom. That'd be nice. And carrots. Throw in a few carrots.'

'Jimmy, please don't go to work.'

'I'll be all right, Carol.'

Carol went down into the greenhouse, picked some mush-rooms, lifted the carrots and went back up to the kitchen, made the pie and put it in the oven.

Now you can never really tell how a mild-mannered girl like Carol Byrne will react. Not when her husband's threatened with violence. She'd either tell him when he got home or run to warn him. I was hoping for the latter. If not, we'd have to figure out some other way to poison that dog. We weren't poisoning the dog just for the sake of poisoning it. We had a good reason. Two good reasons, as it happens. The first you know. Carol would feel bad and blame herself. The second was Byrne. She'd made the pie for him. So if it killed the dog . . . ? The implication was that if Byrne had eaten it, it would have killed him.

The hall phone rang. Regardless of what Toner had told Byrne, the truth was we needed Carol Byrne to know that her husband had been threatened by Ivers. Maguire laid it on in a thick accent, came the heavy. 'Is Jimmy Byrne there?'

'No. Who is this?'

'Con Ivers.'

'Con who?'

'Ivers. Are ya fuckin' deaf!' Made her jump, that one. 'You tell him he'll get more of what he got this afternoon if I don't get the money he owes me.'

'What?'

'Where the fuck is he?'

'I . . . a . . . I don't know.'

'You're lying to protect him. He's at Leopardstown, isn't he? I'll see to him over there.'

Maguire watched her on the monitor. She was worried sick, not knowing which way to turn. She tried Byrne's mobile, got no response. She turned off the oven and drove to Leopardstown races.

Maguire told Mrs Gallagher he was going out for the rest of the day. She had the week's takings from the carpark on her desk and asked him to check it before he left.

'I'm a bit pushed. I'll check it tomorrow. Put it in the safe.'

'I'll need your key.'

Maguire had two keys in his pocket. He gave her one, then left.

Maguire drove to The Cedars, fed the puppy cooked beef and poison mushrooms in gravy, turned on the oven, then went into the living room, opened the safe and put the letter into it – the letter he'd typed the night he was in Tom Hassett's office. The one he had made Tom Hassett sign.

Dusk was setting in when Carol hit the brakes and hurried through the stile to the betting ring. Byrne's clerk was changing the prices on the race sheet.

Carol was in a desperate state. 'Harry, where's Jimmy?'

'What's the matter, Mrs Byrne?'

'I need to see Jimmy. Where is he?'

He shrugged. 'I think he's gone for a quick one.'

She ran to the bar and saw him standing next to an attractive young woman with the most glorious red curly hair. Lou. Lou was wearing a miniskirt and a low-cut top. She was holding her toddler's hand and she seemed concerned by Byrne's battered appearance.

I had orchestrated this little scene, then got offside when

Byrne entered the bar. Lou was a pawn. She knew nothing. She merely thought she had bumped into her landlord. Byrne knew she was a pawn. Toner had filled him in. Toner was upstairs in one of the trainers' boxes. Byrne was happy to play along. *Aching* to play along.

Byrne turned and saw Carol in the doorway.

'Carol, what're you doing here?'

Carol didn't answer. Carol was too busy eyeing the lovely Louise.

'I'd like you to meet Louise Kelly. Louise, meet the wife.'

Lou was all smiles. 'Nice to meet you, Carol.'

Liza tugged her hand. 'C'mon, Mammy. The dodgems.'

'In a minute, darling.'

I was watching all this from the far window. The thing that I liked best was when Carol and Byrne turned to leave, Byrne said 'Bye, Louise, bye, *Liza.*'

It registered with Carol that Byrne knew the toddler's name.

'Bye, Jimmy,' said Liza.

And that the toddler knew Byrne's. Nothing great in that, you might think. But these little things would add up, create a bit of doubt, y'see, when we got around to making Carol think Byrne was giving Lou one. That's what I liked about it.

I watched them leave, then went inside.

'Where did you get to?' Lou asked me.

'The bog. Who were you talking to?'

'My landlord and his wife. She looks dreadful.'

'That's not a very nice thing to say about your landlord's wife.'

'No, I don't mean that. She looks really ill. I felt sorry for her.'

'Probably needs a good tonic. Come on, time for the dodgems.'

* * *

'What's the matter, Carol?'

'A man called Ivers rang after you left. Jimmy, he frightened the life out of me.'

Which frightened the life out of Byrne. He could see the Philistines upon him.

'Why didn't you tell me that was how you got this, Jimmy?' (The battering.)

'I didn't wanna worry you. What did he say?'

'He said you owed him money. He's on his way over here.'

'*Shit!*' He smacked his sore forehead. Then regretted it.

'Who is he, Jimmy?'

'He's a punter. He placed a bet with me. Said it was for a thousand. The ledger said a hundred. He accused me of writing down two noughts instead of three.'

'I thought Harry did the writing.'

'He was away having a piss.'

'We'd better call the police.'

'No! No, we can't.'

'Couldn't you just pay him?'

'Do that and God knows what he'd come up with next. He's a nut. Maybe I can get a restraining order on him or something. I don't know. But I'll have to do something. I don't like the way it's getting to you, Carol.'

'I'm scared, Jimmy.'

Byrne was trying to figure out why Ivers was coming after him so soon after the first kicking. He had expected a few days' grace, at least. Maybe Ivers had found out that Carol was loaded and was putting the frighteners on her to get at him. I couldn't really tell what was going through his mind, other than that he was looking very edgy, trying to figure out how he could get off the course without the crunchers seeing him.

'I don't understand, Jimmy. Why can't we go to the police?'

'It'd be your word against his. Besides, that might only provoke him.'

'By the look of you, he's already provoked.'

'I didn't know he would get this serious. Come on.'

'We'll take yours,' said Byrne, when they reached the car-park. 'I'll pick mine up tomorrow. Ivers'll see it and think I'm still here.'

They sped out of the course and along the Leopardstown road, going east for the main Dublin to Wicklow road.

'Jimmy, how on earth did we get into this situation?'

Byrne lit a panatella. 'You've seen what it's like when there's a big crowd and everybody's clamouring to get money on before a race. It's easy to make a mistake. Even if I get it right, I might be taking that many bets Harry can't keep up with me. I might be saying a tenner to win fifty Mick's Delight, ticket number six-two-two and at the same time taking another bet for, say, forty to win eighty Trojan Princess, ticket number six-two-three, and Harry gets them crossed. Next thing you know the race is over and some punter's handing you a docket that tallies up with a losing bet as far as Harry's ledger's concerned. The punter says he backed Mick's Delight but Harry's got him down as having bet Trojan Princess. Did Harry write it down wrong or is the punter trying it on? He's-lost-his-wife's-housekeeping's written all over his face. He's desperate. He'll try anything. What do you do?'

'Then maybe Ivers *did* bet a thousand.'

'If he did, the takings would have showed nine hundred pound too much. He's trying it on.'

'But what about Harry? Maybe he'll hit Harry.' Typical Carol.

Fuck Harry, Byrne was thinking. *Anyway, who the fuck's gonna bother Harry? I'm the one with all the problems. Carol, please see a psychiatrist. For me.*

It seemed hopeless. 'Look, Jimmy, we've got so much going for us. We don't need a pitch. Why don't we just pull out? I don't think I could stand this happening all the time.'

He tried to look sympathetic, as though the very possibility of anything spoiling their lives together was anathema. 'All right,' he said. 'I'll sell up.'

'I feel terrible now for asking you.'

'Your happiness is more important, Carol. I'll work it till a buyer comes along. Shouldn't take that long. I was a fair punter myself. I can still do that. It'll be for the best. Besides, we've the baby to think of.'

'Jesus!' A mass of smoke hit them as Byrne opened the kitchen door. 'The cooker's on fire.'

'But I turned it off.'

'You stay here and I'll put it out.'

'Ginny! Oh my God, Ginny's in there!'

He held her back. 'Carol, I'll take care of it. Now stay here. I don't want anything happening to you. I'm not going in there till you promise me you'll stay out here where it's safe.'

'Oh God, I can't hear her. Hurry, Jimmy, hurry.'

Byrne did his fire-brigade act. Covering his mouth he went inside, closed the door behind him, trained the extinguisher on the oven, switched it off, grabbed a towel and carried the burnt remains of the pie outside.

He came out coughing. 'She's not in there. She's not in her bed.'

'She must be!'

'Carol, believe me, in all that smoke, thank God she's not. I'll see if she's upstairs; you check down here.'

Byrne came back down and found Carol standing outside on the living-room patio calling out to her dog. 'That door was left open, Jimmy. She *must* have got out.'

'She can't have gone far.'

'Then why doesn't she answer me?'

'Calm down. We'll look for her first thing in the morning. As soon as it's light. OK? We'll find her. I promise you. Now I'm going to take a shower, get the smell of smoke off me.'

The phone in the hall rang and Carol answered it.

It was Maguire. 'So you thought you'd get away from me, did you? I saw you speeding out of the carpark. Well, you can tell that bastard I just slashed his tyres. You tell him if I don't get my money, I'm taking a blade to *you*.' The line went dead. It fell from her hand. She broke down in tears.

In his office in the Hassett building, Maguire opened the safe and took a thousand quid out of the carpark's takings.

Byrne stepped out of the shower and into the bedroom. In the distance, at the far end of the back lawn, he saw a flashlight flickering. He opened the window and heard a faint, cracked voice crying out, 'Here, Ginny, here, girl. Where are you, girl? Mammy's here.'

He closed the window and got dressed. He sat in the living-room armchair that night.

Carol came back in the early hours and cried herself to sleep at the kitchen table. Byrne went outside and emptied the filling from the pie in under the hedge and trampled it in. Then he put the remainder of the pie outside the back door. Next morning he found Carol in the scorched kitchen, cleaning and trying to salvage what she could. On the table lay charred pictures of her parents. Her mother's apron, which Carol had kept on its hook, was in ashes.

'Jimmy. Mammy's kitchen.' She was sobbing her heart out.

'It was an accident, Carol.'

'But it's ruined.'

'We can get a new one.'

'It's not the same. Oh God, Jimmy, what am I going to do? What's happening to me?'

He put his arms around her. 'There, now, don't get yourself all upset.'

Maguire let go of the puppy. It ran up the back garden. Byrne heard it scratching at the door. He went out.

'Hey, Carol. Ginny's back. She's eating your pie.'

Carol's face lit up. She ran in from the hall. The dog jumped into her arms and she made a big fuss of it.

(Kipper, by the way, took three days to die. I figured Ginny would probably last about a day and a half. Ginny was about half the size of Kipper.)

Byrne held up the pie dish. 'Look. She must've been starving. She ate it all.'

The following afternoon, just as the staff were breaking for lunch, Maguire entered his office and asked Mrs Gallagher to open the safe and take out the takings from the car park. She put the cash plus receipts on his desk and handed him back the key.

'Can you please count that cash before you go, Mrs Gallagher?'

'I'm meeting someone,' she said, looking at her watch, which he ignored, telling her to count the cash while he added up the corresponding receipts.

'These add up to six thousand and forty,' Maguire then said, setting the calculator aside. 'Is that how much cash you have, it is?'

'No.' She seemed puzzled. 'It's a thousand short.'

'A *thousand?* God save us. Count it again.'

She did so. 'It's still a thousand short.'

'How many keys are there for that safe, Mrs Gallagher?'

'Yours and Mr Byrne's.'

'And you took mine home with you last night, y'did?'

'Yes.'

'Then Mr Byrne must have taken the missing thousand.'

Maguire put the phone on loudspeaker and called Byrne.

Mrs Gallagher looked mortified, dreading the implications of Maguire asking Byrne outright if he'd been at the safe. If he hadn't, suspicion would fall on her.

'Mr Byrne, you've been in this office since yesterday afternoon, y'have?'

'No. Why?'

'Nothing important.'

Maguire hung up, sat back, joining his hands under his chin, mulling it over. 'Well, I don't know what to say, Mrs Gallagher. I really don't. If you were sittin' in my chair, what would you say? How would you deal with such a huge amount of money going missing? You'd call the Guards, y'would?'

'Well, I don't know. I . . . I can't understand it.'

'You didn't lend the key to anyone?'

'No. I'd never do such a thing.'

'You had it with you at all times?'

'Yes. I hope you don't think I had anything to do with it, Mr Maguire.'

'I'm like you, Mrs Gallagher: at a loss. Enjoy your lunch. Sorry for keeping you.'

'Oh, thank you, sir.'

Bringing her before a court, exposing her as a thief at her age, would have a knock-on effect: her family's good name, grandkids wouldn't look up to her any more. People like Mrs Gallagher would worry about stuff like that. She'd be giving it a good deal of thought, appreciating his attitude. Maguire liked that.

Chapter Twenty Three

I have to say that Ivers was becoming increasingly more interesting to me. I'd never noticed it before, but Ivers and Toner sounded very alike. Which gave me an idea. Whether I'd ever put it into practice was a different matter. But I always like to have as many get-outs in place as I can, just in case things take a turn for the worse. It would mean a bit of voice-mixing, the use of some fancy dubbing equipment, and the kind of recording gear you find in record companies. Still, it had possibilities. So I told Toner to invite him over for a little chat. And to tape it. I wanted Ivers's voice, not Ivers.

Toner calls him in to his games room.

Ivers is wary. He stands there, looking like a member of the Gestapo in that overcoat of his, wondering why the invitation. He respects Toner, only because he's afraid of him. They had a minor run-in once over a prostitute Toner was fond of. She owed Ivers money. He was putting the frighteners on her. Toner stepped in and now Con was absolutely one hundred per cent positive; he never again wanted any more run-ins with Toner.

'Drink, Con?'

'Yeah, thanks.'

'Sit down.'

Toner pours a couple of Jamesons and sits down opposite him.

Ivers takes a sip, then waits to see what this is all about.

'I got a proposition to put to you, Con.'

'Oh?' He's still wary, but a bit less so. Toner's sounding amicable.

'I'm going into the casino business.'

'I thought casinos were illegal in this country.'

'They're passing a law.'

'I didn't know that.'

'I have it on good authority.'

'You'll make a fortune.'

'We'll make five million out of it.'

'*We*'ll make five million out of it?'

Toner takes a drink.

Ivers checks his hearing. 'You said *we*'ll make five million out of it.'

'Five million *a year*. Interested?'

Ivers is all ears. But he's wondering why the sudden generosity.

'You're wondering why I'm offering you this.'

'Are you wanting me to invest in this, Paddy?'

'Not a bean. Another drink?'

Ivers looks like he needs it. He downs what's left of the first. Toner pours a couple more and leaves the bottle on the desk.

'You're good at what you do, Con. And you look right. Dress well. I always thought that about you. And you know how to handle people. Gamblers are always making trouble. I need someone who can keep them in tow, yet happy at the same time. So they'll keep coming back. Barring them defeats the object. I'm too busy to run a casino. I finance it, you run it. A proposition like that interest you?'

'Yeah, a proposition like that interests me. I can't believe this. You're talking about giving me two and a half million.'

'I'm not Father-fucking-Christmas, Con. You get ten per cent of the first five million profit per year, five per cent of everything thereafter. If it only makes two mil you get ten per cent of that.'

'You had me wondering there for a minute. Still, this is one great opportunity.'

'I've bought a big site. Building plans are under way. There's a catch.'

'I thought there might be.'

'You ever been to Vegas?'

'Regularly.'

'You notice the hotels there have private luxury villas on the grounds?'

'They reserve them for the big shots from all over the country.'

'All over the *world*, Con. We could end up making a fortune. Once the casino's up and running, I intend building villas. I'd want you to invest in them. I'd want you committed.' *So do the people who owe him money.* 'That way I'd be sure you were giving it your full attention. So we're talking property as well. You like to own property like that?'

'Yeah, I'd like to own property like that.'

'So you'd like to buy into the property business?'

'Yeah, I'd like to buy into the property business. I'll be getting my money straight back. So where's the catch? I don't see any catch. It'd be the easiest money I ever made. I'd be getting it for nothing. Where's the catch?'

'You'd have to give up all your other businesses. No loan sharking. I'd want you totally focused.'

'I'd be more focused than Kodak, for fuck's sake.'

'We're a lot alike, Con. We both see the angles. Take a look around you. The people who work for us only know how to rob casinos, not run them. And the beauty about this is it's all in cash. Which means the last thing I need is to put in some manager who keeps proper accounts.'

'Fuck that!'

'There's another reason. Security. I'd need you to find the right people. No sozzle-heads. Men who work out, take pride in their appearance, yet, when the occasion demands, do whatever you tell them, without question. Cleanly, so the law would never suspect our hand in it.'

'No problem. I know the right people for a job like this. The law would never suspect a thing. They'd never see our hand in it. Everything'll look like an accident. Any pimps, anybody with a magnet under the roulette, card-sharps – boommmphh!'

'Good man.'

They touched glasses.

Half an hour later and I had as much of Ivers on tape as I needed.

Chapter Twenty Four

<hr/>

I'll tell you something. See this guy Byrne – he's a fucking disaster. If he's not careful, he'll ruin everything. He's running around like a lunatic. People must think his head's on a swivel. Every time you look at him it's on backwards in case Con Ivers is behind him. He's desperate to get Carol to see a psychiatrist.

Anybody'd think that tape was top of the charts the way he's been playing it. Only now he's going overboard. He's edited it. Every time Carol closes her eyes, he's hitting the remote. Her head's swimming in it. He never lets up. And I'll tell you something else – the guy's got no style, no finesse. He charges at everything. I'd worked it out so events would follow on from one another. So everything would look natural, y'know? So it would look like Carol was *gradually* coming apart. With each stage she would be asked to get psychiatric help. If she says no, you heap on a bit more, turn the pressure up. Byrne isn't interested in things looking natural. He's hitting Carol with the whole lot at once.

But the irony is he's getting away with it.

She finds the dog. It's dying. They rush it to the vet. The vet suspects poison. Does his best. The dog dies. Carol goes into hysterics. Blames herself.

'Why are you blaming yourself, Carol?'

'I'm the one who feeds it.'

The vet insists the dog could have eaten fox poison, a whole number of things.

'Look, you'll have to do a post-mortem. My wife's not well. Put her mind at rest.'

The vet has the contents of the dog's stomach analysed. The toxicologist finds beef, carrots and poison mushrooms. The kind that grow under cedars.

She'd weeded in under the row of cedars, she remembers clearly. Picked carrots. Left them in the wheelbarrow. She must have somehow – she doesn't know how it happened. But they got into the pie.

They got into the pie?

'The pie you made me, Carol?'

She's frantic with the implications.

'The pie you made me, Carol? If I'd eaten it, I'd be dead. Is that what you're saying?'

'Oh, Jimmy, I'm so sorry, I—'

'You're sorry? You could've killed me! I don't know what's happening to you, Carol. You need help.'

She won't go.

He piles it on.

Night comes and she's afraid to sleep. She knows what sleep brings. Her head is filled with what sleep brings. But she can't fight it forever. She finally drops off at the kitchen table. Byrne comes downstairs, switches off the light, steps into the adjoining dining room and, watching her through the hatch, hits the remote.

The tape plays down through the ceiling. Carol stirs. Byrne switches it off. She drops off again. He switches it back on. Her father's crying out, water coming in on him.

But the tape's been edited, don't forget, now he cries only *Carol*'s name. 'Carol, help me, Carol.' All that. She stirs. Byrne switches it off. She drops back over. Byrne switches it on. 'Carol, help me, Carol' is resounding in her unconsciousness, working away at her. She stirs. Off on off on off on off on off. He's after a build up. On! Her eyes spring open, but she's only half-conscious, she's in a bad way, cold sweat, awestruck, writhes, she's mesmerized by it.

'Carol, help me, Carol.'

She calls forth: 'Daddy? Daddeeee?'

'Carol, help me, Carol!'

'I'm so sorry. I'm so sorry.'

'Carol, please help me. Carol, help me, Carol!'

'Daddy? Daddy, I'm so sorry. Daddy I . . . I . . .'

'Carol, help me, Carol. Carol, help me, Carol!'

Byrne steps into the kitchen. She swings round. 'Daddy? Daddy?'

'Carol, help me, Carol.' She moves towards Byrne.

'Daddy? Oh Daddy. I'm so sorry. I'm so sorry.'

Byrne grabs her. 'Carol. Carol, what is it? You're frightening me, Carol.' He shakes her. 'Carol, wake up.' She wakes.

She's not even sure it's him. In the darkness she's still half-convinced it's her father in the room. And the tape's still playing.

'What's wrong, Carol?'

'Jimmy?'

'Yes. It's me. What is it, Carol?'

She's hearing voices. 'Can't you hear it?'

'Hear what, Carol?'

'Jimmy, please tell me you can hear it.'

'Carol, help me, Carol.'

'Jimmy, tell me you can hear it.'

'Hear *what*?'

She screams. 'Daddeeee!'

Byrne shakes her. 'Hear what, Carol?' He rushes for the light switch. Hits it. Hits the remote. Silence.

She's fixed on the silence. Entranced by it. Straining for her father's voice.

'What?' he says. 'Hear what? Snap out of it, Carol.'

She withdraws further into herself.

Morning comes and Byrne's cooking his own breakfast. Carol nearly always cooks his breakfast. He's implying he doesn't trust her cooking, that she's losing him. But she doesn't see him.

'Carol, you're going to have to pull yourself together.'

She's staring at the table, or into it, into space, in some kind of mental stupor.

He leads her up the stairs and into a cold shower. She squirms from it. He slaps her. Shakes her. Forces her into it.

He's pushed her too far with the tape. She can't come to a decision about seeing a shrink in this state. He'll have Toner to answer to. He has to bring her out of it.

He holds her till she can't breathe, is choking, spluttering. 'Carol, get a hold of yourself.' She coughs, retches. He stands back, looking at her, fretting, for his own sake, not hers, then sighs as if he's been reprieved, as she comes to, a pitiful sight, her negligee clinging to her, now see-through from the water.

He grabs a towel and dries her, 'Carol, you're gonna have to get a hold of yourself.'

'Jimmy, I'm sorry,' she says, whimpers almost. 'I'm sorry.'

Lunchtime comes. She's listless, but offers to make it. He says, 'I'll make it.' Does. Offers her a sandwich. She won't eat. He eats. Watches her across the table. She's looking contrite.

'Jimmy?'

'Yes?'

'I'll make dinner.' What she's saying is, *Please let me make dinner, Jimmy. No poison ingredients this time, I promise. I'm in control.*

He doesn't answer.

'Jimmy, it'll be all right.'

'Of course it will.'

She's trying to convince him. 'But it will.'

'Of course it will.'

'Six o'clock?'

'Fine.'

He goes out.

She makes his favourite. He always loved her cooking. He still loves her cooking. She'll make things right. He loves *her* Chinese. She's making him Chinese. Sets the table, bottle of his favourite red wine. She inspects every ingredient minutely. No mushrooms. She won't take the chance. Can't. Nothing must go wrong. She wants his trust back. He's all she has and she's letting him down. She loves him. She didn't mean to poison him. But she didn't poison him. But she didn't mean to anyway.

She checks the pots, the pans, the oven. It's not overset. She's checked. She has a hot shower, gets dressed, goes back and checks the plug: it's not in the plughole, she's double-checked. She's certain. She's certain the bath tap isn't running. But she didn't have a bath. Doesn't matter. She's taking no chances.

It's six. Jimmy will be home any minute. She waits, strumming the table, for the sound of his car.

He'll really love this meal.

It's seven. The meal's simmering. The clock's ticking. *He'll really love this meal. It's all right. I checked.*

It's eight. The clock's ticking. *He'll be home in a minute. Must have got held up.*

It's nine. The house is silent. The meal simmers. The clock ticks. She's still watching it.

Ten.

She jumps up, nervously fidgets with her fingers, looks out across the hall to the front door, hears his key turn in it, sees it opening, Byrne entering, head low, looks tired, a lot on his mind. She moves forward, 'Jimmy.' Hears the lethargy in his voice.

'Oh hello, love.'

'Busy day?'

'Not bad.'

Feels for him; he's so down. 'I've made your favourite. Chinese. It's all ready. Bit dried up but . . . I was expecting you earlier . . . it's all ready.'

'Not hungry.'

'But I . . . I . . . thought.'

'I had something out.'

'Oh? OK. A glass of wine, then. It's your favourite. I bought it specially.'

'I think I'll just go on up.'

'Oh, right, well . . .'

'Night, Carol.'

She watches him go up, 'Night,' round the landing, then, glancing back up, goes into the kitchen and sits in silence broken only by the clock ticking, alone.

She goes to bed, lies awake, hopes he'll wake up, wants to tell him everything will be all right, wants him to come to her. He lies with his back to her.

Dawn breaks. She drifts off, then wakes. He's gone. Without even coffee. It's all proving too much for him. She's losing him.

Byrne piles it on. Gives her the silent treatment.

She cooks. Treble-checks. Byrne stays away, morning till night. She stops cooking for him.

The postman comes. She opens the envelope and sees photographs of Byrne with Louise Kelly and her toddler. The toddler is in the saddle. All three smiling. Looking like a happy family. One photograph shows Lou and Byrne outside a bank. Money is changing hands. The enclosed note says 47 Finster Avenue. It's not signed.

Maguire's watching and taping this on the monitor.

He rings her. 'Mrs Byrne, Kevin Maguire here. Is Mr Byrne there?'

'No.'

'He was dealing with money that went missing from the carpark takings. One thousand in cash. Has he decided what to do about it yet?'

She hates Hassett Property. Doesn't respond, or care. Hangs up.

Looks at the photographs. Sees they were taken at the horse sanctuary.

Maguire has Mrs Gallagher ring. 'Carol, is Mr Byrne there? He was due here to discuss an insurance policy for the horse sanctuary.'

Carol's puzzled. 'Why is my husband involving himself with the horse sanctuary?'

'Horses broke loose.' (Our doing.) 'Mr Maguire is worried about the company being liable. Mr Byrne insisted he'd deal with it personally.'

What does this mean? She's muddled. *Is Louise Kelly involved in the horse sanctuary?*

'Mrs Gallagher, you know that house we have in Finster Avenue?'

'Yes.'

'Who's renting it?'

'No one.'

'You're sure?'

'Your father had it renovated, but it's never been let.'

Carol arrives at 47 Finster Avenue. It's fully furnished, the garden well kept, a bucket and spade in a child's sandpit next to the swing. She rings the bell. No answer.

She goes round the back, looks in through the window. Chinese takeaway cartons beside unwashed dishes are on the table next to the ashtray. It contains panatella butts.

At The Cedars Byrne lights a panatella and sits down. The photographs of him with Louise are on the coffee table. He's weary, looks as if he's had enough, that whatever Carol has in mind for the photographs it will not surprise him, given the things she's been putting him through lately.

She's ready for crying. 'Do you love her?'

'You're being ridiculous.'

'But you're seeing her.'

'Look, Carol, those photos don't say that.'

'But you're giving her money.'

'Yes.'

'And she's living rent-free in a house that belongs to me.'

He sighs. 'Yes.'

'Where last night you were having a meal with her?'

'Yes.'

'Is her daughter yours?'

224

He again sighs wearily – as if he wants to answer but something is preventing him. 'Her father was the best man I've ever known.'

She sobs. She wants to believe him but so many questions remain unanswered.

He gets up. 'Carol, I can't go on like this. I don't know you any more. You need help. If you won't get help for yourself, at least think of the baby.'

'You think I want this baby! I *don't* want this baby! I don't *deserve* this baby! Don't you see?'

He's dazed. He'd been using the kid as leverage. 'No, I don't see.'

'Annie's dead because of me! She was to have her baby first! I *can't* have my baby first! I can't have a baby knowing I'm responsible for the death of Annie's! I don't deserve my baby!'

She had taken the guilt upon herself far more than any of us had realized.

'Carol, I miss them too. But I can't watch you destroy yourself. If you won't get help for yourself, get it for us.'

She shakes her head.

He leaves. But is he leaving for good? Are they finished? She's not sure. But she's determined not to seek help.

'This is to be expected,' the psychiatrist I had visited said.

'Why?'

'The guilt she feels over the deaths of her parents and sister is, to her, strange as it may seem, to be borne, to be *suffered*. Professional help would benefit her. She feels she deserves to be punished, harbours a hard and fast belief that she is worthless. The traumas that she has endured, the loss of her husband, she subconsciously welcomes: she wants him, yet in her mind she is, to a lesser degree of course, voluntarily suffering that which she had put her brother-in-law through, namely the loss of his wife. These are her penance.'

'So how do I get her to go to someone like you?'

'Change her perspective.'

'How?'

'Make her question it. Introduce in her a plethora of emotions. This will either push her over the edge, in which case her husband will have grounds for involuntary commitment in the interests of the unborn child, or force her into facing the fact that she can no longer cope, that she *has* to seek help. For instance, she cherishes her father's memory. He was all things to her. Break that. Create ambivalence, an unconscious anger towards him. Make her feel that her father wronged her mother. Make her feel that she herself has wronged her husband. Evoke in her additional feelings of pity, of compassion for her husband. Currently she is in a limbo of self-blame. In some patients, events that follow on from the initial trauma in themselves create this additional plethora. It is plausible, psychologically, that she will then seek help.'

She did. When the man came to open her father's safe, in which the 'plethora' (his word, not mine) that I had arranged, lay. The letter Maguire forced Tom Hassett to sign.

She goes to see a psychiatrist. He hears all that she has been through.

She reads the letter:

> My daughter Carol asked me to loan this land to a
> horse sanctuary. Through this I met Louise Kelly.
> But a close employee of mine, a Mrs Gallagher,
> whom I now know to be responsible for money that

has been going missing from the takings from my carpark, found out about the affair by tracing a monthly direct-debit maintenance payment of £800 to Ms Kelly, who now lives with our child in my house in Finster Avenue. Mrs Gallagher has taken photographs of myself and Ms Kelly with our daughter and my fear is she will forward them to my wife if I expose her. Though, regrettably, I suspect my wife already knows. I dread to think what this is doing to her in her present condition. If I don't expose Mrs Gallagher, my son-in-law, who is now running the business, and who strongly disapproves of the affair, yet appreciates my financial obligation to Ms Kelly must be met, might find out about the thief sometime in the future: she may steal again, and she might try similar tactics on him to stop him going to the police. She might send similar, though in his case innocent, photographs to my daughter Carol and wreck her marriage. Since he is innocent in all this, my concern is that he is kept out of it as much as possible, and it is this that I wish to discuss with you.

I enclose the photographs Mrs Gallagher took of myself with Ms Kelly.

The police must not be involved in this.

Tom Timothy Hassett.

'The last line is in Daddy's own hand. And it is his signature. It is addressed to Arrow Investigations. Dated the day before his death. But never sent. I found it in his safe. It hasn't been opened since his death.

'The sanctuary was my idea. I'm responsible for bringing

them together. I'm responsible for the affair. It's there in Daddy's own hand. My husband knew what it would do to me if I found out and kept it from me, even though it meant I would think the worst of him. I drove him away. I should have trusted him. He deserved that, at least. But no, I saw four innocent photographs of my husband and Ms Kelly and made an adultery case out of it. I should have found out who was behind it.'

She had sacked Mrs Gallagher that morning. She had served eviction on the horse sanctuary that morning. Mr Maguire had said to leave it to him. All she had to do was sign.

Everything she'd held dear was wrecked. Everyone she'd held dear was dead. The man she loved she'd driven away.

She broke down, crying that she couldn't live with herself if her mother had died knowing her father had cheated on her, blaming herself for having brought it about.

As the psychiatrist helped her out of the consulting room, the pain struck deep into her abdomen. The receptionist rushed to her side. Carol collapsed.

She lost her baby.

Byrne was ecstatic. Byrne was over the moon. She'd gone to a shrink. Her time had come. When would we kill her was all he wanted to know.

'The weekend, Jimmy. I want you out of the country. Alibi. Know what I mean? Just in case something goes wrong.'

'No problem, Paddy.'

We were into the final phase. What had at first looked like an impossibility was nearly over.

See me? I'm a fucking genius!

Chapter Twenty Five

See me? I'm a fucking idiot!

My solicitor rang. 'Gerd, it's Michael.'

'Morning, Michael.'

'Gerd, we need to get together and go through our approach to your divorce hearing.'

'OK, what have you got in mind?'

'Well, there's the question of custody. Sinead will fight for custody just as hard as you will. The art of litigation, Gerd, is anticipating your opponent's questions and having all the answers ready. Sinead will try to blacken your character. We have to be prepared.'

'I've nothing to hide.'

'Gerd, let me speak frankly. I can act in your best interests only if I am in possession of all the facts.'

'I've nothing to hide, Michael.'

It came like a sledgehammer. 'You're sure Sinead hasn't hired an investigator?'

'An investigator?'

'It's not uncommon. You've been estranged for months. An investigator could have had his camera on you. Know everywhere you've been. All on record. You'd never even have noticed him.'

Nah! Not Sinead. She's not that smart. She wouldn't have.
'Are you there, Gerd?'
Shit!
Was this why Sinead hadn't bought all that crap I'd put around about Bawn? Her investigator had had concrete evidence to the contrary all along. Was this what Molly meant that night in my place when she said she had proof that we weren't having an affair?

If you think about what I'd been up to over the previous few months, you'll realize why Michael almost floored me. It never occurred to me that right under my nose Sinead was gathering evidence for a custody battle, that an investigator had been following me all along, talking photographs of me with Lou, of me buying a Secret Safe identical to Bawn's, of me picking the lock of that house in Wicklow, where dope was then found, of me throwing Kipper into the septic tank. He'd have a record proving that I'd used a key to go into Tom Hassett's office late at night, that I'd talked to Christy McDermott, cased their cottage, visited The Cedars, the horse sanctuary, the forensic pathologist, the psychiatrist. With a listening-in device, he'd have heard every word they said.

And that's what puzzled me.

If he'd been on my tail, he'd have made the connection once the Hassetts turned up dead, given Sinead his report, and turned me in.

So why hadn't he turned me in?

More to the point, why hadn't Molly? She knew what he knew. Sinead would've told her.

Or did she?

For the first time in my life my activities with Toner had

become entangled in my private life. I hadn't seen it coming. But now that it had, how damning would it turn out to be? The answer had to lie with Sinead. To get that answer, I needed her back on my side.

Not a prospect I relished.

Chapter Twenty Six

───────◆◆◆───────

Now, if you were in my position you'd be shitting yourself. Right? I mean, you'd be saying to yourself, 'Fuck me, what am I gonna do? I'm fucked.' Yeah, well, I'm made of sterner stuff. Not for me the packing of the bags and heading for the hills as though the Lone Ranger were after me with that half-baked Indian. Always look on the bright side. That's me. Y'know why? Because I'm smart. OK, Sinead slipped one in while I wasn't watching. But what had worked for me for years would work for me again. All my expertise, know what I mean? Just because this is new territory for me doesn't mean I can't go on the defensive as well as the offensive. In other words, I'm gonna defend myself from her Dick while leading him into a trap. Know your opponent. Then confuse the balls off him. But just as important, appreciate his view of you.

Right now my guess was that this private investigator of Sinead's was afraid of me. Oh, no doubt he had some hare-brained scheme in mind – blackmail, probably. But fear would still come into it. He'd seen what I'd brought about under the noses of the law, and not a peep out of them. He knows what I'm capable of. He comes at me, he knows he'd better watch himself. If I'm any judge, he's the one who's

SEAMUS SMYTH

shitting himself. He's biting his nails trying to figure out how to approach me and watch his back at the same time. His mind'll be running away with him. He'll be feeling like a guy in a horror movie watching the shadow of the killer creeping up the stairs. One wrong move and I'll be upon him.

Then there's due process. I tell him to fuck off, he goes to the law, they arrest me, fair enough, but they also wanna know why Dick here didn't come forward at the time.

'*He* blackmailed me, officer, that's why.'

'Oh, *he* blackmailed *you*?'

Dick would be weighing that up, too. Even a small detail like that.

Then there's Carol Byrne. Dick was watching me, not her. He probably knows nothing about her little adventures. No one else does, so how would he? So there's no risk there. He'll find out, of course, when Byrne cops it. Put two and two together and make the connection. Maybe he'll join Byrne in that septic tank. Keep each other company. They'll even have Kipper, y'know, man's best friend.

He's wondering what to do next, I'd say.

I've a way of helping him come to that decision.

Get him the sack. Get Sinead to call him off. Once that happens, he'll know I'm *definitely* on to him. Then he'll come forward.

Sinead had taken a job in a clothes shop, y'know, to make ends meet because I'd cut her off without a penny. What applied before still applied as far as she was concerned. She'd be missing the kids and her comforts. The kids were my way back in. She visited them every lunchtime. So I told them to tell her I wanted to see her.

She came out of the school gates, saw my car and got in.

She looked in bad form, by the way, as if I was the last person she wanted to see.

Now you take me, for instance – I never see the point in arguing. I like to sit down with people who are being unreasonable and discuss my differences rationally, y'know, totally disarm them by the power of my intellect, drawing on all its resources. Even if it means lying. A lie is a resource, isn't it? But Sinead, well, you heard the way she spoke to me in the police station.

She likes arguing. 'You could have sent a note. But then you knew I wouldn't have come.'

See what I mean? Implying I'd used the kids as leverage. She could tear up a note, but not ignore the kids' pleas to come. She was right, of course.

'Why do you look for ulterior motives in everything I do?'

'Experience has taught me to.'

'Sinead, I don't want to argue.'

'What *do* you want?'

'I want you to come home with me.'

'You must be joking.'

'I want to have a talk with you. Then, if *you* decide, I'll drive you back to work.'

'If *I* decide? What's that supposed to mean? We can talk here.'

'I want to show you something.'

'Show me it here.'

'It's at home.'

She flew off the handle. 'What are you playing at?'

This was a very good sign. She hadn't used her ammunition. I suspected she didn't even know she had any. It was a theory I was working on. Oh, her Dick might have thrown her a few scraps to justify his fee come the court hearing –

Lou was one – but I suspected he was holding out on her, saving the *really* damaging stuff for me.

This one would definitely get her going. She hadn't heard it in a while. 'I think about you, Sinead.'

'Fuck you!'

Still no ammunition. Things were looking up already.

'Sinead, I miss you.'

'If you keep this up, I'm getting out of the car.'

'I want to apologize.'

'Then apologize.'

'I apologize.'

'Good. Is that it?'

'I apologize for everything.'

'I meant, is that why you wanted to see me?'

'You don't believe me.'

'Why should I?'

'If I dropped the custody claim, then would you believe me?' No custody claim, no need for Dick's report to go to court. Remove the small hurdles and the big ones will take care of themselves.

'What are you up to?'

'The kids miss you, Sinead. So do I. It's not the same.'

'You're not getting round me. Not this time.'

'I'm asking you for an hour of your time. If you don't like what you hear, see, we'll forget about it. Please.'

'See' puzzled her. It also interested her. She's a woman. Nosy. Can't help herself.

'For the kids' sake.' Always gets to her, that one.

'If you're messing me about, I warn you.'

'Sinead, when have I ever messed you about?' I said it as a joke. She wasn't laughing. But it melted her a little bit. Sinead always had a good sense of humour. And one of the things she loved about me was mine. So far I'd offered to drop the custody suit, apologized, and dangled. She was coming round. Which convinced me her Dick hadn't told her about Kipper, my picking locks in Wicklow and all that. If she'd known, she'd have battered the face of me with it. 'What harm could an hour do?'

She gave me one of her 'Don't think it means you got round me' looks, then cocked her head. 'Come on.'

You see, already, by staying cool and assessing the problem, I'd figured out that Sinead wasn't a threat. I won't say she wasn't a threat *after all*, because she was still in a strong position to *become* a threat. But if I could get her back on my side, or at least get her to call off the divorce, she'd sack her Dick. (Makes him sound like some sort of paid penis. I'm sorry but I didn't invent the vernacular. I'll call him her PD, for Private Dick, instead.) And that would bring him out into the open, plus get the divorce off my head. I didn't have time for it now, with all this other stuff hanging over me. Getting Sinead back on my side would be easy. Then when things got back to normal, I could give her grounds for divorce again. Send her back to her clothes shop. I was getting used to living by myself, y'see, just me and the kids: gives you a lot more freedom to have women over.

The first thing I wanted to show her was her new car. She got out of mine, had a look around the place, y'know, had a lot of affection for it, missed it, like a homecoming.

Anyway, the remote brought the garage door up and there it was. Just like her own, but spanking brand new. Gleaming pink. 3-series BM, pink seats with white trim. Suit her light hair. Hard luck, Lou. I'd bought the car for you.

'Here,' I said, handing Sinead the keys, as if it was a

foregone conclusion that the car was hers, regardless of the outcome of the talk we were about to have.

She looked at it. Cagily, you know. What's he playing at?

'I didn't sell your car, Sinead. I bought you a new one. I wanted to pep you up, but, I dunno, things just got out of hand. I didn't mean them to. Anyway, I'm sorry.'

She was still wary.

I took the keys back off her and pulled the car into the drive, closed the garage, and put them gently back in her hand. Still she was wary. Took her hand away.

I smiled. 'I want to say something to you, Sinead: I'm a bastard. I want you to know that I know that. You were always good to me. And I've always loved you for it.'

She sat against the boot, wondering what to make of all this.

Dead easy. 'I want you to consider something. Don't answer now. In fact, don't answer at all. What you do over the next few days will tell me your decision. The kids miss you. They need their mother.' Getting her in the chest here; she was fighting back a lump coming to her throat. 'I know you don't want me here any more. And that's fair enough. I don't blame you. But I can't be without the kids. I will if you insist. But it won't be easy for me. So if you could see your way clear to coming back, I'll sleep in the spare room. You won't get any shit from me. You'll be rid of me. I'll just be sleeping in the same house, that's all. For the sake of the kids. Neither of us want to put them through a divorce.'

I let it go at that. Her eyes were filling up. I didn't want her to think I was thinking she was softening towards me. Her pride, y'know, crap like that. All I said was 'Take care, Sinead,' kissed her cheek, then got in my car and drove off.

Course, her new car was also in my name.

And, naturally, PD would have been watching all this. The kiss was for his benefit. She'd drive away in a new car. He'd weigh it up and know he was being taken off the case.

Chapter Twenty Seven

Course, there was always the possibility Sinead's PD hadn't followed me to England. If that were the case he would have a lot less on me; he wouldn't know about the specialists I'd seen there.

A little detective work would soon tell me. A check back through my bank statements to about five weeks after Sinead had left me showed a cheque had been made out for two grand, which my bank confirmed had been made payable to Tony Coyle Investigations. Up-front money, probably.

I rang the ferry ticket office, quoted the details of the day I'd caught the ferry to Holyhead, and said my name was Tony Coyle. 'I paid by cash,' I told the girl. 'But my credit card statement says you also debited my account.'

'Our records show you paid for your ticket by credit card, Mr Coyle.'

Which told me Coyle had been on that ferry. So he *had* followed me. He knew I'd seen the specialists.

Which brought me to Sinead. What information had Coyle given to her?

Sinead, as I knew she would, made the right decision. She picked the kids up from school and moved back in. The air between us was still a bit strained. For the kids' sakes we carried on as if everything was back to normal. I carried her bag up to our bedroom, her bedroom now, and found a typed letter from Coyle in amongst her things. It told her I'd been seeing Lou, and that Molly had 'visited twice, once in the early hours', complete with photographs, places and dates. But there was no mention of my other escapades. He'd left them out on purpose.

What it did say, though, was: 'Wide-ranging investigation ongoing'.

Cute. 'Wide-ranging', indeed. He'd figured I'd find a way to get a look at this. He was letting me know he *knew*. OK, so he knew. But *what* did he know? He had parts of a jigsaw. But not all the parts. He was biding his time until the rest of the parts showed up. Once Carol Byrne was dealt with, he'd have a fuller picture. But he wouldn't have motive on my part. And he still didn't know of Toner's involvement. But when the time came to deal with Byrne, Coyle would then know that Toner was involved. He would also know that I was in it with Toner. He'd know everything.

Which gave me an idea.

I altered the game plan.

I had to see Toner.

'I've thought of a way to bring this forward, Paddy.'

'How?'

'Byrne's not inheriting after all.'

He laughed. 'Can *I* tell him?'

'It'd be worth it just to see the look on his face.'

'Why the change?'

'You know me, Paddy. Things go along in a certain

242

direction, then I see a better option. Now I see us wrapping this up by Sunday.'

Course, Toner knows me only too well. He sensed something else was up. But he would never insult me by questioning my judgement. He looked at me, knowing I knew what he was thinking. Then he smiled. 'Smoke, Gerd?'

'Thanks.'

'So how do we get Hassett Property, if we're not gonna buy it from Byrne?'

'Buy it from Carol.'

'So what was all that driving-her-nuts bit for?'

'That *was* necessary. Now it isn't.'

'You're kidding? She went through all that for nothing?'

'This way she doesn't die.'

'Fair enough. No point killing her for nothing.'

I told Toner what I now had in mind.

It was Thursday. We were gonna buy Hassett Property Saturday.

Chapter Twenty Eight

Naturally we didn't tell Byrne the game plan had been changed.

When Saturday morning came, Maguire picked up Byrne from a flat he'd been staying in near the city centre and drove him to the airport. Byrne, I have to say, was afraid of Maguire. He'd seen what he was capable of. This, plus the fact that the job was finally coming to an end, made him a bundle of nerves. He was also feeling cocky, if you can imagine that. A big man, with all that money coming to him. He believed. Naive bastard.

Maguire, being Maguire, started winding him up. Though he had another reason for doing it. Here he was: 'You're givin' me a bonus for this, Byrne, y'are?'

'I wouldn't have been able to do it without you.'

'I can name my price, I can?'

'Name away.'

'How does ten percent grab ye?'

'That's a million quid!'

Maguire smiled to himself. Byrne hadn't twigged that, in keeping with the deal he'd made with Toner, he should have said half a million. 'It's too much for you, it is?'

'Fuck's sake, Kev, I'd end up skint at that rate.'

'Sure I'll leave it up to you. You won't insult me.'

'Aye, no problem.' *Some chance!*

'You're gonna invest, y'are?'

'Me?'

'I'd buy a niteclub.'

'Nah. You get the wrong sort in niteclubs.'

'I'd be your bouncer. Half gate.'

'Half gate?'

'Aye. Straight down the middle.'

'We'll see.'

'Then there's charity. Once they hear you've got a few bob, they'll be banging on your door.'

'They can bang away.'

'Let them fuckers in and they'll plague you to keep throwing to them.'

'Some fucking chance!'

'You'll be tortured day and night. How much is it you'll be worth, Jimmy?'

'Ten.' Now he twigged. 'Five.'

Maguire had again led him into it. Byrne was gonna sell out to the supermarket.

Byrne shifted in his seat, hoping Maguire hadn't tippled. He changed the subject. 'How you gonna do it?'

'What?'

'Carol.'

'Bottle of Valium. Be all over by the time you get back.'

'Thank fuck.'

'You'll miss her, y'will?'

'Aye, no doubt.'

'No feelings for her at all, no?'

'Wise up.'

'What made you marry her?'

'Not her looks.'

'Found out she was loaded and zoomed in?'

'Wouldn't you?'

'How'd that come about?'

'I was in having a pint. Her old man saw a bookie's docket fall out of my pocket and handed it to me. We got talking.'

'Was it a winning docket?'

'No. But it turned out to be.'

They were calling Byrne's flight as they came in.

Maguire told him to go and check in. 'And lend me your phone. I've a call to make.'

Byrne handed him his mobile, then went over to the British Midland desk. Maguire stayed in the middle of the concourse and made a polite call to Carol Byrne.

'Good morning, Mrs Byrne, Mr Maguire here. Is Mr Byrne there?'

'No.' She sounded down.

'I see. He said he'd meet me there at three. Is that still on?'

Which pepped her up. 'Jimmy said he'd be here at three?'

'He did. I got the impression he wanted to be there when you sign, advise you, whatever.'

'Sign what?'

'The contracts.'

'What contracts?'

'For the sale of Hassett Property.'

'You've got a buyer?'

'Of course. I thought you knew. Mr Byrne said something about doing the deal, then taking you away for a few days. He seemed worried about you, after you losing the baby. I was sorry to hear about that, Mrs Byrne. I know how much it must have meant to you.'

'Thank you.'

'Well, look, you'd better give him a ring. He should be on his mobile. The buyer is expecting to do the business at three. He's paying the full asking price, in cash. The solicitor's had the contracts ready for months in case a buyer showed, as you know. It's only a matter of signing.'

'I'll see you at three, then. I'll talk to Jimmy in the meantime.'

'There's one other thing, Mrs Byrne. Your solicitor might insist on hiring an armed security guard to man your safe – with all that money, and the banks not opening till Monday morning. Would you be happy with that?'

'Yes.'

'Good. This buyer's leaving the country tonight. He'll be away for several months. He wants this finalized today. You can have your solicitor ready for three?'

'That's no problem, Mr Maguire.'

'Great. I know how much you want to sell. Bye, now.'

'Bye.'

Maguire switched off the phone. Carol would be trying to contact her husband on it. He slipped it into his pocket and brought out an identical one, the one I had told Toner to tell him to buy.

He handed it to Byrne. 'I'll pick you up in the morning when you get back in. And make sure that worried look's off your face when the law comes to tell you your dear departed's body's been found. I don't want them reading something into it.'

'No danger of that happening.'

'Right. I'm away.'

'Kev?'

'What?'

'Thanks.'

'All part of the service.'

In the carpark, Maguire rang Toner on Byrne's phone and told him Byrne had gone to get his alibi. 'By the way, he was intending to inherit, then sell that land to that supermarket and cut you out. You'd have ended up with sweet fuck all.'

Toner laughed. 'You can't trust anybody these days.'

On the way back to Dublin, Byrne's phone rang repeatedly. Maguire didn't answer it. It had to be Carol.

Chapter Twenty Nine

———— >◦◦◦< ————

Three came and Carol Byrne was waiting for her husband. Telling her Byrne was coming had been Maguire's idea. He knew it would put her in the right frame of mind for the sale. It wasn't necessary. She'd have signed anyway. Maguire knew that. It suited his perverse sense of humour to have her suffer. He got a kick out of seeing her standing there, all done up, looking her best for the man in her life who she believed . . . well, you could tell she was hoping for a reunion.

She was wearing a polka-dot dress Byrne had bought her. He'd said he liked her in it. She was also nervous about seeing him, fidgeting when the doorbell rang, glancing over Maguire's shoulder to see if it was Byrne, hiding her disappointment when it wasn't.

It was the buyer.

Maguire did the introductions. 'Mrs Byrne, I'd like you to meet Mr Toner.'

'Mrs Byrne.'

'And Mr Nugent, Mr Toner's solicitor.'

'Good afternoon.'

A car pulled into the drive. Carol craned and saw that it wasn't Byrne's. Her solicitor came in and the introductions were gone through again.

'Shall we go through, Carol?' said Carol's solicitor.

'What? Yes, Sean.'

In the living room, Toner and his man put down the attaché cases and they all sat around the coffee table, Carol staying in the hall, waiting, watching.

Then a van arrived and a uniformed security guard with a two-way came in.

'Mrs Byrne?'

'Yes.'

'I'd like to run through the procedure with you, if that's all right.'

'Procedure?'

'The way this works. Which callers I can let in and—'

'Fine. Fine.'

'May I close the door?'

'I'm waiting for my husband.'

'I'm afraid he'll have to knock.'

Her solicitor called her in.

'Right, Sean, coming.'

The guard manned the closed door.

'Let my husband in when he comes. That's him,' she said, proudly pointing to their wedding photo on the wall. 'Let him in the minute he arrives.'

'No problem.'

Maguire went outside to his car. Then he came back and knocked on the door.

The guard asked: 'Who is it?'

'Mr Maguire.'

He was let in. Maguire did this for a reason. He wanted to make sure the guard would remember him.

'Carol, I need to explain these documents to you,' her solicitor said as she came in.

'No need, Sean. I'll leave everything to you. Would you like something to drink?'

'Yes, please.'

'Mr Maguire, would you mind?'

'Of course not. What'll you have?'

'Nothing for me, thanks.'

She went out past the guard and walked up the drive to the road to watch for Byrne's car, standing there, arms folded, on edge, worrying if she looked nice, if Byrne would be pleased to see her, not knowing how to react on seeing him, anxious not to overdo it, desperate to save her marriage. Fifteen minutes later they called her in to sign the documents. She didn't even want to see the cash.

Eventually she showed Maguire and Co out. 'He did say three, Mr Maguire? My husband. He did say three?'

The clock said half past.

'Yes. Caught in traffic, I'd say.'

'Ah, yes, yes. I expect so.'

Toner shook her hand, thanked her.

'Right, Mr Toner, bye.'

She opened the safe and left it to her solicitor to put the money in.

'I'll be going now, Carol. That was a good bit of business.'

'Right, Sean, thanks for coming. On a Saturday. You know, short notice.'

'Think nothing of it. Bye, Carol.'

'Bye-bye.'

The transaction was as straightforward as that.

She went upstairs and sat by the bedroom window, watching for Byrne.

Chapter Thirty

———◦◦◦◦———

By six, I was watching Coyle through a pair of binoculars; he was parked along the road from my place. Sinead had called him off several days earlier. He was now tailing me on his own time.

Making use of Byrne's mobile for several hours – a use which I had not foreseen until now – I rang Coyle four times between then and half-seven; hanging up each time he answered. Then I drove to Hassett's office and rang him again.

'This is Gerd Quinn. You want to see me. Come on up.'

When he came to the door, I threw him down the key. On the same keyring was the key to The Cedars.

Maguire rang Carol Byrne that night, right about the time me and Coyle were having our little discussion. The fact was we needed Carol out of the house. We needed her alive to tell the police what had happened that night – or what she believed had happened. Maguire figured he'd *spin* her a yarn that Byrne wanted to see her downtown. Get her out that way. She'd have jumped at the chance. But the security guard said she was upstairs asleep. Maguire couldn't wait. He had to go in then. She would see him. He'd have to kill her after all.

He drove to The Cedars.

The security guard asked: 'Who is it?'

'Mr Maguire.'

The guard let him in.

'Is Mrs Byrne in?'

'She's still upstairs.'

'Thanks.'

Maguire had the revolver out just as the guard closed the door. Two shots to the head and he fell to the floor. Maguire looked up, expecting the gunfire to bring Carol. It didn't. He went up.

Carol Byrne had rung Christy McDermott that morning and told him that she planned to bring in a man to look after the garden, a housekeeper to take care of running the things, cooking, and so on, that had caused her to lose face; that way her husband wouldn't think it was an issue any more when they got back together. This was based on what Maguire had told her; that she'd see Byrne that afternoon. She believed it offered a new chance. That she could build on that.

But she had watched for his car from the bedroom window until dusk. When he hadn't showed, she still had hope: something unforeseen might have kept him away.

But Byrne had had a lot of time on his hands in England. And he got to thinking, had he covered every angle? He was supposed to be estranged from his wife, so why were some of his clothes still in their wardrobe? That bothered him. The way he saw it, she was committing suicide, for reasons you know, and partly because there was no hope of reconciliation between them. The clothes weakened that. In his eyes, anyway. Probably he thought the police might say: 'But you didn't leave her. Your clothes are still there'.

Exactly what he was thinking we'll never know. In any

case, he rang a friend on the hotel phone and had him go round and collect his clothes. Which told Carol there was no hope.

She had decided to take her life among the things that were important to her and had gathered all her soft toys from when she was a child. They were neatly laid out on the bed. Photographs of her parents, of Annie, of her husband, were arrayed on the tallboy.

She had taken the pills, then wrote: 'Jimmy I love you. Forgive me,' closed her eyes and waited for the end to come.

Maguire opened the door and saw her in the chair.

And saw the note. She still had a pulse.

This was better than we could have hoped for.

He went downstairs, smeared blood from the guard's body into a plastic bag, then went into the living room and emptied the safe.

Thirty minutes later Maguire was in the warehouse. He had told Ivers to come alone.

Ivers believed that Byrne would be there. He wanted to see him.

'Where is he?'

'Here.'

The lights were off, but in the moonlight coming in through the perspex roof panel, Ivers turned and saw the revolver aimed at him.

'Kev, what're you doing?'

Maguire cocked the trigger.

'Kev, for fuck sake! Kev!'

'See ya, Con.' Two bullets entered just above the eyes. Maguire emptied Ivers's pockets, lifted his body up over his shoulders and carried him into the field. He removed the timber from the top of the septic tank and lowered Ivers in, watched him go under, replaced the timber, edged the sods back over it with his foot and was gone.

He drove to Byrne's flat, opened Byrne's BM, smeared the guard's blood on the front side of the seat, daubed it with a rag so it would look as though it had come from Byrne's calf, then drove to Toner's.

Toner was in his games room. He poured two whiskeys. He didn't have to ask if it had gone to plan. The attaché cases told him it had. He sat back in his swivel chair. They touched glasses.

Hassett Property hadn't cost us a bean.

The five million that Toner had paid for it that very afternoon was in the cases.

And I was having a chat with Sinead's private investigator. As I'd suspected, he had some notion in his head about blackmailing me.

But *I* blackmailed *him*.

Chapter Thirty One

Picture a parasite with a weeping-willow haircut and round wire spectacles and a you've-no-choice-in-the-matter attitude – 'You ask a forensic pathologist and a shrink how to murder three people and drive their daughter to suicide, for your *book*, and then it happens in real life. Yeah, I think that's worth fifty grand' – and you have Coyle. All twenty-eight years of him.

My problem with him was that if he turned up dead the law would find out I was the last person he'd been paid to follow. I needed to confuse them into thinking he was mixed up in something else, some business that had nothing to do with why Sinead had hired him – something big that had made him take off with the proceeds.

First I had to frighten the bastard into handing over what he had on me.

And, if I was reading it right, he didn't know who was behind me. It was the only thing that made any sense.

He watched me write down a phone number, dial it, and hit the loudspeaker button.

Toner answered. 'Yeah?'

'Did you arrange that, Paddy?'

'Two men are outside now. They go in on your say-so.'

'I'll get back to you.'

I hung up.

I'd arranged this for Coyle's benefit. He eyed the door, then shrugged as if he didn't give a fuck who was outside. He was in the blackmailer's chair. He hadn't a thing to worry about. He was a little edgy with it nevertheless. Phone calls affect some people that way.

'Smoke?'

'I don't.'

I lit a Players. I was back on the non-tippeds.

'So you got lucky and now you're making the best of it,' I said. 'Well, if I were you I'd do the same.'

'I'm glad you're seeing it that way.'

'What did you think I was gonna do – start screaming abuse? It's my own fault. If I hadn't let that wife of mine catch me playing away from home, you'd never have caught on to me. Drink?'

He shook his tree. I had a flask of Jameson. Just took the one sip. Don't like drinking too much when I'm at work.

I spun him a story I'd concocted for the occasion—

'My problem is this, Coyle. It's not the fifty. It's that guy I just phoned. He knows about you. He's wondering why you'd even go to the law about me, when that pathologist and shrink who can identify me would be being identified by the time they got to them and you'd be sitting in their favourite chair explaining why you didn't come forward day one and save the lives of three innocent people, instead of blackmailing me with it. He reckons you're looking at this based on what you have on me and ignoring what we have on you.'

He spoke in italics. '*What you have on me?*'

The key Coyle'd let himself in with, plus the one to The

Cedars, on the same keyring, lay on the desk. With a pencil I edged them into an envelope and put it into my inside pocket.

'My very words. "What have we got on Coyle, Paddy?" I said.

' "Well, we can tie Coyle in with killing that security guard and helping himself to five million from the safe at The Cedars tonight, Gerd," he said. "How, Paddy?" I said. "The cops'll blame Byrne for it," he said. "They'll be looking for Byrne by tomorrow night, find the guard's blood on the driver's seat of Byrne's car, along with the keys with only Coyle's prints on them, make a few inquiries, find out Byrne's mobile was used to ring Coyle five times around the time of the shooting, think Byrne, not you, Gerd, rang him on it, and wonder what it all means, what was Coyle doing with keys to The Cedars the night of the robbery, stuff like that. Byrne will have disappeared by then. Coyle'll be all they have to go on." "But Coyle'll put them straight, Paddy," I said. "How, Gerd?" he said. "He'll have disappeared too".'

Coyle's glasses were taking on a whiter background. *Where t'fuck did this come from* was coming under review.

' "But if Coyle disappears, his stuff goes to the law, Paddy," I said. "He'd have made provisions. He's not stupid." "Gerd," he said, "what Coyle has on you only stands up if he's around to corroborate it".' Make that a sickly background. ' "With Coyle as their tainted star witness against you in destinations unknown, unhelpful or unwilling or unsomething to come forward and clear up the question of the guard – why, if he's nothing to hide? – and take the stand and tell who killed the Hassetts – which even Coyle doesn't know – even his own report on you,

Gerd, will prove you didn't kill them since he himself was following you and only saw you setting it up, all they'll have is unsubstantiated allegations. Better to pay a lawyer to prove it's Coyle's word against yours, which is what it'd come down to, than have him hanging over us. It's the best I can come up with at such short notice, Gerd".'

Yeah, 'sickly' definitely describes it.

'So, I said to him, "Paddy," I said, "I don't think Coyle knows who he's dealing with here." "I'm amazed he's coming up against me too, Gerd," he said. "Y'know, Paddy," I said, "my guess is he took that long-range listening device he pointed at those two specialists into that hide after me and from way back in the tunnel couldn't tell who was in the tack room with me, only hear muffled voices through the wall crackling from his earpiece and, hearing me call you by your first name only, made the mistake of thinking you're just another guy called Paddy. The country's full of them. He obviously thinks all he has to do is put the squeeze on me and I'll pay up to get him off my back, because what's fifty compared to the ten mil I'm in on? He just thinks you're my partner in all this, that you'll be as scared of him as he thinks I'll be and give him what he wants." "I think you're right, Gerd," he said. "Why don't you ask him?" "That's what I'll do, Paddy," I said. 'I'll ask him if he knows it's you he's really dealing with here".'

I opened the phone book at names beginning with T, handed Coyle the piece of paper I'd written Toner's number on, said 'Put a name to that and see who's worrying you,' and watched as he looked down the column of numbers and stop at a match and trail it across the page and light on Toner, P, The Hacienda and his own stupidity dawn and pull a face that only people in trouble pull, when they realize that turning people in includes people you don't wanna turn in because their own private victims' support group see to it you never live to testify.

—Incidentally, this story I'd concocted: Toner didn't know a word about it. The only part of it that was true was the bit about setting up Coyle; so's the law'd have something important to go after him for instead of me. Like Toner never said: It was the best I could come up with at such short notice.

Now Coyle's face was in his hands and a distracted 'Toner? Toner's behind this?' was coming through his fingers. He now knew that all schemes were possible except the one he'd walked in with.

He had a decision to make. He wanted that drink after all. He swigged, tried to get a hold of himself, then swigged again. My guess was he was wishing I'd brought a bigger flask. Oh, and that 'Fuck you' attitude he'd come in with? He'd disowned that; no doubt cared to leave the stage, bow out while his bow was still in working order.

'Look,' he said, in his new non-aggression-pact mode. 'Call Toner. Tell him he can call off those two men outside.'

'They're outside your place.'

'Oh Jesus!'

'Deep down you must've known we'd go for your weaknesses. You squeal, your family join in.'

'But I'll never say a word.'

'Toner doesn't know that yet.'

'What do I have to do to convince him?'

'Be convincing.'

'Look, I'll give you everything I have on you. We'll go to my office. Most of it's on file. The rest is in my e-mail. I e-mailed it to myself.'

'Codeword?'

'Annie.'

'Your daughter's name?'

He nodded, hoping he'd see her again, probably remembering another 'weakness' called Annie.

'What about other people you've been following? Anything he could use? He'd take it as a sign of good faith.'

'I'll do whatever it takes.'

'Come on.'

'Where are we going?'

'To put your case. I'll do what I can for you.'

He thanked me all roads and directions.

'He'll want to weigh you up face to face. He won't come here though. I know a place.'

I knew a good one. We took my car. He was shaking too much to drive.

'Remember this warehouse?' I asked, when we arrived. 'You must have followed me here.'

'You-u pu-oot some thing in the sep-tic ta-nk out in the fi-ield there,' came out like most everything else he uttered from then on – in pieces. Like him.

'My kids' dog.'

'Why in there though?'

'To get the bacteria working. This place is being let soon. Inside.'

'What's the rope for?'

'Hands behind your back. You wait in here and I'll bring Toner.'

'You don't have to tie me.'

'If Toner thinks you're at liberty after that conversation we've just had, he'll question my judgement. He's liable to kill us both.'

'Not too tight.'

'Sorry.'

'You don't have to tie my feet as well.'

'Don't act naive. There. Now, let me see . . .'

'Hey. What're you doing?'

'I'm carrying you out into the field.'

'But why?'

'A precaution.'

'But—'

'It's for the best.'

'*For the best!* Hey! What the fuck—'

'Stop wriggling.'

'Look—'

'We're almost there.'

'Quinn, I—'

'Trust me. There now. Put you down here for a minute.
Won't keep you. Just taking the lid off this tank.'

'Jesus Christ! Why?'

'Take it easy. Lie there and be quiet. I'm only measuring
it.'

'For what?'

'Look. It's full of piss, right? A concrete tank full of black
piss. I can't see into it. Y'see this rod? This'll tell me how
deep it is. I measured it before. But I can't remember if it's
big enough.'

'For what?'

'You'll see in a minute. I have to hook this rod into
something and pull it out.'

'Jesus! Who's that?'

'Con Ivers. Come on, Con. Jesus, you're a heavy bastard,
Up you come. Christ, what a stink! I'll have to have a shower
and change my clothes. Before I clean out your office,

y'know? Wouldn't want it smelling of this stuff. There now, Con, just put you down here beside our friend. You know Con?'

'AARRGHH! Move him away.'

'All right, all right.'

'You're not putting me in there. Please tell me you're not putting me in there. I swear to God I'll never say a word.'

'Calm down. Calm down. Come on now, calm down. Are you calm?'

'Yes.'

'Good. Now let me explain the way this works. Maguire, you know Maguire, don't you? Kevin Maguire?'

'I know of him.'

'Well, he put Con here in there. See those bullets in his head? Maguire did that. Now, tomorrow night, he'll be coming here with Jimmy Byrne. To put him in, y'know?'

'AARRGHH!'

'Look, I can't talk to you if you keep screaming at me. Now be quiet.'

'All right! I'll be quiet, I'll be quiet.'

'Good. I'm just making sure there's room for Byrne. That's all I'm doing. Maguire'll have a fit if he can't get him in. You with me?'

'Yes! I'm with you.'

'Good. Now, let me explain further. Maguire doesn't know about you. When he comes to open this, if he sees your leg sticking up, he'll wonder what the fuck's going on. He'll wonder who you are. He'll think everybody's moving in, like it's some sort of squat.'

'AAARRGHHH!'

'But if you go in first, then Con here goes in on top of you,

266

he won't see you. That way he won't ask any questions. Now get up.'

'No no please you can't put me in there please I won't say a word I won't please.'

'Stop getting all flustered. There, we're nearly there. Just drag you over a bit more. That's it. In you go.'

'Wait wait please wait.'

'What now?'

'Please.'

'Please what?'

'I want to say a prayer.'

'You want to say a prayer. Are you fucking serious? An hour ago you were trying to destroy me and now you want to say a prayer?'

'I want to say a prayer please let me say a prayer I have to say a prayer.'

'What kind of prayer?'

'An Act of Contrition.'

'An Act of Contrition? Oh all right. Fair enough.'

'Help me kneel.'

'OK. There. Pray.'

'I confess to Almighty God . . .'

'Feel better now?'

'Let me bless myself.'

'What?'

'Please.'

'I'll do it. I'll make the sign of the Cross on your forehead with my thumb. Will that do?'

'Yes.'

'There. How's that?'

'Thank you.'

'You're welcome.'

'Tell my wife I love her.'

'What?'

'Please tell me you'll tell my wife I love her.'

'*Me?* You're asking me to tell—'

'And my daughter. Please tell me you'll find a way to tell my wife I love her.'

'All right. Is she nice-looking? Shit. Too late. All the best. Well, at least you won't be sending Sinead any more bills. Now, Con, in you go on top of him. Atta boy.'

Chapter Thirty Two

———◦◦◦◦———

See that fucker Maguire! He nearly ruined everything. We were getting round to the real reason for having used Byrne's mobile (no point telling you about it now, you'll see why later, but it had fuck all to do with why I'd used it to get something on Coyle – I hadn't even known about Coyle when I dreamt it up), and the bastard started acting the cunt.

He picks Byrne up from the airport the following morning, swaps phones, so Byrne now has his own mobile back on him, then drives him back to his flat.

Then he starts enjoying himself.

Byrne's all questions. He's believing he's now single again and the new owner of Hassett Property, and he wants to know everything.

Obvious ones, like 'You're sure she's dead?'

'I gave her enough pills to kill two of her.'

Then: 'Where is she now?'

'Where I left her, for all I know. She might be lying there for days before anybody notices. You go back to your flat and wait till the law comes with the bad news. Tell them you were out of the country when it happened and collect your inheritance.'

Maguire should've left it at that. But no, he's only getting started. Byrne wants details. Byrne wants to revel in details.

And Maguire's only too happy to concoct a few. 'I held her mouth open and fed her the bottle one at a time,' he says.

'Did she know?'

'Nah – I told her they were Smarties! What the fuck are you talkin' about? How could she not know?'

'Did she know I was behind it, I mean?'

'Not at first.'

'What did she say?'

' "Mr Maguire, why you doing this to me?" Crap like that. I looked at her like she was some kind of moron. "What kind of daft cow are you?" I said to her. "Haven't you twigged yet your husband's behind this? He put me up to it." Should've seen her face. I think she was hoping for a reunion.'

'Fuck that!'

' "I'm the one who fucked your old girl down the stairs", I said. "Then drowned your da and that sexy sister of yours." That went down worse than the pills. You shoulda heard her.'

'Was she crying?'

'No law says you can't cry when you're committin' suicide, Jimmy.'

'Pity we couldn't figure out a way to leave a note.'

'I'll drop you here.'

'Why?'

'The law might already be at your place. No point in lettin' them see me. The walk'll do you good.'

Maguire drove off, then doubled back to keep an eye on Byrne. Now if it had ended there, it would've been all right. But it didn't.

Carol Byrne began to come round in hospital. No problem; we knew she would.

And the law goes to Byrne's flat. No problem there, either. But I had expected a Detective-Sergeant Paul Rice to visit him. Rice was the cop who was with Molly that day at the hospital. He had once caught a guy based on mobile phone records. And it was his knowledge of how they could be traced that I was counting on. I'd expected Rice to ask Byrne a few questions, not suspecting Byrne for the robbery at this time, you understand – that would come later – and during their conversation, Maguire would ring Byrne's mobile, this would register with Rice – it may not sound like much, but it was crucial to the way I'd planned things. Then Rice would leave, having told Byrne his wife had survived, and Byrne would contact Maguire with this disappointing news, and Maguire would take him to see Con Ivers. And that would be it.

But Rice sent two uniforms.

And he couldn't have sent a worse pair. They were a couple of agony aunts. Full of sympathy.

'Your wife tried to take her life, Mr Byrne,' they told him.

And insisted on accompanying Byrne to the hospital; they would get him there quicker, they explained. And they weren't taking no for an answer.

'The signs are good, Mr Byrne. They say she'll recover. She might even be conscious as we speak' they're consoling him with.

And Byrne's going '*Marvellous*,' piping in with his 'I was in England last night' alibi. 'I'd no idea she was this down.' Knowing Byrne, he felt like telling her off for ruining his celebration. What exactly was on his mind at that particular point, I couldn't say. His bowels probably.

But the scenario I had envisaged with Rice was no longer in play. From here on in it could have gone drastically wrong. Maguire was no longer in control. He was relying on luck. Byrne was never supposed to go near that hospital, especially not with that pile of shit Maguire had told him in the car. Byrne's face alone could've given him away. He wasn't looking distraught because of his poor wife, he was looking *terrified* because of her.

The uniforms even accompanied him along the long corridor to where a Garda constable was standing, and opened the door for him.

Byrne went in alone. It was a ground-floor room. He went in hunched over, like he'd come cap in hand to beg forgiveness for trying to have her done away with.

Carol was sleeping on her back.

No doubt he considered using that: *She's asleep, officer, I'll come back later. The drip? What would pulling her off that do? The pillow? Smother the cow.* Anything, just to get the fuck out of there.

Or any minute now she'd sit up screaming and the law'd run in and wrestle him to the ground under a tirade of accusations.

Then she did see him.

And 'Carol. Carol, there's something . . . Carol, I want to explain. I had nothing to do with this,' croaks out of him.

And she sobs 'Oh, Jimmy, I'm so sorry.'

And he stops dead.

'I know you didn't,' she assures him.

'Wha'?'

'It wasn't your fault.'

'Wha'?'

'There's no reason to say anything. You're not to blame. I couldn't stand it if you blamed yourself.'

Then Paul Rice knocks and politely asks Byrne for a word.

And Byrne's standing there with his mouth open wondering what the fuck's going on. Why isn't she accusing him?

And comes out not knowing what to think and follows Rice along the corridor to the window overlooking the car park, Rice going 'I'm sorry about your wife,' and Byrne trying to appear as if he is too.

When I heard about this, I nearly had a fit. How Byrne came through it, under that type of pressure, God knows.

Anyway, Rice gets down to it. 'She left a note. So her suicide attempt was genuine.'

'A note?'

'To you. Asking you to forgive her. Presumably you're living apart, her losing the baby . . . all adds up.'

'I'd no idea she was feeling so down.'

'No one ever does, sir. Pity. How much do you know about last night?'

'The Guards who brought me here told me what happened.'

Byrne was now breathing a lot easier. My guess was he was asking himself: had Carol, for some mad reason, refused to believe Maguire when he'd told her that her husband was in on it? Had she regained consciousness after Maguire had tried to kill her and wrote a note exonerating him, then called her own ambulance? Whatever he was thinking, if she was behind him – and she appeared to be – he was safe. Rice was being sympathetic – great sign – talking away, Byrne no doubt reminding himself that the inheritance possibility was back in play, until he heard Rice say 'new owners'.

'New owners? What new owners?'

'Your wife sold Hassett Property yesterday.'

'Carol sold Hassett Property?'

'Yes. And the transaction was in cash.'

Then Byrne's mobile rang. 'You're there, y'are?' said the person he wanted to talk to most. But he couldn't talk to him now. Not with Rice there. Maguire, outside with field glasses, did this to draw Rice's attention to the mobile. This was what I had envisaged happening, but in Byrne's flat, not here.

'I'll have to get back to you,' Byrne says, then hangs up.

'You have that phone with you in England, Mr Byrne?' Rice says.

God bless him. He asked exactly what I'd wanted him to ask.

'Yeah, why?'

'Just routine. I'm sure it will check out.'

'What will?'

'Ruling out suspects, that's all.'

'Suspects? For what?'

'I'm talking about the security guard.'

'What security guard?'

'I thought you said you knew about last night. A security guard was killed at The Cedars.'

'What?'

'He had instructions not to let anyone in. Only people your wife would have told him were OK. Anyway, whoever he let in shot him, then, presumably, went upstairs to do the same to your wife, saw her unconscious, and emptied the safe. That's another thing.'

'What?'

'The safe wasn't broken into.'

'It wasn't?'

'No. The killer knew the combination. Who else knows the combination?'

'Don't know,' said Byrne.

He could hardly say Maguire did.

'Ironic, really, when you come to think about it,' said Rice.

'What?'

'The guard was due to call in every two hours. When he didn't, the alarm was raised. That's what saved her. Only for that, she might not be alive today. Even though she doesn't want to be. Crazy, isn't it?'

'Definitely.'

'The killer went to kill her and ended up saving her life.'

'Mad.'

'You're not planning on going anywhere over the next few days, are you?'

'No.'

'Good. I'll want to talk to you again. I'll let you get back to your wife. Then I want a word with her.'

Byrne went in, sat on the edge of the bed, and took her hand in his. 'How are you feeling?'

'I keep thinking about that poor security guard.'

'I know. It's terrible. And the money.'

'I don't care about that. I never wanted anything from that company. I hate it. I was glad when Mr Maguire said he was talking to you about it and suggested I talk it over with you. I must have rung your mobile a hundred times.'

'Who bought it?'

'A man called Toner.'

He knew the answer to this one already, but just had to ask. 'How much?'

'The asking price. Five million.'

Now, as I say, we were running on luck here. Who knows how it might've turned out. Byrne might've fallen apart and given the game away.

Maguire, who'd been outside getting the gist of this with the binoculars and a Long Ranger – although I read a word-for-word account of it later on from a different source – couldn't resist putting Byrne through a touch more of the same, just to see the look on his face when he came out of that hospital.

He headed for the taxi rank, when Maguire pulled up and got out. 'It went well, Byrne, it did?'

'Fuck you!'

'What the fuck kinda talk's that? After all I've done for you!'

'I don't believe this.'

'It was hard identifying the body, it was?'

'What fucking body? She's not dead!'

'Get in the car, Jimmy. This is a bad place to talk.'

'I'm not going anywhere with you.'

Maguire pushed him behind the wheel. 'Get in the car till I find out what you're talking about. Drive.'

They headed out towards the warehouse.

'What d'you mean, she's not dead?'

'They pumped her out.'

'They pumped her out? Fuck me! We're in for it. She told them everything, she did?'

'Would I be here if she did? She never mentioned anything you said.'

'She must've got a dose of amnesia. A shock can do that. I remember reading it somewhere. Or maybe she's covering up for you.'

'Are you bonkers! Covering up for me? After what you did to her?'

'This is Toner's doing.'

'I never mentioned Toner.'

'Didn't you? I thought you did.'

'She said you arranged for Toner to buy Hassett Property.'

'She must have me mixed up with an estate agent.'

'Fuck you, Maguire.'

'Wait a minute. Something's wrong here. I told her to talk to you about it, yeah, no problem on that score, but that's all. Did she say she actually saw me yesterday?'

'I didn't ask.'

'Then Toner's pulled a stroke. He believed you were going to sell it to that supermarket outfit and cut him out. That's what this is all about. The bastard! He got to it first.'

'Are you saying you weren't in on it?'

'Here's the gun, Jimmy.'

'What?'

'If I did the dirt, would I be giving you this?'

'What the fuck's going on, Kev?'

'Fuck knows. But I'm gonna find out what this is all about, if it's the last thing I ever do on this earth.'

'It's about the fucking money. The five mil. It was stolen. Toner stole it.'

'What? So that's his game. He bought the company, then stole the money back. The fucker. Go right here.'

'Where are we going?'

'To see Toner.'

'No way. I'm not going anywhere near him. That's what he wants. I'll become a missing person.'

'He won't touch you with a gun in your hand, Jimmy.'

'Wait a minute. What are you getting all concerned about? I'm the one who lost the money. How come you're on my side all of a sudden?'

'Ooops! Can't answer that one, Jimmy. You've caught me out. I've run out of answers.'

'What?'

'I was bullshitting you, Jimmy. Winding you up. Couldn't resist it. Give me that gun, you daft bastard. Cut that out. Give it to me or I'll beat the skull of you with it.'

'Fuck!'

'No need to get upset. Pull in at that warehouse.'

'What're we doing here?'

'Get out of the car.'

'Why?'

'Get out of the fuckin' car! Con Ivers wants a word. Face to face.'

'Ivers? Shit! What does he want? Is he here?'

'Maybe he wants you to move in with him. Move.'

'Where?'

'Over there.'

'Where are we going? Where's Ivers?'

'I'm taking you to see him.'

'But it's a field, for fuck's sake.'

'It's where he sees people these days.'

'But—'

'Not much further. There. Move that grass away.'

'Why?'

'Do it. Do it, Jimmy. Do it. That's it. Now pull up those timbers.'

'Jesus! What a stink! What *is* that?'

'A septic tank. See that pole? Lower it in. Hook first, till you feel it hook onto something.'

'No fucking way! What the fuck's going on here?'

'Do it, Jimmy. Do it. That's it. You've found something, y'have?'

'It's caught on something.'

'Pull it up.'

'Oh God. It's Ivers. It's Con Ivers.'

'Con, you're keeping well, y'are?'

'Jesus Christ!'

'Con wants to know where his money is so he can rent a better gaff. Tell him, Con. Tell him you want to rent a better gaff and you want Jimmy here to rent this one. Cheap, of course.'

'No, no, oh my God, you're not putting me in there.'

'Get in, Jimmy.'

'AAARRGGHH.'

'Get in, Jimmy. Jimmy, get in. Don't make me shoot you, Jimmy.'

'You're fucking mental!'

'Get in, you bastard.'

'No. No, please! Kev.'

'Don't make me shoot you, Jimmy!'

'AAARRGH!'

'There. See what you made me do. You made me shoot you.'

'AARRGH!'

'Why are you being so unreasonable? Why didn't you just move in with Con?'

'AARRGH!'

'You must be fond of bullets, Jimmy. Here's another. Shit – all gone. C'mere, y'bastard, get in there. C'mon now, I haven't got all day. Stop wriggling or you'll waken Con. Sorry about this, Con. Thanks for lending me that money, by the way.'

'AARRGH!'

'That's it. Down you go, Jimmy. That's it. You'll enjoy your stay, y'will?'

Chapter Thirty Three

Well, that's about it. That's how we took Hassett Property.

All that was left was the police and Molly Murray.

Paul Rice knew that Toner was in on it, of course. No problem. That was to be expected. He also knew he'd be wasting his time asking him about it. Still, he had his little routines to go through.

'A likely story' was written all over his face before Toner had even begun to answer his questions.

Dopey questions like, 'Do you often buy businesses in large amounts of cash on a Saturday afternoon, Mr Toner?' When a cop starts asking you crap like that, you know he's got sweet fuck all.

'I wanted to pay by cheque. I sent a cheque to Tom Hassett before he died. His solicitor sent it back. Mr Byrne then contacted me. Asked me did I still wanna buy it. I said only if I can put my associate in to see if it was still worth the money, now that Hassett wasn't running it.'

'Your associate?'

'Mr Maguire here.'

'I see. So now you're a property expert, Maguire.'

'*Pardon em whaaaa?*'

Maguire loved helping police with their inquiries.

'Like I was saying, Rice, Mr Byrne then rang me last Saturday morning, said he could put the deal together for that afternoon, said he was leaving the country. Would I pay cash? Ask him yourself. He'll verify every word.'

He'd already spoken to Carol Byrne. She told him that a man called Ivers had repeatedly threatened her husband. Said he owed him money. No doubt Rice wondered if Ivers had found out about the robbery and gone after Byrne to get his money back.

No doubt he wondered whether Byrne had even robbed the safe. The security guard's blood in his car indicated he'd shot him. But then Byrne couldn't have shot anybody. He'd been in England. Hadn't he?

Then Rice spoke to Eircell. They told him what he already knew: mobile phones emit a periodic signal, for billing purposes. That the signal tells them where every phone is, within a thirty-mile radius. That Byrne's mobile never left Ireland. Proof Byrne didn't go to England. He'd been in Dublin all along, the lying bastard.

Then he checked Byrne's mobile phone records. They said he repeatedly rang Tony Coyle's number around the time of the robbery. Rice then checked the unknown prints on the keys found in Byrne's car and matched them to prints in Coyle's own car.

Routine stuff.

Then carried on investigating.

He needed to bring Coyle, Ivers and Byrne in for questioning. Get to the bottom of it. Wrap up the case. Once they showed up.

Rice was scratching his head. His investigation was ongoing. Nowhere.

Exactly what I had planned for: the 'blame' factor pointed to those who, on the face of it, had scarpered. Why would they do that if they were innocent?

Confusion.

Which brings me back to Molly.

Confusion's all well and good. But I never leave it at that. Most villains would celebrate at this point. To them the job would be over.

Not me.

In life I fear tenacity above all other things. If a person has it in her mind to come after you regardless of all consequences, you know it's time to take stock. But there's an art in taking stock. Anticipate. Take it long before you need to. Wait until you need to and the chances are it's too late. Identify your own weak spots. Have it in your mind that your opponent will also identify them and come after you. Say to yourself: 'If I were an investigator, what would I do next?' Because you already know how you could get caught, you are in a prime position to prevent it. But only if you already have your diversions in place. And never, ever shirk. Do whatever it takes. Don't find yourself in a cell kicking yourself for having been complacent.

Before the sale of Hassett Property, I told Toner to bug our weak spots: Christy McDermott's home and garage; the homes of Mrs Gallagher; Louise; Coyle's widow I myself bugged. Every word they said was recorded onto equipment in that warehouse. The monitor had been moved there. Maguire had his radio scanner on the law, and his eye on Molly Murray wherever she went. Miss Tenacity herself. Even her car was bugged, as was the word processor in her office.

In her professional life Molly faced the lowlife of Dublin: the AIDS junkies who threaten with needles; the pimps who run twelve-year-old girls; the pimps who run the girls who wear bobby socks so they look like twelve-year-old girls to kerb crawlers; the gay pederasts, the gunmen, the whatever-you-can-think-ofs. All for the story. The story meant everything. Even Toner, who hated her, respected her grit.

For years she had tried to get something on him. She'd been described more than once as being on a crusade against him. She'd do anything to jail him.

Naturally, she, like the law, knew in her bones that he was behind this. But what she knew in her bones wasn't proof.

The first of our weak spots she tries is Carol Byrne. But Carol isn't talking. So Molly tries again. She rings the hospital and finds out when Carol is coming home.

Christy McDermott brings Carol Byrne home. He's the only family she's got now. He knows she's broke. She owns The Cedars, but that's it. McDermott offers her half his garage. He feels it's the decent thing to do, given that Tom Hassett had given it to him. He'll run it, she'll also get half the profits to live on. She won't hear of it.

Then the doorbell rings. It's Molly. She wants to talk to Carol.

McDermott tells Molly to wait in the hall.

So Molly's standing there in the hall and, being the nosy reporter she is, has a look around. She sees a letter on the telephone bureau. It's addressed to Carol Byrne, marked 'Private and Confidential'. The cow couldn't resist nicking it. If Carol wasn't gonna help herself by talking to the press, the press had no alternative but to use every dirty trick at their disposal.

McDermott comes back.

'I see you've had the hall redecorated. The last time I was in here it was different.'

'Carol had a little accident. Flooded the place.'

'New kitchen, too.'

'She set the cooker on fire.'

'And the garden? The last time I saw it it was beautiful.'

'Carol accidentally sprayed it with weedkiller.'

'I see. Is she usually so accident prone?'

'She's been under a lot of pressure lately.'

'Of course.'

'She's still too upset to talk. Sorry.'

'OK. Thanks anyway.'

That's how it went.

So me and Toner met in the tack room.

This is the point I hate. Where all your planning has worked, then *bang*! Big problems.

You can see why I take stock. There's always some fucker who hasn't held his end up. Still, thank fuck I had my diversions in place.

'The letter Molly stole was from Carol's shrink,' Toner explained. 'He returned the letter Maguire made Tom Hassett sign. Plus the photos of Hassett with Louise and her little girl. That fucker Byrne was supposed to have destroyed them. Sorry, Gerd. Carol must have dropped them in her shrink's office. Who could've foreseen that?'

'How do you know it's the same letter?'

'Molly went to see Louise.'

'What did they say?'

He had a recording of it:

Molly: 'Would you mind answering a few questions about Tom Hassett?'

285

Louise: 'I only met the man once.'

'But you're living in his house.'

'Jimmy Byrne rented it to me.'

'So *Byrne* rented it. Not Tom Hassett. OK. I have some photographs. This one, for instance, of you with Tom Hassett?'

'Who took these?'

'You didn't know they were being taken?'

'Jimmy Byrne introduced us that day. That's all I know.'

Byrne again!

Molly: 'And this one, of you outside a bank with Jimmy Byrne. He's giving you money.'

Louise: 'I remember that day. But he wasn't giving me money. I was giving him money. Rent money.'

'And you weren't receiving a monthly direct debit of £800?'

'Hah! I wish I was.' End of conversation.

'I'll take it from here on in, Paddy.'

'What are you gonna do?'

'Follow her. Tell Maguire to stay away from that warehouse. I'll be using the equipment that's in it.'

Molly knew my car. I rented another and tailed her to Christy McDermott's garage. The Long Ranger picked up most of what they were saying, the full text came from the equipment in the warehouse. They talked in his office.

'What sort of man was Tom Hassett?' she asked him.

'The best.'

'You liked him?'

'Tom was a gem.'

'A ladies' man?'

'Three – his wife and daughters.'

'No others?'

'Carol told me about the letter, if that's what you're referring to.'

'It also says Mrs Gallagher was blackmailing him before his death.'

'You know Mrs Gallagher?'

'Do you?'

'Ms Murray . . .'

'Molly.'

'Molly. I'll put you a question. Is your father alive?'

'He died six years ago.'

'If I was to say he'd been guilty of something you know him to be innocent of, how would you convince me otherwise without hard evidence?'

'I knew him.'

'I knew Tom.'

'Fair enough. But I asked you about Mrs Gallagher.'

'One cancels out the other. Tom wasn't playing around. Therefore Mrs Gallagher had nothing to blackmail him with. Therefore she didn't. Talk to her. She's OK. I can't prove that, of course. But if you can't see it in her, that'll tell you more about yourself than it will her.'

'You're bitter.'

'I am now.'

'Your wife.'

'Yeah, my wife. I loved her. I *love* her. I respected and admired *both* her parents. But I've also been talking to Carol. She's been telling me what's been going on. She's in bits. Tom worked and provided for his family his whole life. Now it's all gone. Bitter isn't the word.'

'The day after the accidents, you told me you'd received a breakdown call.'

'Why are you asking me about the accidents?'

'I'll come to that. You said you got a breakdown call.'

'I did. But my truck broke down.' (Maguire's handiwork.)

'Who called you out?'

'Never got to him to find out.'

'What direction were you called out in?'

'Towards Ballinraa. Why?'

'If you'd been called out in the opposite direction, you'd have broken down on the same road as Tom Hassett was coming in on. You'd have seen him.'

'But I wasn't.'

Convenient!

'What time did you get back home that night? Or that morning, I should say?'

'Dawn. I walked back as far as the far side of the lake. I sometimes keep my boat there. It has an outboard. I crossed over, the bow hit . . . well, you know what it hit.'

'You didn't see it go in, from where you were, no head-lights approaching?'

'I told you that at the time. Everything happened while I was out.'

Convenient.

'Then what happened?'

'I've been through all this with you before.'

'Go through it again.'

'Why? Why is it important now?'

'I'll come to that.'

'Look, my boat hit Tom's car. The roof was just inches below the surface. The driver's door was open. Then I saw . . . I couldn't tell it was Annie, at first . . . I suppose I thought it was the driver, trapped trying to get out. Then I saw her hair, flowing up toward the surface. Annie had lovely long red hair. I waded in and I . . . I found Annie.'

'I'm sorry to make you go over it again, but during the course of the next few days, did you notice anything unusual? Anything, however unimportant it might have seemed at the time.'

'Nothing.'

'You're sure?'

'Nothing. Well . . .'

'What?'

'Well, Annie loved her garden. She kept it nice.'

'It's still nice. I saw it on the way over. So?'

'I keep it nice now. I try to, anyway. For her. I know she's gone. But—'

'I understand. Go on.'

'Well, she always watered it from a rain barrel. After the funeral, I noticed the hose had been left out. Annie rarely used it. In any case she'd been at her mother's the day before she died, helping her pack. She hadn't used it to water the garden, is what I'm saying. Even if she had, she'd have reeled it in. She hated things lying around. So who left it out? That's it. I told you it wasn't important.'

'It was important enough for you to notice.'

'Now will you tell me why you're asking me these questions?'

'Because, at the time of the accidents, I, and the police, saw accidents. No motive. Last Saturday that all changed.'

'What are you saying?'

'I'm saying that you're right, Christy. Sometimes knowing a person is reason enough. You *knew* Tom Hassett. Well, I *know* the man who bought his company. That changes everything.'

* * *

McDermott had suggested that Molly should visit Mrs Gallagher. She'd have visited her anyway. I would have. It was the next logical step. It was a warm summer evening. The chances were they might talk in the garden. Which meant the bug that Toner had had a pro plant in one of Gallagher's ornaments in the living room would not pick up their conversation.

I drove to Gallagher's street, parked the car outside her semi, the Long Ranger connected to a battery-powered recorder concealed in a fine-meshed rabbit hutch on the back seat, pointed at the garden furniture, then watched from the bar on the corner.

Molly arrived an hour or so later. They talked across a wooden table in the shade of a large multicoloured parasol.

'Mrs Gallagher, what kind of man was Tom Hassett?'

'Tom was a prince. I was dying about him.'

'Did you work for him long?'

'Fifteen years.'

'Mrs Gallagher, I'm going to say something to you. But before I say it, I want you to know that I believe it to be false.'

Gallagher knew immediately what was coming. Out came the hanky.

'I don't mean to upset you, Mrs Gallagher.'

'I know you didn't, dear. It's just that, well, I tried to hide it, you know, I was so ashamed. But then my husband, well, he knew something was up. And the kids, of course. Thank God the grandchildren didn't suspect. They thought I was just feeling under the weather. I don't think I'd have been able to cope if they'd found out.'

'It must have been terrible for you.'

'It was. I've always paid my way, you know. Tried to do what was right, set a good example.'

'Am I right in saying that during all the years you worked for Mr Hassett, money never went missing?'

'Never, oh never. Never as much as a penny piece. It was only when Mr Byrne came to work there.'

'I suspected as much.'

'Then when Mr Maguire started, the same thing happened again. I felt very bad about it.'

'So money went missing only while Mr Byrne and Mr Maguire were running things.'

'That's correct.'

'Did you notice anything unusual about the way Mr Byrne or Mr Maguire ran the office?'

'They were hardly ever there. And when they were there, they didn't do any work that I could see. They never dictated letters, never looked into the general running of the business. They were both a bit on the formal side, I remember. Strict about staff entering without knocking. And even when you did knock, they kept you waiting.'

'And when you eventually did go in, they weren't doing anything unusual?'

'Not that I could see. Reading the racing paper, mostly.'

'Did Gallagher mention the monitor, Gerd?' Toner asked me later.

'No, she didn't.'

'Then all Molly has is that letter she stole, of Hassett saying Gallagher was blackmailing him. No pressure there.'

'I wish that were the case, Paddy. Molly asked Gallagher to identify Hassett's signature on it?'

'So? He signed it, didn't he? What's there to get excited about?'

'He's signed it Tom "Timothy" Hassett.'

'So?'

'Gallagher told Molly that in fifteen years she'd never once seen him sign his middle name. He didn't like it. Never used it. I heard Hassett say as much myself the night I was watching them having dinner. Fuck! This is bad, Paddy. This is bad!'

'I still don't get it, Gerd.'

'Molly was trying to prove the letter's a forgery. But she's done even better. And she'll read into it what I'd read into it. If only I'd looked at it. But I didn't. That was my mistake. I would've zoomed in on the name Timothy and saw it for what it was. It would have been destroyed before Carol got a look at it. If she hadn't been demented at the time, she'd have seen it herself.'

'Seen what?'

'Signing "Timothy" was Hassett's way of letting people know something was up. The letter was dated the day before Hassett died. Obviously he hadn't bought that yarn Maguire had alluded to that night, about Mrs Gallagher being behind it. It was never a strong runner. But Hassett buying it one hundred percent hadn't been that important then. Anyway, whatever the reason, Hassett must have sensed something. Deep down he must have sensed it wasn't a robbery, or a ransom, but that Maguire was going to kill him. And that hadn't been that important then, either. But that letter's out in the open now. That changes the whole fucking equation. Molly has her character picture. She now knows Hassett was a decent man, that the letter is a pack of lies, that he wouldn't have put his name to it. Signing "Timothy" was his way of saying he'd been forced to sign it.'

* * *

Course, you know me. I'm a stickler for my own personal security. I'm a behind-the-scenes man. I'm just another face in the crowd. Nobody's mentioning my name. I'm all right.

But Molly's only getting warmed up. She goes to see Rice in his office.

Now these two are friends. They'd traded information over the years. It was Rice who arrested the guys who'd robbed those safes named in that invoice book Toner told me about. Sean Connors had sold that information to Molly, you'll recall. She had passed it on to Rice. So they knew one another well. Worked well together. And, like Molly, Rice longed for the day when he could shove a warrant under Toner's nose and lead him off to the calaboose.

So she asks Rice if Byrne has any previous.

'Until now Byrne was a grain of salt. Small-time. We suspected him of working the tracks for Toner, but nothing ever led to his arrest.'

'But you have his prints. Or, at least, what you think are his prints.'

'They weren't in that safe, Molly, if that's what you mean. We found four sets in it: Carol Byrne's, her solicitor's, her father's and her mother's. We needed to eliminate the obvious. So we asked Carol Byrne was there anything with her parents' prints on it. She told us her father was an avid collector of crystal. She'd kept it just as he'd left it. His prints were on it. They matched those we found in the safe. We eliminated Mrs Hassett's the same way. Then Carol's. Then her solicitor's. Byrne must've used gloves.'

'To rob his own safe? Why would he do that?'

'This case is one big maze, Molly. Anyway, why the sudden interest in Byrne's prints?'

Out came the letter.

Rice read it. 'Where did you get this?'

'It was given to Carol Byrne. To make her believe Tom Hassett was having an affair, and that Mrs Gallagher was a thief. It's a fabrication.'

'But Hassett signed it.'

'He was forced to.'

'What have you got, Molly?'

'Have it checked for fingerprints.'

'Why?'

'If he was forced to sign it, somebody had to hand it to him. Byrne maybe. Maybe Maguire. They both had access to his office. They're the ones we're talking about.'

'Maguire's not stupid enough to leave his prints lying around on a letter like this.'

'What else have we got to go on?'

The letter lay under a light in the lab and the technician who had run the test pointed his pencil to each grey print, explaining who they belonged to. It contained five sets. Carol Byrne's shrink's. They'd taken his and eliminated him. Molly's, Rice's, Carol's and Tom Hassett's. Not Maguire's. Not another set, which might have pointed to Byrne.

'Too bad, Molly. It was worth a try.'

But Molly saw something Rice didn't. 'Point out Tom Hassett's again,' she told the technician.

He did. 'Those near his signature. Those are Tom Hassett's.'

'You're sure? None of these other ones up the page are his?'

'No.'

Molly turns to Rice. 'This is a pretty personal letter. Hassett says he doesn't want anyone else involved. Not his daughter. Not his wife. Not Byrne. Not even the police. He must have typed it himself.'

'So?'

'He couldn't have. If you type a letter, you leave your prints on the sides of the page. His are only on the bottom. Somebody else typed it, then handed it to him to sign.'

'He could have had someone else type it, Molly. Someone he trusted.'

'Then that person's prints would be on it. They aren't.'

If the coroner had had the letter at the time of the accidents, they wouldn't have been seen as accidents. Now they were being seen for what they were. Things were mounting up. A murder investigation got into full swing.

Years ago in Belfast when my old man disappeared, my mother didn't know whether she was coming or going. Was he dead? Had the Loyalist killer gangs taken him? Would he turn up? Deep down she knew he was dead. It was against his nature to just disappear. But she was praying to God that for the first time since she'd married him, he was acting against his nature. Whatever he was doing, good or bad, at least he'd be alive. So she was in a state of *not knowing* if he was dead or alive. That was hard for her to bear.

Teresa Coyle was like that. Not knowing. Praying her husband would turn up safe and well.

They sat at the table by the window in the kitchen-cum-dining room, yours truly watching from the hired car and listening via the bug I'd planted.

'What was your husband like?' Molly asked her.

'*Is* like. I have to keep believing that. It's the only thing that keeps me going.'

'I'm sorry. Tell me about him.'

Out came the smokes. Teresa Coyle's nerves were getting to her; she had a job holding the lighter steady. 'Tony was, is, well, he's just a man starting out, trying to do his best, always talking about getting us out of this place, y'know, full of big ideas. But a good man. Decent.'

'Did he ever talk about his work?'

'Tony wasn't proud of what he did. He hated spying on people. He'd spend days maybe trying to get a shot of an accident victim so some insurance company could prove fraud, divorce, whatever. It made him feel like a snitch. He got into it because he thought it would be exciting. Instead it was just sordid. He used to say something big would come along that he could maybe sell to the papers, then get out. Try something else.'

'Did he say what he'd been working on?'

'Whatever it was, it scared him. He wasn't sleeping well. Hadn't been for a while. Started taking a couple of whiskeys to get him over. That wasn't Tony. When I asked him about it, he wouldn't say. Then one night, in the early hours, I came down and found him in the chair staring into the fire. He'd drunk nearly a whole bottle of whiskey. I asked him again what was bothering him. It was as if he was afraid to tell me. Eventually, he said he'd been hired to follow a man for one reason, then he found out he was into something else, "setting up something else" was how he put it.'

'You've no idea who the man was?'

'Just that he went to extraordinary lengths to avoid being seen. Tony said he followed him out into the country and photographed him going into an old hide.'

'Hide? Did he say where?'

'All he said was he went in after him, but he disappeared.

Then he heard voices, but he couldn't tell where they were coming from. So he taped it. Tony had a lot of expensive equipment.'

'He taped what they were saying?'

'He often taped conversations. The man he'd followed was being asked to set up something to do with a property company. Tony said he was the smartest man he'd ever come across. A behind-the-scenes fixer, he called him, who planned things that others carried out. Nobody even knew about him, except the man he was talking to. Not even the police.'

'Did he say who this man was talking to?'

'He said he later saw a blue Merc, but it was too far away to tell who was driving it.'

'Did he describe the man he followed into the hide?'

'He started to. He said he had a cut on his head; stitches. Then he fell asleep.'

'Did he mention the name Paddy Toner?'

'That was all he said.'

Course, there was always the danger something like this might happen. You can never safeguard against what a man will tell his wife. And to think that I'd promised Coyle I'd find some way of telling his wife he loved her. I'd kept that promise, by the way.

'Did you tell all this to the police?'

'Tony rang me the night he disappeared. He rang me to tell me he loved me. I knew right away something was up. That maybe he was about to go somewhere, see somebody, and didn't know how it would turn out. I don't know if that's right or not, but you know how you just get a feeling? Anyway, I sat up all night waiting for him. By the time the police came, I was so worried I just answered the questions they put to me. Then when I read what you'd written, that maybe Tony had unwittingly been caught up in that robbery, I called you. Do you think he's alive?'

'I wish I could tell you, Mrs Coyle.'

Maybe there was an insurance policy on him and she couldn't collect without the body. Nah, only joking. Then again, you never know. There's nothing like a visit from the Man from the Pru. Nice-looking woman, Mrs Coyle. Boy's haircut, dark, nice figure . . . What she'd said here, of course, was very disturbing news from my point of view. Not the cut on the head. I'm not talking about that. I couldn't see that leading Molly to me. That didn't bother me. What bothered me was that I'd have to figure out a way to kill her if it turned out that Molly later came across anything that might lead to Mrs Coyle taking the stand. Couldn't have that. Know what I mean?

'Did your husband keep what he was working on anywhere else besides his office: notes, undeveloped film, that photograph and tape you mentioned?'

'Everything was in his office.'

I'd emptied that.

'Or on computer.'

I'd emptied that as well.

'Or in his e-mail.'

'His e-mail? He kept stuff on e-mail?'

In Coyle's office, Molly switched on the computer and went straight for whatever it was Coyle had been hiding in his e-mail. His wife and young daughter stood watching.

Dated and timed the night he'd gone missing, she read:

Byrne called. Wants to do deal for V-A R in vacant flat at 22 The Mews, Dundrum.

I love you, Annie. And I love you, Teresa.

Sentimental shit, I know. But I always keep my promises. This was my way of telling Coyle's wife he loved her.

Molly looked up and saw a tearful Mrs Coyle hugging her daughter.

It was knock-down-the-door time at number 22. Or rather, Molly called out a locksmith and told him she'd locked herself out. He drills a hole in the cylinder lock where the key goes with his cordless, lifts the crossbar, and she's in.

She goes into the bedroom, kitchen, et cetera. They're all empty. Not a stick of furniture in the place. She searches the fitted units. Nothing. So where did Coyle hide his voice-activated recorder? Under the floorboards? Nah. They'd mask the sound. The only likely place is the vents. She puts her ear to the one in the kitchen, then says something, so her voice will set it off and she'll hear the low whirr as it clicks on, find it that way. Nothing. Eventually she gets round to the living room. Puts her ear to the vent, speaks, and hears it come on. She'd found it. She pries the vent off and there it is.

She takes it out, rewinds it, then hits play.

And it plays: *'Yeah, a proposition like that interests me. You said we'll make five million out of it.'*

'Hassett Property's worth five million. Once her old man goes, that leaves her mother, her sister Annie and Carol in the will. With her mother and Annie out of the way, that leaves Carol. She inherits. Then with her out of the way it falls to me.'

'This is one great opportunity.'

'So you're interested?'

'Yeah, I'd like to buy into the property business. You're talking about giving me two and a half million back. Where's the catch? I

don't see any catch. It'd be the easiest money I ever made. Where's the catch?'

'You'd have to carry it out. Kill Carol's parents and her sister. Then Carol.'

'No problem. I know the right people for a job like this. The law would never suspect a thing. They'd never see our hand in it. Everything'll look like an accident.'

The tape crackled and went fuzzy. Then it finished with:

'Like I said: Can just see myself in the winner's enclosure, cracking open a bottle of champers! OK, I'll see you at the Hacienda when I get back.'

I'd planted this for such an eventuality. The flat belonged to Hassett Property. To be honest, way back when I'd told Toner to tape himself talking separately to both Byrne and Ivers, I wasn't quite sure if, or how, I'd ever use the results. Coyle's part in this had presented me with the answer and I'd simply made the best of what I had to work with once Molly got hold of that letter. I'd mixed what Molly had just heard using recordings of those conversations, omitting Toner's voice off both, of course.

This is what I meant about Ivers and Toner sounding very alike. It was a gamble, I grant you. But if Molly came out thinking she'd just heard Byrne talking to Toner – instead of Byrne talking to Ivers, which was what she had actually heard – and acted on it, without first having it analysed, we were safe.

Her enthusiasm didn't let me down.

She couldn't resist gloating. She called Toner on her way back to her office and hit the loudspeaker. 'I've got you, Toner. I've got you on tape. I've got you, you bastard.'

'Who the fuck is this?'

'Twenty-two The Mews. Ring a bell?'

'Fuck you.'

'You didn't know you were being followed? Hah! The great Paddy Toner! You're going down!'

'You got nothing.'

'No? Listen to this.'

She played the tape. 'Yeah, a proposition like that interests me . . . we'll make five million . . . yeah, I'd like to buy into the property business . . . you're talking about giving me two and a half million back . . . where's the catch? . . . you'd have to carry it out . . . kill Carol's parents and her sister . . . no problem . . . everything'll look like an accident . . . I'll see you at the Hacienda when I get back.'

'Back off, Murray!'

'And miss your day in court?'

'You'll never live to see that day.'

'Fuck you. I'm just getting started, Toner. I know everything. I know about that guy in the hide. Your Mr Fixer. I always suspected you weren't smart enough to pull off a job like this by yourself. Now I know why. This story will be on the streets by tonight. I'll go nationwide. I'll find that hide. I'll find this . . . *third man*! I'll see you, him, and Maguire in the dock. Want to know how I'm going to write it up? I'm going to begin with the word *Sinister*. That's you, Toner. Sinister.'

She called Rice. He wasn't available. She left word for him to be contacted immediately, to go to her office. Urgent. I told you she was determined.

And that's how she got herself into this mess.

Which brings us back to where we started.

Chapter Thirty Four

———◇◦◦◦◇———

I put the second question to her.

Her son was in goal. Behind him was the white box van. The question was simple. Yes, he dies, No, he lives.

She could kill her own son or hand over the tape that she believed would convict Toner. And Maguire. And, eventually, yours truly.

'Yes or no?'

It came hard. 'No.'

'Take that microcassette out of your top pocket. Pull the tape out of the cassette and throw it into the road.' My voice, though muffled by a gadget I'd made out of a gas mask, was on that tape. I wanted it destroyed. She threw it out.

'Now the one from The Mews.'

She reached for it, pulled the tape out of the cassette, and threw it out also.

The kids were playing up the field towards the net and the ball was kicked and young Liam saved it and got up all smiles and waved proudly to his mother, who was coming apart inside at the thought of his father lying dead on the lawn and how the boy would cope with that, and the circumstances which had brought it about, for which Molly herself was responsible, because she'd refused to back off. That's how the boy would see it.

The white van started up, slowly pulled away into the side street and was gone.

The teacher blew the final whistle.

Molly got out of her car and made for Liam. She hugged him harder than she'd ever hugged him, at the thought of having nearly lost him. Then she took his hand. 'Come on.'

'Where?'

'Come on, Liam. Quick.'

She led him back to her car.

She had a look of defiance on her face, a 'Fuck you!' look, as she scanned the rooftops and the windows in search of me. Failed to find me, of course. Then she picked up the tape and held it up knowing I would see it. Then put the phone to her ear. 'This is a blank. The Mews tape is with the police. I've got Toner. I've got Maguire. And I'll get *you*, you bastard!'

Rice, racing to the scene of the explosion, saw her and pulled up. They talked. Then Molly nearly fainted. My guess was Rice'd told her about that tape. That he'd had it voice-analysed, before getting a warrant for Toner's and Maguire's arrest, and found that it wasn't Toner Byrne was talking to on it after all, but Ivers. Toner'd been in for questioning over the years. I'd say they still had the interview tapes and compared it to them. Con Ivers. He'd been interviewed over the years as well. The other voice had to be Byrne's, given the content.

Molly was devastated. The shock of having gone after Toner, only to find out that she'd brought about her husband's death for nothing, must have got to her. She had nothing on Toner, after all. Ivers's car would be found nearby later, with listening-in equipment in it tuned into a mike in Molly's car, which would point to the fact that he'd overheard Molly phoning Toner, knew she had the tape, which had his, Ivers's, voice on it, and that this little explosive episode would be put down to Ivers, his way of trying to get back the tape that could send him away for life.

Well, at least Rice knew that once he finally got his hands on Ivers, he'd be able to put him away for this and for killing the Hassetts. There'd still be a lot of unanswered questions, of course. But that's what confusion is all about. That's the beauty of it. Course, he'd be able to put Byrne away for it too. Smart cop, Rice.

These vans, incidentally, had been put in place as soon as Molly got her hands on that letter. It was bound to make her dangerous.

How close it would have led her to a courtroom, I couldn't say. But let me put it this way: she was closer than she'd ever been before. Halfway there, even. If someone's halfway there, act.

The evidence she had from Coyle's widow had not been dropped into her lap. If it had, she'd have questioned it. It would've been too easy. She'd have seen straight through it.

So she had to come across it through her own ingenuity. Only then would she believe that that e-mail of Coyle's, and the follow-up, were genuine.

What I'm saying is this: I had to make her believe she'd solved the Hassett case. Then, as I said, I had to make her pay for her own vanity. Demoralize her, ruin her. Turn her into a guilt-ridden emotional wreck. Make her question her own abilities from this day on. Neutralize her. Before she actually did come across a piece of evidence that might uncover the truth of it all.

I couldn't have that, know what I mean?

Serves her right for going around nicking people's letters.

Chapter Thirty Five

I went to see Molly a few months after all this had happened, to tell her Sinead had got two years – for dope pushing, y'know. We sat in her conservatory. She actually insisted I join her in a G&T. It was a nice night. Young Liam was up in his bedroom, playing on his computer. I was waiting for him to take himself off to bed. I was working on a 'I think about you, Moll', y'know, get the leg over. She hadn't had any for a while and my guess was she was dying for it. You never know. Always worth a try.

Here she was – she was tipsy, glass tilted, slurring, I'd a job making her out, but the gist of it went something like this: 'You know it's funny, Gerd, the things that come into your head.'

'Oh, what's that, Moll?'

'Well, Sinead told me she'd paid Coyle to follow you. I even read the report he gave her on you. Then when I started digging into your background, to counter all that bullshit you were going to tell about me in court—'

'Said in the heat of the moment, Moll.'

'You're full of crap, Gerd. You meant every word. Anyway, as I was saying, I kept remembering what a man called Sean Connors had told me. He had this theory that way back in the seventies, when the O'Neills and the Dunnes wiped each other out, there was this unknown guy working behind the scenes for Toner. This happened round about the time you came to live in Dublin. Toner then went on to bigger things. All of a sudden the jobs he pulled became more . . . labyrinthal' (her word, not mine) 'though no one could prove he'd pulled them – and things started to click into place. They coincided with dates you'd bought into certain businesses. I won't bore you with the details now, but when I later heard Coyle had gone into a hide after a man who was behind the Hassett murders, or was thought to be behind them, I'm not sure any more, I again thought of you. I thought he'd been following you, because Sinead had paid him to, and, contrary to his report, that he'd inadvertently found out you were Toner's Mr Fixer.'

'Me? Christ!'

'Crazy, isn't it?'

'What made you "again" think of me?'

'Seemed a bit of a coincidence that Coyle had been following *two* men, both of whom wore bandages in the same place. I mean, that's a bit of a coincidence, Gerd, you have to admit.'

'I know you have a low opinion of me, Moll, but that's taking it a bit far.'

'I told you it was crazy.'

'What convinced you of my innocence?'

'You have your faults, Gerd, but young Gerd goes to St Martin's Primary and Steven goes to St Vincent's. He was playing football that day with Liam. Not even you would put your own sons under that kind of risk? I mean, you're a bastard. But you're not that bad.'

Well, you have to make it look good, don't you?

'How's Sinead?' Molly asked me.

'She's not doing too well. She was hoping you'd be in court.'

'Couldn't face it, Gerd.'

Molly'd been too busy facing the bottle, by the look of her.

Liam went to bed. Molly got even more drunk. I'd caught her at a weak moment. My guess was I could have had her there and then. But the idea of fucking a has-been had suddenly lost its appeal. Her life was in a mess, y'know, ruined. She started talking about her late husband. Blaming herself all the time. Got a bit depressing after a while. So I left her to it.

Though I have to report that she finally did get herself back together. She actually went on to write a book about the Hassett case. *Six Murders and a Suicide?* she called it. Notice the question mark. Much of it was speculation. And much of it was correct. Not a bad read, though, all the same. It stated what I knew: how she'd nicked Hassett's letter, and stuff like that, and what I'd put together myself: how she'd interviewed Coyle's widow, then, later, Carol Byrne, who'd told her what had happened regarding her attempted suicide, Byrne visiting her the following morning, what had transpired word for word between herself and Rice when they'd fingerprinted that letter; a lot of first-hand detail that I'd had to extrapolate from the bugs we'd planted at the time.

She also wrote that she'd paid Sean Connors to tail Toner, that he'd followed him to a barn, that he'd seen a man with a bandage on his forehead going into a nearby hide. Alas, Connors died before he could identify the man.

Lucky for me the man had been in England at the time researching a book. Then again, as I always say, I'm a great believer in luck. Naturally, I haven't used the hide since.

Other than that, life was back to normal. Little Lou was still keeping me warm. Then there was a new barmaid in Hugo's. Lou found out about her, but she didn't say anything. For the sake of the relationship, y'know. I like that in a woman.

I popped into McDermott's garage, by the way. Carol served me. She looked all right. Had put on a bit of weight.

McDermott came over. 'I'll do that, Carol,' he said. 'You know how you hate having the smell of petrol on your hands.'

It was the way he said it. Fussing over her. Put a smile on her face anyway, made her blush. I like a happy ending.

Never did get to use that wasps' nest. Still, it might come in handy in the future, when Toner contacts me with another little bit of business.

Know what I mean?